D1096395

ANCIENT RETRIBUTION

ANCIENTS RISING SERIES

KATIE REUS

Ancient Retribution

Ancients Rising Series

Copyright © 2022 Katie Reus

Cover art by Sweet 'N Spicy Designs
Editor: Julia Ganis

This book is a work of fiction. The names, characters, places, and incidents are products of the writer's imagination and are not to be construed as real. Any resemblance to persons, living or dead, actual events, locales or organizations is entirely coincidental. All rights reserved. With the exception of quotes used in reviews, this book may not be reproduced or used in whole or in part by any means existing without written permission from the author.

Also, thank you for not sharing your copy of this book. This purchase allows you one legal copy for your own personal reading enjoyment on your personal computer or device. You do not have the right to resell, distribute, print or transfer this book, in whole or in part, to anyone, in any format, via methods either currently known or yet to be invented, or upload this book to a file sharing program. If you would like to share this book with another person, please purchase an additional copy for each person you share it with. Thank you for respecting the author's work.

RETURN TO THE ACTION-PACKED
ANCIENTS RISING SERIES...

A dragon princess once lost...

Juniper hunts down the most dangerous criminals on her black ops missions—and she's good at it. A dragon shifter who was raised by wolves, she doesn't know her birth clan and gave up trying to find them a hundred years ago. Since The Fall, when rogue dragons razed half the planet, she's spent her days hunting down supernaturals who think they can escape justice, delivering her own. During a dangerous mission, she falls into the claws of a sexy warrior dragon adjusting to the modern world—and from the start she knows she's in trouble.

Is now found...

Dragon shifter warrior Zephyr doesn't fit into this new world. He doesn't feel like he fits in anywhere—until he meets Juniper and her crew. He knows from the moment he sees the sexy and brave female dragon that they're destined to be together. Unfortunately, life just got a whole lot more complicated. Not only are they in the fight of their lives against an overwhelming enemy force, but she's royalty and her long-lost clan has come to bring her home. Even as they fight side by side to save hundreds of humans, he knows that winning her heart will be the hardest and most pivotal battle he's ever waged. Juniper doesn't want to get mated, doesn't trust anyone with her heart—but this is one battle Zephyr will never stop fighting.

For my mom and sister, the two strongest women I know.

PROLOGUE

125 years ago

Juniper crept along the tree branch, careful to balance her weight so that it didn't move. Her natural camouflage as a dragon shifter came in handy—like now when she was spying. She wasn't even sure why she was bothering.

She already knew what she'd hear. The Alpha of the wolf pack she'd been pseudo adopted into wanted her gone. And her "parents" were going to agree. She couldn't even be angry at them. The kind healers had taken her in out of the freezing cold a year ago and they tried so hard with her.

But...she knew she'd pushed them to their limits after this morning. It wasn't her fault though. Some stupid wolf had thought he could pick on a younger, weaker wolf.

So, she'd set his tail on fire. And she wasn't sorry. The big bastard had tried to come after her then, thinking that just because she was fourteen she was easy pickings. He found out fast that she fought back.

Now she was about to get kicked out of her pack. Which wasn't great. This place was freezing, with mountains and snow surrounding them in every direction. She wasn't sure where she'd go now. Something in the back of her brain told her that the cold weather was similar to where she was from but she didn't know for sure.

She couldn't remember her true home. And every time she tried, it was like blades pierced her skull, only to be followed by nosebleeds that wouldn't stop for hours. So she'd stopped trying to remember where she came from, or anything else about her past. If she had actual family, they sure hadn't cared enough to come after her, to find her.

From her perch, she had a decent view of the Alpha and her adopted parents in a clearing where sometimes the pack had a big bonfire and gatherings. Right now the pit they stood next to was unlit and no one was around for at least a mile. She'd be able to hear or scent them if they were.

"She is too wild for the two of you," Valentin said, frustration in his voice as he stood in front of Milana and Andre, the two gentle healers who'd shown her nothing but love and understanding.

"Respectfully, Alpha, we disagree." Milana spoke softly, her gentle voice perfect for her petite frame. Her dark hair was pulled into a long braid that fell down her back, over the thick coat she wore.

Juniper was already taller than her by a few inches.

"She set Stephan on fire!" Valentin snarled. "Attacked him like a feral animal. She's not like us. I'm not saying I'll kick her out, but she needs to be with a stronger family. Someone who can rein in her impulses."

Andre growled low in his throat, the first aggression Juniper had ever heard from him. She blinked in surprise. "If you try to remove her from our home, we will leave the territory with her. I respect you as my Alpha, but I will not respect this decision. Juniper doesn't need to be toughened up. She needs care and understanding."

"She doesn't remember where she comes from," Milana continued right when Andre paused. "If you place her somewhere else, she'll run. Of that I have no doubt. And make no mistake, we *will* follow her. So don't even think about separating us. We love that girl and won't abandon her."

2

Juniper blinked again, taken so off guard by the heat in Milana's voice, and the fact that she wasn't just going to...abandon her. Her throat tightened as unwanted emotions bubbled up. So she ruthlessly squashed them.

"We know our worth to the pack," Andre continued. "We're two of the best healers. We receive offers annually to leave your pack. Something we've never considered."

"Until now." Ice coated Milana's words.

Valentin was silent as he looked between the two of them. "If she sets anyone else on fire—"

"Did you ask why she set Stephan on fire?" Milana asked quietly, a diminutive figure who stood as solid as a mighty oak in front of the overly tall and broad Alpha.

He blinked. "What?"

"It is a simple question. Why did she set Stephan on fire? Because I guarantee she had a reason."

There was a slight rustling below Juniper and she froze, thinking she'd been caught. She'd rolled around in ferns for an hour, covering her body in the smell, and had soaked her hair in native berries so she knew no one would catch her natural scent. No one should know she was here.

She looked down and spotted Ren and Griffin, two members of Valentin's pack, hurrying through the snow, just as their earthy scents reached her. They were the same age as her. Ren was a jaguar shifter and Griffin was a wolf, like the majority of the pack. He was small for his age, but he was a scrapper. And he was a good tracker.

"What are the two of you doing here? This is a private meeting." Valentin stepped forward, frowning at the two youths.

"If you're going to kick Juniper out, that's garbage!" Ren snarled, taking Juniper by surprise. He was always so easygoing, so relaxed that she often heard some of the wolves call him a lazy feline. But he wasn't. He just...didn't get riled up by anything. Ever.

Valentin started to respond, then Griffin stepped forward, hands on his hips. Griffin's father was huge, a "small mountain" she'd heard him called before. She'd also heard his father assure him that he'd

3

grow into himself, and even if he didn't grow as big as him, that it did not matter. "Your worth is not in your size," his father had said more than once. The older wolf was a gentle giant, one of the few wolves in the pack that Juniper liked, other than her adoptive parents. He'd taken Ren in as well and was raising him.

"Juniper stood up for me when Stephan was attacking me," Griffin said.

The Alpha scoffed slightly. "I'm sure he was just toughening you up."

"No. He is a grown wolf who thought it was okay to attack me, a thirteen-year-old." Griffin's tone was all pragmatic. "He made sure to do it when no one else was around and it's not the first time he's done it. Juniper was just defending me."

"Does your father know about this?" the Alpha asked.

"He does now." There was no pragmatism in his tone. Just satisfaction in those three words.

Oh, no. Juniper had no doubt that Griffin's father was now currently having a "talk" with Stephan. *Good.* The wolf got away with everything, simply because he was Valentin's cousin.

The Alpha simply looked between the two youths for a long moment. "Thank you for coming to me. Now leave us."

The two boys ran off, but for a moment Ren looked up at the snow-covered branches and she could almost swear he saw her. Mainly because he winked once. Such a weird shifter.

Juniper stayed immobile, almost afraid to breathe.

"Just make sure she does not set anyone else on fire," Valentin murmured as soon as the boys were far enough away that they couldn't hear. "But I've got my eye on her. If she causes trouble, she's gone. Don't think to threaten me with your healer status." He growled low for a long moment.

Fire tingled at the back of her throat, ready to lash out and blast the Alpha for daring to use that tone with her...with Milana and Andre. But she held on to her control, reined in the impulse because she knew that attacking an Alpha was just plain stupid. She might be a dragon, but she could sense how powerful Valentin was.

"She will not cause any more trouble," Milana said quietly, with Andre nodding his agreement.

The Alpha stalked off, his steps agitated, his whole body vibrating with rage as he headed back toward their village.

Once Valentin was well out of earshot, Juniper started to move, to jump down and tell them she was there, when they turned to each other. She froze as Milana continued.

"We need to make plans to leave soon. Before the next full moon," she said quietly. "I don't think she'll be safe here much longer and I won't let anyone hurt her or take her from us."

Andre nodded. "We'll say we're planning a trip to see your parents' pack."

"Then we'll head southeast instead. They'll take all of us in, and be happy to have new packmates and healers. It'll be a fresh start for all of us."

"Griffin Senior and Griffin Junior will want to come too," Andre said.

Which meant Ren would come too, Juniper knew. The jaguar shifter lived with the two of them.

Milana nodded. "Then it's settled. I'll speak with Griffin later tonight."

Juniper wasn't sure where they would be going, but she was glad they'd be leaving. She didn't like the way some of the wolves in this pack looked at her, as if she was less than them. And others looked at her with something...uglier. But she couldn't believe her adoptive parents would make such a big move for her. Sure, they'd told her they loved her. But people said stuff they didn't mean all the time. Milana and Andre, however, showed her how they felt more than anything.

Those unwanted emotions shoved up to the surface again, threatening stupid tears. She refused to cry. Couldn't. Didn't want to let the floodgates open for reasons she wasn't quite sure of. She knew she'd lost something important, something she couldn't remember. And she couldn't even cry about it because she didn't know what it was.

She waited until Milana and Andre were long gone before finally dropping down into the snow. She made a vow then and there that she wouldn't do anything to shame Milana and Andre. She knew that she had impulse control issues, but no matter what, she would be the best daughter for them. They were willing to leave their pack and move to a new territory to keep her safe.

And she would never let them down.

She would also never forget the way Ren and Griffin had stood up for her.

CHAPTER ONE

Present day

J
uniper dove toward the demon-covered roof of a parking garage, her dragon wings beating in quick, sharp bursts as she arrowed directly at the hellish sight before her—pun intended.

Because some dumbass had clearly decided to open a Hell gate nearby. It was bad enough that a year ago a bunch of loony dragons had attempted to take over the world. Yeah. *Take. Over. The world.*

Instead, they'd destroyed half of it.

They'd failed in what was now known as The Fall, but they'd altered the direction of the world forever. Supernaturals no longer lived in the shadows.

Which, she had complex feelings about.

She wished she could be surprised that someone had decided to allow demons free roam in somewhere…Tennessee? She wasn't actually sure where they were right now.

Didn't matter anyway.

She and her crew had to stop this.

A couple dozen demons were all huddled around something,

screaming and moaning like banshees. Whatever they were doing, it wasn't good.

Letting out a wild stream of fire, she incinerated five full-blooded demons with razor-sharp teeth, red skin, mostly humanoid bodies, and black, depthless eyes. At least these weren't the gray-skinned Akkadian demons—those things stank worse than anything.

Half the demons turned at her blast of fire, baring rows of teeth as they rushed at her, their claws clicking across the concrete.

As she neared the rooftop she shifted forms, let her human body overtake her as her feet slammed into concrete. Unlike most dragon shifters, she could shift with her clothing so she wasn't butt-ass naked right now fighting a bunch of demons. She had no idea how it worked —she didn't know a lot about her dragon heritage—but she liked not having to constantly change clothes like her shifter friends.

Releasing two long, glowing chains born of magic deep inside her —also an oddity for *any* being—from her hands, she whipped them around, slicing off the heads of the nearest demons in a whirlwind of movement.

One of the creatures broke away from its pack, drooling and snarling as he raced at her on his hands and feet, running like a crab. He ducked, rolled, missed her magical chains and sprang off the pavement right at her face.

Fire burned the back of her throat, ready to blast him, when a glowing arrow bolted straight through his head.

The demon screeched right before it turned to ash. The arrow clattered to the concrete.

"Thanks, Ren!" she shouted above the cacophony of snarls and screams. She wasn't quite sure where he was, but she knew that had been his save for sure. The jaguar shifter loved his magical arrows.

Suddenly a roar rent the air and fire blasted outward from the huddled demons. Ash coated the air as they incinerated and…a naked male stood, panting hard, blood running down his arms as he held his bloody open palm against a Hell gate opening.

Oh goddess, the Hell gate opening was right *here*. No wonder there had been so many demons huddled together. A glowing slash that cut right through the fabric of reality spilled out red light as this guy did his best to close the gate. He had to be magical—or a dragon shifter if he was going to successfully close the gate.

She had to help him.

"Guys, cover me!" she shouted as she called on her chains, ordering them to disappear. She'd been working with Ren, Hyacinth and Griffin in black ops for a long time and knew they'd have her back.

Juniper raced up to the male as demons exploded to ash one by one all around her thanks to her crew.

She sliced into her palm as she reached the big bearded male with scars on his face and body.

He turned to look at her, his gray eyes almost glowing as he held his palm against the illuminated seam that looked as if someone had taken a jagged blade to it and just sliced it open.

This wasn't her first time dealing with a Hell gate and clearly it wasn't his either. With a foot separating them, she pressed her palm on the opening as he continued chanting an incantation she'd heard before. She sliced her other palm open and pressed it against the opening as well.

He chanted faster.

She joined him, repeating the words even as she had to cut her palms again due to her healing capabilities.

Behind them, she heard scuffling, but forced herself to trust her team to protect her.

That had been decades in the making, being able to trust someone enough to allow them to have her back. Literally.

The red light spilling out of the gate dimmed faster and faster the more blood they smeared.

Suddenly a blast of light shoved out at them, like hands trying to attack, before the gate sucked in on itself and disappeared in a burst of smoke. Now a crumbled wall stood in its place, revealing the decimated buildings next door to the garage.

At the sudden silence that descended, the adrenaline that had been punching through her dipped low.

She swiveled to face her crew to make sure everyone was okay just as the male next to her collapsed.

Moving lightning quick, she reached for him, caught him in her arms before he could slam into the pavement face-first. The male was huge and solid. Yeah, he was a dragon.

Gently she eased him down as the others hurried over, all covered in dead demon dust. They'd done a damn good job of clearing off this rooftop. There would likely be demons who'd escaped, but she'd worry about that later.

"Oh, crap," she breathed as she realized the male had a wicked-looking blade sticking out of his right rib cage. She hadn't seen it before, but it had been embedded deep.

"This dude's a dragon so it's gotta be tipped in poison to take him down like this." Ren knelt on the male's other side, gripped the handle slightly. "We need to pull it out."

Hyacinth whipped her backpack off, was unzipping it even as Juniper said, "Do it."

When they were working missions, they had to make snap decisions. Sure, it could be a mistake to pull this blade out, but they had to risk it. Humans and shifters healed differently so keeping this in the guy could do irreparable harm if it had poison on it.

They didn't have access to a healer right now, but they did have very strong blood and antibodies they could inject this dragon with.

And she had no doubt this male was a dragon shifter. First, he was huge, and second, dragon blood was one of the only things that could open or close Hell gates.

The male's body jolted, though he didn't open his eyes as Ren eased the blade out of him. A black liquid coated the end of it. She winced. She'd seen this before. Thankfully it wouldn't be deadly if they got enough of her blood into him. She could see that the wound was already fighting to knit itself closed so that was good too. He was clearly powerful, but he'd have just expended a lot of energy closing that gate while fighting off demons.

Hyacinth, a vampire who was part of her crew, pulled out a few syringes and got to work as Griffin said, "I see a few tangos running away. They're about a mile out and moving fast."

She glanced over at Griffin, saw he had binos up to his eyes as he scanned the surrounding area. The sun was about an hour from setting so unfortunately they'd be hunting them in the dark. "We'll get them later." Juniper held on to the dragon male's hand, watching him suck in a sharp breath as Hyacinth injected him with the second syringe. "Come on," she murmured, willing the stranger to open his eyes. This male had been out here trying to shut a Hell gate all alone, facing an overwhelming enemy force. And from the looks of his battered body, the demons had been going at him hard before he'd blasted them with his fire. His chest and thighs had gouges, mostly healed, but they'd still be painful.

Hyacinth had pulled out the third syringe when his pale gray eyes opened.

He looked around at them, his eyes not focusing.

"You're going to be okay," Juniper said. "We're giving you blood." Her blood, actually. "It's got healing properties." Unlike humans, they didn't have to worry about blood types for transfusions or injections. And right now, the stronger the better to get him up and going.

He blinked, then looked at her, his eyes focusing a bit more as he stared.

"Give him another injection," she ordered Hyacinth without taking her eyes off his. "You'll start feeling better soon. Promise."

His gaze fell to Juniper's lips as Hyacinth injected him. He didn't react, except to reach out and drag one of his big, callused fingers over Juniper's bottom lip and murmur something she couldn't make out.

"Okay, buddy." She gently grasped his wrist and moved it down to rest on his abdomen as he closed his eyes.

"He's in a natural sleep now. He'll be all right," Hyacinth said as she started closing up her bag. "We need to move him."

Though she was loath to drop this stranger's hand, Juniper did and joined Griffin by the edge of the rooftop, looking out over the destroyed city. This place had clearly been hit hard during The Fall and had never recovered. Half the buildings had been charred, the tops of them looking as if they'd been sawed off. Which they technically had been—with dragon fire. The rest of the buildings hadn't fared much better.

She could see exactly two roofs still in decent shape, but everything else had been torn or burned off. After a year of these places all being open to the elements...she didn't think anyone human would be living here now. But they'd still check for signs of life. Later, however, because they needed to get this dragon to safety.

"I'll shift and carry him back to our rendezvous point. Everyone head there now. If you spot any tangos, eliminate. Otherwise, see you guys in a bit."

She stepped back as the others hurried off, and called on her dragon, shifting immediately before she scooped up the male who smelled like the deep, unspoiled forest on a winter's day.

The scent woke something inside her, the dragon half of her purring with anticipation.

CHAPTER TWO

Zephyr felt warmth surrounding him even as the sound of a crackling fire filtered in the background. He kept his eyes closed as he listened to murmuring from…four individuals.

Two males, two females. And one of them smelled like heaven.

Where the hell was he— The Hell gate. A tall dragon female had helped him close it. She'd been…*magnificent*.

"You can open your eyes now," a sultry voice said, her tone dry.

He cracked open his eyes, wiped away the grittiness and sat up. *Ugh.* He should have paused and taken stock before jolting upright. He bit back a groan as he shifted against the sleeping bag they'd stretched him out on. He was naked, but someone had wrapped a blanket around his middle.

If these people had meant to kill him, they'd had plenty of chances already. For the moment, they weren't his enemy. And he really hoped the female with the bicolor eyes watching him like a predator would never be his enemy. "Where am I? And who are you? And what happened to the Hell gate?" He vaguely remembered it closing, but he needed to be certain.

"You're about five miles from that now-closed Hell gate," the female with the sexy voice said.

Zephyr was aware of the three others. Very aware. They all exuded power that rippled around them, but there was no menace, no malice in the air, so he rolled his shoulders once, keeping his gaze on the female. "What's your name?" Because he needed to know that more than anything.

Goddess, she was stunning. All long legs stretched out in front of the fire, her hair covered in a sort of bandana so that her unique eyes stood out against her tanned skin. One gray, one the color of the Mediterranean. And he could scent right away that she wasn't mated. Wasn't claimed by anyone. No, she smelled like wild, untamed magic. It was exhilarating, and he had to force himself to not be obvious and lean closer to inhale more of her. Dragon females were the deadliest of creatures, and this one? Oh, she was dangerous. In more ways than one.

His dragon side purred in pleasure at the knowledge that she wasn't mated, his beast rumbling under the surface, very, *very* interested in this female. He wondered if she tasted as delicious as she smelled.

She narrowed those eyes at him, as if she read his thoughts. "What were you doing on that parking garage?"

He snorted softly and looked around, taking in his surroundings more. They were in a clearing in the woods with sleeping bags set up. If he scented right, one male was a feline of sorts, the other male a wolf, and the other female...a vampire, if he had to guess. "Fairly certain it's obvious what I was doing there. Anyone have any water? I'm parched. Pants would be nice too." He stood then, not caring that his blanket fell away.

As a dragon he was unconcerned about nudity. And...he wanted her to see what he could offer her.

The vampire, a female with light brown skin and short, tight curls pulled back in a headband, smothered a laugh and looked away.

Laughter at his naked form? That was a new one. *Ouch.* At least the female with the enticing scent hadn't laughed. He lifted his arms over his head and stretched as the female dragon—definitely their leader—

stood across from him, hands on hips. Her expression was a mix of curiosity and maybe exasperation.

"Here." The dark-haired, bronze-skinned male he was certain was a feline handed him a giant bottle. "I'm Ren, by the way."

"Thanks. I'm Zephyr," he said as he took it, his eyes still pinned on the sexy female. Not smelling any poison, he chugged it in a few swallows, feeling immediately better. But he needed more. Needed actual sustenance. Food.

"You going to answer my question?" the sexy female demanded.

"After you tell me your name. Or I can just keep calling you 'sexy female' in my head."

The vampire snorted and Ren cough-laughed as he stepped back.

The female's jaw ticked once, but she responded. "Juniper."

Juniper. He rolled it around in his head. *Juniper*, his dragon half purred. *Mine*.

He ordered his dragon half to shut the fuck up. Maybe he'd gotten hit on the head or something.

The other male, the wolf, tossed pants at him with a grunt before bleeding back into the shadows and stalking off to the edge of the forest.

"Thanks," he called out as he tugged them on. "And I was closing the Hell gate." His gaze was drawn back to Juniper, and he was once again struck hard as their gazes connected. It was like a sucker punch straight to his abdomen when he looked at her.

He wasn't sure what was going on with him, but his dragon half really, *really* wanted to get closer to her. To run his nose along her neck, nibble on that sensitive spot where her neck and shoulder met.

He shook himself and continued when she just stared at him. "There were rumors that a couple witches with no sense decided to open a Hell gate. I was sent here with orders to see if it was true, then report back. But I decided to close it because far too many demons were escaping. And when I started closing it, they rushed it, trying to overpower me with brute numbers and force." He winced, looking down at his chest.

Faint white lines crisscrossed his chest and abdomen and he had no doubt they were all over his thighs and back too. Raging demons had carved him up good. He twisted side to side, stretching more to check his mobility. He felt fine. Rejuvenated, even. And he liked that her eyes were on him.

"Who ordered you to check out this area?" Juniper asked, her dragon in her eyes as she stared at him.

"The Alpha of the territory I live in."

"That's an oddly specific way of phrasing it. Is the person not your Alpha?"

Zephyr paused. He liked King, respected the male, but he was only recently escaped from prison in a Hell realm and his dragon hadn't decided if he'd follow King yet or not. Hadn't decided a lot of things.

He weighed his answer. There was no reason to lie to these people. Not yet anyway. "King, Alpha of the New Orleans territory, ordered me here. And I haven't decided if he's my Alpha yet. I live in his territory and I respect his rules." Not to mention Zephyr's brothers lived there and had given King their allegiance. But he wouldn't talk about his family to these strangers. "I'm not certain yet if I will call New Orleans my home, or if I will move elsewhere."

The female watched him cautiously, curiously. "Why are you not certain? From all accounts, King is a good leader."

"He is. I'm...a long way from home. I haven't been in this realm for a long time. Until recently. I'm still adjusting to things." It was vague enough, but still true.

Seeming to relax at his answer, she pointed back at the sleeping bag, silently ordering him to sit as she sat. Both the vampire and Ren did the same.

So Zephyr eased back down onto the fluffy seat, savoring the feel of the fire. As a dragon, he ran hot, but whatever he'd been poisoned with had weakened him. He needed to shift to his beast form to accelerate his healing, but found he was enjoying talking to these strangers. One stranger in particular. "What are the four of you doing here? There is no claimed territory here. No Alpha."

"We're tracking down...someone," Juniper said.

"Who?"

"Traffickers of humans," Ren bit out, disgust in the male's voice.

He recoiled at that. "Someone is trafficking people?" He knew it happened—humans had been trapped in the same Hell realm he'd been trapped in because of trafficking.

"Calm down there, big boy," the vampire said, and he realized smoke was coming out of his nose.

He cleared his throat, met Juniper's gaze again. "Who are you working for, then? Or are you just hunting down traffickers for your pack? Or clan?"

There was a long pause and he thought they wouldn't answer, which was well enough. He was intrigued by this female, but he did need to leave soon. Or at least he needed to get in touch with King and update him. He'd left his small pack with his cell phone in a secret cache he intended to retrieve. And there was the matter of the demons that had escaped before he'd gotten to the gate to close it.

At that, his stomach rumbled—he also needed to eat something and replenish his strength if he was going to hunt them down. So if these supernaturals weren't going to be open with him, then it was time to leave. He shifted slightly, getting ready to stand.

"August McGuire," Juniper said into the quiet.

He blinked, surprised. But then, maybe he shouldn't be. He'd heard enough from his brothers and Prima over the last year about McGuire.

"You know him?" Juniper asked.

His expression must have given him away. "I know of him. I'm friends with the female he…" He cleared his throat, unsure how to continue. He was aware that McGuire was in a relationship of sorts with an old friend of his. But as far as he knew, they weren't mated. "I'm friends with Mira. And her twin."

There was a collective settling among them at his words. Juniper looked at Ren and Hyacinth and they seemed to have a silent conversation.

Then Juniper looked back at him. "We worked for August before The Fall and we still work for him. Just because the world went to hell doesn't mean all the baddies have disappeared."

Baddies? His lips curved up slightly at her vernacular. He was still adjusting to modern language and had not heard that one before. "So he's ordered you to hunt down traffickers?"

"It's a group of them. Vampires, mostly. We think they were doing this before The Fall, and with the chaos... We can't be sure, but we think they're using the chaos of everything, the completely lawless territories, to kidnap humans with abandon. Some vampires and shifters too. Younger ones. Less powerful."

"So this is organized?"

She nodded, her expression grim. "Yes. We've gotten a few tips that some of these guys are headed to New Orleans, to test out the waters there. See how strong King is or if he notices people going missing."

Zephyr's dragon prowled under the surface. He liked the territory of New Orleans, liked what the Alpha wolf was building. And all three of his brothers cared deeply for human females. One was mated to one. And Zephyr liked the little human as well—she was bossy and took care of his brother. "Do you need help?"

They all looked at him, mostly with faint surprise.

He shrugged. "I owe you. Thank you for helping with the Hell gate." He'd had it under control, but...he might not have recovered enough to get all that poison out of his system once he'd closed it. He would have been vulnerable lying there on the top of that parking garage. "What did you guys do to me anyway? Are you a healer?"

Juniper shook her head. "We injected you with blood." She cleared her throat slightly. "My blood, since I'm a dragon too."

He had her blood inside him? His dragon definitely purred now, liking that a whole lot.

"We might be able to use your help," Juniper finally said. "I'll have to talk to August and Mira, see if you're who you say you are. If you're trustworthy." The glare she gave him said she'd cut his head off if he wasn't.

And that was...hot. Yes, that was the right word. He'd heard his brother Cas use it before and it applied here.

He nodded and stood. "That sounds good. Now, I'm hungry and need to hunt." He'd scented some deer before he'd ended up on that parking garage roof battling for his life. He regretted not eating first because he was far too weak right now. And he knew better. It wasn't as if he'd been out here with a partner. He knew better than to go off alone like that, but he'd been feeling reckless. "And then I plan to hunt down any demons who escaped."

The others stood then but he paused as he scented the tinge of blood in the air.

"It's just Griffin," Juniper murmured, turning around and looking into the dark forest behind her.

Zephyr narrowed his gaze and spotted the shadow of the wolf loping through the thicket of trees, dragging a dead animal with him.

Seemed they had the same idea. Zephyr jogged back from the fire and shucked his pants. He needed space to shift. "I'll be back," he said before anyone could protest, and shifted to his beast form. Not like he was asking for permission anyway.

He stretched his wings out and did a slow spin, showing off all his gorgeous scales. The most primal part of him wanted to preen for Juniper like an obnoxious peacock.

So he gave in to the impulse.

He'd been told that his scales looked like a million shimmering diamonds. He hoped she liked what she saw.

"Pretty sure that beast is showing off for you," Hyacinth murmured, her voice barely loud enough to carry.

"Doubt it." Juniper's voice was just as quiet.

But he was. He was also going to bring her back food from his hunt as well.

Might as well make his intentions clear up front. He wanted this female. Badly.

CHAPTER THREE

One week later

"This is quite the party." Juniper eyed the melee around them as she and Zephyr strode across the grass yard of a private residence—a three-story mansion in New Orleans. The sun had set a couple hours ago and this place was lit up everywhere, with lights strung up in all the trees as well as spotlights set up where people had decided to carve out areas to dance.

Zephyr had contacted King earlier in the day and had been informed that there was a huge celebration going on. Apparently a lot had happened while Zephyr had been gone the last couple weeks, including King officially mating. Zephyr told her that he wasn't surprised about the mating, said it had been a long time coming apparently.

This party had spilled out into the street and down a couple blocks.

Being around so many people had Juniper's dragon on edge, right at the forefront. She was used to operating in the shadows so she was accustomed to being around others—but that didn't mean she had to like it. She'd infiltrated countless places—shifter packs in the dead of night, government institutions all over the world, cartel compounds, exclusive clubs. But this was a party.

For *fun*.

She didn't care for it.

There were far too many supernaturals around that she knew nothing about. There were dancing bears, in shifted form, acting like they had no sense at all. And of course there were wolves and all sorts of felines in various states of undress. Some were engaging in sports games, in animal form. Not to mention all the humans dancing, laughing, drinking. There were just so many of them. One human male in particular had looked at her as if he'd seen right through to the heart of her. As if he'd known she was a dragon.

She hadn't cared for that insight either. There had been no malice in the man's dark eyes, but it had still unnerved her.

"There they are." Zephyr's voice was quiet, steady as he nodded across a makeshift dance floor underneath a giant oak tree. Strings of lights and paper lanterns were hung up everywhere as a DJ blasted some song that sounded vaguely familiar.

She looked in the direction he indicated and saw the Alpha couple —King and Aurora. Juniper watched them carefully, saw the way the wisp of a female laid her head on the male's broad shoulder, their hands intertwined in a clear symbol of unity.

But it was the way their bodies curved up against each other, the way they both angled in to each other in silent affection, that made Juniper turn away. The moment felt almost private. And it brought up a yearning inside her she didn't want to acknowledge.

She'd never had that connection with anyone. Sex, yes. Love and affection? No. At least, not the kind shining from that couple as bright as a star.

As they approached, King stepped forward and held out his hand for Zephyr. "I'm glad you're back," the Alpha said. The male was tall, but only an inch taller than her.

His dark hair was cropped close to his head and he had memorable, ice-blue eyes that seemed even brighter against his dark brown skin. Juniper had seen his picture before, courtesy of her boss August, so she would have recognized King without Zephyr.

She'd seen a picture of Aurora before as well, but the picture hadn't done the petite female justice. Her dark hair was pulled back into a braid and she had a soft, serene smile. She practically glowed, her entire being emanating an inner light. A year ago, Juniper had watched a video clip of Aurora in her phoenix form as she battled a dragon, so she was very aware that this was not a female to underestimate. Juniper smiled politely at the Alpha female as Zephyr and King greeted each other in the way of warriors.

"Glad to be back." Zephyr stepped back and motioned to Juniper. "This is Juniper."

She nodded again as he introduced the two of them, formally. She was a warrior as well, but King wasn't her Alpha so she didn't greet him the same way.

"It's a pleasure to meet you both. Thank you for allowing me into your territory." She kept her tone polite, deferential. She was about to ask for permission to be in this Alpha couple's territory. She quickly looked at Zephyr, taking his lead now. This was his territory, and he knew these people.

He nodded once, then turned back to the couple. "I took care of that thing you asked me to and...that's how Juniper and I met. She works for August McGuire. He's—"

"I know who he is." King's voice was a low murmur as he glanced at Juniper. She couldn't read his expression as he turned back to Zephyr. "Is he in my territory?"

"No," Juniper answered. "He's up in Montana. His base is with the Petronilla clan. But...I think you know that?" August had been clear that King was an ally, but had wanted her to introduce herself to the Alpha, to make way for their operation.

King simply nodded.

"I worked for him before The Fall and I still do," she said, even though the Alpha likely knew all of this as well. "We're still doing what we did before. Right now I'm hunting down traffickers and it's led me here, to your territory. I would like permission for me and my crew to stay here until we've found them."

King looked at Zephyr, clearly to see what he thought.

"They saved my ass from some rogue demons," Zephyr said immediately. "And they're good people. I vouch for all of them. And I'd like permission to work with them while hunting down these fuckers."

Juniper had asked her crew to hang back until they got the official okay from King. Besides, it made more sense for just her and Zephyr to approach the Alpha, not all of them at once.

"I'll need more details, but that's acceptable," King said, his expression still opaque. "Just let me know where you're staying. And I'll want to speak to all of your crew. They will obey all my laws while in my territory." He shot her a hard look as he spoke.

"Of course," Juniper said. Her people were here to do a job. Then they'd leave.

Though...the thought of separating from Zephyr left an odd ache in her chest. One she didn't want to examine too closely.

He was confident in the way of most dragon shifters she'd met. She shouldn't be surprised, but she hadn't grown up with other dragons. And they were so different from wolves. They loved to strut around as if they were kings of the world. And when Zephyr strutted, she liked it. Aaand, she locked that thought down. But he was a truly stunning specimen of raw masculinity. One she wanted a taste of. So did her dragon half. *Ugh.*

After they thanked the Alpha couple, they headed back across the party until Zephyr stilled.

"What?" She went on alert, ready to shift or release her chains and attack any threat.

"Ah, nothing. Just, those are my brothers." He nodded toward a group of three huge males standing with three females—all human, if she had to guess. They weren't tall enough to be dragons anyway.

"You have brothers?"

He shrugged and gave her a lopsided smile that she felt in places she did not want to be feeling. "Yep. Come on, let's go meet them."

Juniper just wanted to get out of there, away from all these damn people and the noise, but...she was curious about Zephyr's family. Zephyr's everything. She'd already seen the male naked, and sweet goddess, he was gorgeous. So no surprises there. But he'd been tight-lipped about anything personal.

All three males turned, almost as one, from where they were congregated by a small table littered with drinks and plates of food. Two of the females, a redhead with pale skin and a dark-haired one with bronze skin, didn't seem to notice her and Zephyr's approach as they stared and giggled over a couple wolves playing soccer. But one of Zephyr's brothers had his arm securely around a big-eyed, curvy female who watched their approach cautiously.

"Brothers, this is Juniper. Juniper, this is Mikael, Ivyn and Casimir —or Cas."

"Or," the one named Mikael said as he held out a hand, "you can just call these two dumbasses."

"Or, she can just watch as I kick both your asses," Cas said as he held out a hand. "Nice to meet you."

Ivyn nodded politely and murmured a greeting, but didn't take his arm from the curvy female, who gave Juniper a shy smile.

Juniper grinned as Cas challenged Mikael to a fire-breathing contest.

Around that time the other two females had turned around and the dark-haired one simply rolled her eyes and nudged both of them back. "There will be no fire-breathing, no stripping naked, no hand-stand contests, no...acting foolish. Just act like Zephyr and you'll be fine," she said as she gave him a big hug.

Juniper watched as he gently patted the small female's back.

"This is Avery," Zephyr said. "She keeps my brothers in line. And her own brothers," he added, looking around. "Where are they?"

"Who knows?" she said as Mikael placed a possessive arm around her shoulders.

All the brothers had similar gray eyes, but Zephyr's were more striking, more vivid.

Juniper shoved her hands in her pockets. She could make small talk on missions, could blend in just about anywhere, but this wasn't a mission. This was Zephyr's family, and while she'd only known him a little while, she found herself wanting to make a good impression. Or at least not come off like a weirdo.

It was an odd sensation, caring what someone else thought about her. She internally frowned at that. As she stood there, trying to think of something polite and normal to say, she sensed movement out of the corner of her eye—and grinned when she spotted an old friend, Christian, approaching.

The male was dressed in a suit, complete with a vest and fancy shoes. He always made her feel a bit like a slob, in anything she wore. Today was jeans, scuffed-up boots and a faded T-shirt. So...yeah. "Christian," she said, delighted.

His smile was reserved but charming as he eyed the dragons around her. "I had no idea you were in town."

"Just arrived an hour or so ago." She gave him a hug and blinked in surprise when she heard someone growling behind them.

Christian quickly stepped back, eyebrow raised as Zephyr stepped up, his earlier easygoing smile gone as he basically bared his teeth at Christian like a feral animal. "I'm Zephyr."

"And I'm Christian."

Her vampire friend held out a polite hand and Juniper nudged Zephyr when he just stared, looking as if he wanted to bite her friend's hand. She shouldn't have worried about being a weirdo at all, not when he was being like this.

"So what brings you to this territory?" Christian asked his question quietly, low enough for only the three of them.

Juniper took a small step away from the others, not that it really mattered. They'd started talking about who could breathe fire the farthest and weren't paying any attention. "Work. I'd planned to stop by and see you regardless, but I'm hoping you might be able to help."

"Anything you need, I'm here." He shot Zephyr an arch look then, perfect eyebrow raised. "I'm not interested in Juniper."

Zephyr blinked in surprise, but still just stood there staring. Then he said, "Good. You get to keep your head."

Uh, what. The. Hell. She didn't look at Zephyr. Didn't trust herself to. He couldn't mean… No. He simply couldn't. And she wasn't going to respond to that at all. Or think about it. Much. Was he just screwing with her head?

"I'm headed out, but I'll stop by tomorrow night if that's okay?" she said to Christian.

Christian nodded, his gaze straying to a lion who was allowing two children to ride him like a pony, complete with making whinnying sounds. Something flickered across his expression, something almost wistful, before he looked back at Juniper. "Perfect. You know where I live." He purred the last part, shot Zephyr a smug, purely male look before he stalked off.

Before she realized she'd moved, she reached out and gripped Zephyr's forearm. And oh, what a forearm it was. His muscles flexed under her iron grip, but he remained immobile.

"He is an old friend and a very helpful contact," she said quietly. "He doesn't belong to a coven and has connections everywhere. He's well liked. So be nice to him. We need him."

Zephyr shoved out a breath, and she could feel the tension leaving his body. "You're heading out?" he said, referring to her earlier comment to Christian instead of talking about the fact that he'd just acted like a mated male toward the vampire.

There was no way she was bringing it up—not a conversation she wanted to have. *Nope.* She would just ignore what had happened like she ignored all things that bothered her. Healthy coping mechanisms? *Also nope.* Drove her very evolved healer parents who wanted her to talk about her feelings mad. But it was what it was.

"Yeah. Want to get back to the others." She shoved her hands in her pockets again.

"Okay. Let me say goodbye to my brothers."

She wanted to tell him that he didn't need to come with her but… she was glad he was. Standing to the side while he hugged his brothers, she scanned the crowd, looking at the happy faces. She'd heard some of what had happened while Zephyr had been gone and it was *a lot.*

No wonder the territory was celebrating. From what they'd heard and seen on their way in, the partying was everywhere. And seeing all these truly happy people, it said a whole lot for the Alpha and the other leaders of New Orleans.

Because she'd seen firsthand how bad some places had been hit, how the "leaders" in charge didn't take care of their people. This…was amazing. And she'd be damned if she let traffickers in here to hurt more people.

"You ready?" Zephyr moved up beside her, as quiet as a wraith.

She nodded, inhaling that wild mountain scent. Her dragon prowled under the surface, liking everything about this male. *Ugh.* Her beast side was so annoying sometimes.

"You didn't have to come with me," she said once they'd cleared the gate of the property.

It wasn't much quieter out on the street. All the surrounding streets were closed off for a couple blocks with people partying in the streets. And some humans had actual grills out in the road and were handing out various foods as people passed. It was basically a giant tailgate party.

Zephyr snagged a couple hot dogs and handed her one. "I wanted to. We need to plan for our next move."

The way he said "we" warmed her from the inside out. She knew he was just helping out because she and her crew had saved him from poisoning, but still. He'd jumped feetfirst into this mission with them.

"Besides, I feel kind of awkward around my brothers and their mates."

She swallowed a bite, turned to him in surprise as they stepped up onto the sidewalk. "Why?"

He shrugged. "I was gone for a long time. When I escaped that realm…" He cleared his throat. "When I returned to this realm, everything was different. *Is* different. I feel like I don't know them anymore. I love them," he added, glancing at her. "I'd do anything for them. But I just feel like an outsider sometimes, I guess. They've been together, the three of them, for a while, and I don't know…" He shrugged, looking uncomfortable suddenly.

"I grew up in a wolf pack," she said, some deep-buried part of her wanting to put him at ease. He'd just made himself vulnerable and she respected that. "I have no idea who my blood family is. They abandoned me." She shrugged too, but doubted she looked as casual as she tried to play it off. Because that shit still hurt over a hundred years later. The cut of being discarded like that... It was bone-deep. Her own family hadn't wanted her, hadn't bothered to look for her.

"I'm sorry." They turned onto another street, this one a whole lot quieter.

It was as if someone had turned the volume waaaay down and the sudden change in noise had tension buzzing through her. It had been easier to be open when they were surrounded by other people and distractions. Now, with just the two of them on this tree-lined street...it felt too intimate. She cleared her throat. "I still sometimes feel out of place when Ren, Griffin and I go back home." Though not because of her pack—everyone made her feel welcome and loved. She knew it was her own baggage. Still didn't change anything.

He nodded. "I can imagine." Thankfully, he didn't let silence stretch between them. Instead, he said, "So Hyacinth obviously isn't from your pack. How did you guys end up teamed up together?"

"Through work. Ren, Griffin and I got recruited at the same time. And August thought Hyacinth would be a perfect fit for us. He wasn't wrong," she said on a laugh. He rarely was. "We've been working as a team for over fifty years." Though she'd been close to Ren and Griffin a lot longer. They were like brothers to her. The three of them had been wild in their youth, getting into trouble together, being there for the others during first heartbreaks. They might not be related by blood, but they were her family.

"It's clear you all work well together."

"We're looking for another member to join us," she suddenly blurted, then internally winced even as she kept her expression the same. What the hell was she vomiting out now? What was wrong with her?

He glanced at her, his gray eyes flickering with surprise as they reached the park they'd chosen as their spot to shift and fly out of. "Yeah?"

She nodded, because she'd already put the offer out there. August had wanted to know what Juniper thought of Zephyr during this mission, if she wanted to offer him a spot on their team. He hadn't told her to actually offer him a job.

"I'll keep that in mind," he murmured, his gaze trailing to her mouth for one long, very hot moment.

Oooh no. Just no. She could not do anything with this male. Not even fantasize. Well, too late for that. But no more after today. She didn't do relationships. Sure as hell wasn't looking for a mate. And it wasn't as if she could hook up with a male who might be on their team. No way. That was just asking for trouble. So she would keep things strictly professional.

She looked away from him, glad to find the park empty. It wasn't well lit, but with her extrasensory abilities that didn't matter.

Right about now, she was glad for her ability to shift with her clothes still intact. Because the thought of getting naked in front of Zephyr, of making herself vulnerable? *No thanks.*

She didn't look at him as she heard him start to strip. Because professionals didn't peek on their teammates while they were getting naked.

Dragons do what we want, her inner dragon purred.

Ugh.

CHAPTER FOUR

Two weeks later

In the cozy kitchen, Zephyr watched as Josephine, the grandmother of Cas's new human mate Jo, gently patted Cas's hand and handed him a platter of fried chicken.

A year ago Cas, his second to youngest brother, had fallen hard for Jo, a human female. And in the few weeks Zephyr had recently been gone, he'd mated with her. Now Cas lived with her, her two sisters and grandmother. And Cas was happy in a way Zephyr had never seen him. Settled.

Mikael was the same. Ivyn too. It was disconcerting seeing his warrior brothers completely settled with delicate human females.

He was happy for all of them, but he couldn't help but be aware of how very vulnerable mating made them. And to mate with a human made his brothers even more so. If a dragon died so did their mate, and vice versa. But it was clear they wouldn't change a thing.

"Help me out?" Cas asked him.

"Of course." He grabbed a couple more trays of the fried chicken, impressed with how much food the elder female had cooked. He hoped she hadn't traded too much to provide all the food for them, and made a note to ask Cas if they needed to bring over more live-stock to replenish the food here.

As he stepped onto the back porch with Cas, a cacophony of noise rolled over him: laughter, music, talking.

"Food, finally!" Grace, one of Jo's sisters, grabbed a chicken leg from his tray and gave him a cheeky grin as she hurried off.

"Oh, classy," Luna grumbled, eyeing the tray as he set it on one of the long bench tables. Unlike her sister, she didn't pounce on the chicken.

Outside there were multiple long fold-out tables with colorful tablecloths covering them, and a lot of festive string lights hung up in the trees similar to the ones he'd seen all over the city. It seemed they were in everyone's backyard.

"Don't even," Zephyr growled as Ivyn approached, hand outstretched. "Grab a plate."

Ivyn simply grinned, looking very much like the youngest brother he remembered from his youth. Many millennia ago. Seeing his face so relaxed, the way his eyes crinkled slightly at the corners from amusement, was a sucker punch. Zephyr had missed his brothers so damn much when he'd been stuck in that Hell realm. He'd never thought to see them again.

"You sound so much like Mom," Ivyn said, snickering.

Juniper strolled up then, a drink in hand, and snickered along with Ivyn. But she didn't say anything, just eyed the array of food with interest in her bicolor gaze.

The last two weeks had been both heaven and hell. He'd been working with her and her crew, hunting down leads that had all turned out to be dead ends. Or if not dead ends, the vampires they were hunting had gotten spooked and simply not shown up to the places they were supposed to.

Which was good and bad. Good because no humans were being taken. Bad because they'd simply move to another territory if they couldn't easily grab people here. And Zephyr wanted to stop them completely. Burn the entire operation to the ground. Literally.

There would be no prison for traffickers. They would all die—and serve as a warning to any other beings who would dare think of committing such atrocities in the future.

He enjoyed working with Juniper, but sleeping under the same roof as her, being surrounded by her wild scent, seeing her every day… He had new respect for his brothers and how long they'd waited to mate with their humans.

"I would like to make an Irish toast," Jo called out, Cas right next to her, a shadow who rarely left her side. "To our new friends; may your mornings bring joy and your evenings bring peace. May your troubles grow less as your blessings increase."

"Sláinte!" Grace held up her glass of wine.

Everyone else followed, including Juniper, who lifted her own glass and took a sip. He stared at her lips as she licked them clean, imagining her licking him instead. Anywhere she wanted.

"And thank you to Josephine for cooking all this food," Mikael added, lifting his own glass again toward the elder human female.

Which led to everyone else drinking again.

Then, everyone descended on the food like a pack of rabid animals. Zephyr wasn't immune either because everything smelled so damn good and they'd been eating junk for the last two weeks. Now he slightly regretted putting off Cas's invitation to come over here these last couple weeks. He and the others had been busy, yes, but he could have made time to come here.

He'd just been avoiding his brothers because of his own baggage. He knew that.

Now, looking at the chicken, cornbread and something called gumbo that he'd never had before—but couldn't wait to try—his mouth watered.

It was a free-for-all of grabbing food, and he waited until Juniper got her plate filled then sat next to her. Because yep, he was just as bad as his brothers. He wanted to guard her always. Scare away any other males who might come sniffing around. Luckily the males on her crew were like brothers to her. Family. And, he liked the guys.

"You sure you got enough there?" Juniper eyed his plate and the almost overflowing bowl next to it, eyebrows raised.

"I would not want to insult our hostess."

She snorted, but her mouth curved up slightly at the corners as she shook her head. Getting her to laugh or even smile had fast become a favorite pastime of his. She'd loosened up slightly over the last couple weeks, but she still had all sorts of walls between them.

He planned to tear each one down.

Everyone talked quietly among themselves as they ate, but he noticed that Juniper was simply eating. And watching. She did that a lot, just watched people—covertly—as if she was memorizing everything. He imagined it made her good at her job.

But now, as she popped a piece of cornbread in her mouth, he saw something flicker in her eyes as she observed Josephine talking to two of her granddaughters, laughing at something one of them said. Clearing her throat, she murmured, "Be right back."

Zephyr frowned as she headed into the house and glanced over at Ren, who'd been staring at Grace. He shrugged at Zephyr and went back to stealthily watching Jo's sister.

Zephyr's frown deepened until Griffin caught his attention. Griffin jerked his chin at him, then nodded toward the house, silently telling him to follow Juniper.

Oh. Zephyr stood and hurried after her.

He followed her scent all the way through the house and out the front door to find her sitting on the swinging bench on the front veranda. "Everything okay?" he asked as he sat next to her, the wooden slats creaking under his weight.

She lifted a shoulder, took a drink of the vodka she'd brought with her.

He let his head roll back. The air was crisp, cold, rolling over him. There were a few neighbors who'd had the same idea as them, and he could hear the various people laughing and eating together in their backyards. A very good thing.

"You can go back. I don't need a nanny," she grumbled.

He wasn't sure what a nanny was, but could infer the intent. "I don't want to be your nanny. But I do want to be your friend." And a lot more. Although she seemed to need a friend right now.

She shoved out a sigh and stretched out her gloriously long legs next to him, effectively making the swing stop. "Just feeling edgy right now. I want to catch these vamps. And this...whole scene, just reminds me of home. That's all."

She'd told him that she'd been abandoned, but she'd also told him that she'd been adopted by a wolf pack. One she loved. "Is that good or bad?"

"Both. I don't know, I've been thinking of my parents lately, missing them."

"How long has it been since you've seen them?"

An extended pause stretched out before she cleared her throat. "Ten months." She ran a hand over her navy blue bandana, something she always seemed to wear. He'd seen peeks of what he thought was blonde hair beneath it, but couldn't be sure. Her eyebrows were an almost silver color, but her eyelashes were brown so that didn't help him either.

"Is that normal?"

"No. But we've been busy since The Fall. Cleaning up a lot of shit. And they've been busy too. But I miss them." She sighed then, something so heavy filling the air he could almost feel it pressing against his skin. He hated seeing her lonely, missing her family.

"Call them. Go visit them after this job."

"I will." She closed her eyes, let her head fall back.

He traced his gaze over the long column of her throat, forced back thoughts of what it would be like to run his nose and teeth over that sensitive skin.

"I was a half-feral thing when they took me in," she said into the quiet, surprising him.

Zephyr stilled, wanting to hear everything she had to say. He wanted to know everything possible about this female.

"But they never gave up on me. They even left their pack because their Alpha had a problem with me. Ren and Griff—and Griff's dad— came too. We joined a new pack, one I actually like. But I still got into trouble." She opened her eyes, looked right at him.

"You were a teen. Teenagers do dumb stuff." Whether human or supernatural, it was like a rite of passage. Just one of those things. He had been a very foolish youth himself.

She gave him a wry smile. "I burned down a barn once by accident. I didn't mean to, had been flying too fast, showing off like a jackass and…" She shook her head and looked away, out into the quiet neighborhood. "I thought for sure they'd kick me out then. I mean, I knew it was coming. I'd convinced myself of it. They didn't, of course. But…" She blew out a breath and stood suddenly, a mask falling into place. "Sorry, didn't mean to dump on you. You're a sneakily good listener." There was almost an accusatory note in her voice.

"You can talk to me any time." He would always be there for her.

She simply gave him a jerky nod, then gave him her back as she stalked inside.

He followed her, drinking in all her long, lean lines that jeans and a T-shirt couldn't hide. Her long hair was covered in the same navy blue material as the bandana over her head, sort of wrapped around it. But his gaze was snagged by the most perfect ass in the world.

He also realized that he was going to need to take a different approach with her. Dragon females weren't like human females, but Juniper hadn't grown up around dragons. And it was clear that she needed him to be more straightforward in courting her.

She was going to expect him to give up, to walk away when things got tough. That much was obvious.

He needed to make his intentions clearer. Keep her on her toes. Break down her walls—show her just how amazing she was.

And how incredible they would be together.

CHAPTER FIVE

R en slid onto the bench seat next to Griffin, nudged him in the shoulder. "What was that?" Because he'd seen Griff wordlessly tell Zephyr to follow after Juniper.

Griff shrugged, wiped his hands on his napkin.

"Gonna need an audible response, Griff." Ren loved Griffin like a brother; they'd grown up together in the same house. But when the male did not want to talk, he simply didn't. Which was pretty much ninety-five percent of the time.

Another shrug. "I like him."

Ren didn't need Griffin to clarify who he meant.

Zephyr had been with them for only a couple weeks, and Griffin had said like five words to the guy. So he was at his entire quota of words for the year. "I do too," Ren murmured, surprised. He'd never thought he would like anyone enough to hope that they would mate with Juniper.

Because he loved Juniper like a sister. Blood didn't matter where they were concerned. She was his family.

"You think he's tough enough to hold on to her?" Ren asked. The party was going on around them, people having gathered together in groups of two and three as they talked and laughed. He liked Zephyr's brothers, liked this whole group of people. And he really liked the way Grace smiled. Sexy, alluring... He sighed.

"Maybe. Quit staring at that human," Griffin said under his breath.

"Can't help it. She smells good."

"Yeah, well, she's Zephyr's sister-in-law, so cut it out."

"I'm just looking," he muttered.

"Last time you 'looked' like that, you almost got your heart cut out."

Ren winced—because Griffin was being literal. He rubbed his chest absently even though the scar had healed and the physical pain was long gone.

"Doesn't look like Juniper bit his head off, so there's that," Griffin said as Juniper and Zephyr stepped onto the back patio. Then Griffin got a mischievous look on his face, a rarity for the wolf.

Oh no. "What's that look for?" Ren kept his voice almost subvocal. Whenever Griffin got that expression, *things* usually happened.

"Hey June bug, grab me a beer, will you?" Griffin called out.

Surprise flickering in her eyes, Juniper turned to glare at him. Ren covered his face. She *hated* that nickname and now Griffin had announced it to everyone. He dropped his hands just in time to see a bottle of beer flying straight at Griffin's face.

Ren grinned slightly as Griff caught it midair and saluted Juniper. He was so going to pay for that later.

His gaze immediately went back to the soft, curvy human, Grace. She'd barely noticed him, which definitely rankled. Ren wasn't full of himself or anything but he never wanted for female attention. Yet to her, he might as well be invisible.

He watched as she suddenly kissed her grandmother on the cheek and then said something to her sisters.

And he definitely heard the word *date*.

Frowning, he moved around the table, ignoring Juniper as she stomped over to Griffin, grumbling at him. Instead, Ren quietly made his way closer to the human sisters under the guise of grabbing another beer. It had been brewed at a local place that was still open, still flourishing.

"So who is this male you're going on a date with?" Cas asked, arms crossed over his chest.

Grace lifted an eyebrow as she looked at him. "Excuse me?"

"Yes, who is he?" Suddenly Mikael and Ivyn were there as well. Then Zephyr fell in line with them, frowning down at her.

She blinked in surprise and laughed lightly as she looked at Jo. "Apparently we signed up to have an army of big brothers when *you* mated a dragon?"

Jo gently nudged Cas. "Leave her alone. She's free to date who she pleases."

The males grumbled and Ren found himself annoyed that they weren't demanding more information. Dragon males were *known* for being over-the-top and obnoxious, and now these four chose to pull back? What was wrong with them? They should be demanding details.

"Ask her where she's going," Ren murmured as he slid up to Zephyr.

Zephyr shot him a surprised look—but he actually did what Ren said and strode over to Grace.

"I can't really tell you why we are working in the city right now," Zephyr said quietly to Grace. "But I can tell you that it has to do with humans potentially going missing. So would you please let me know where you're going to be tonight?" He was all polite about it which made Grace smile indulgently at the male.

And Ren felt that smile like a sucker punch right to his sternum. He wished it had been directed at him. Wanted it all to himself. Her smile lit up the entire backyard. Hell, the block. The whole territory. This female was stunning. Her auburn hair was pulled up into a pony-tail, showing off her big green eyes and smile. *That smile.* It would be his downfall, he was certain. She was petite and curvy, but her diminutive stature didn't do anything to negate her vivid presence.

"Fine." She huffed out a laugh. "I'll write down the address if it'll make you feel better. It's just a bar. He's a vampire and it's totally not a big deal. We're just having drinks. The place will be filled with tons of other people."

Zephyr's shoulders stiffened slightly at the word vampire, but he nodded at her, all polite charm. "Of course. Just humor me and my brothers. Or one of them is likely to follow you."

She snorted slightly and promised she would write down everything for Jo.

"Are you following your human?" Griffin asked as he slid up to Ren, whisper quiet.

Damn wolf was almost as quiet as Ren. Hell, quieter, his jaguar half grudgingly admitted. "Maybe."

"Not tonight. I just got a tip," Juniper said as she moved up next to them. She punched Griffin in the shoulder once for the beer bottle incident.

He just grinned at her because the wolf had a death wish apparently.

Ren cracked his knuckles once. He was intrigued by Grace, hated the thought of her with another male, but he was glad for the tip. It was time to get to work, to hunt down these bastards and stop them for good.

CHAPTER SIX

"You guys know the drill," Juniper murmured to her crew—which now included Zephyr, at least for the moment—as they approached the entrance to the private vampire club. She wasn't sure how she felt about him being there.

Okay, that was a big fat lie. She liked it waaaay too much. Liked *him* too much. He was kind and a good listener and that was dangerous. He was sucking her in with his deep, intoxicating voice and big gray eyes that threatened to drown her. And his scent? Oh, she wanted to bathe in it. Not to mention she'd seen the male fighting off demons so she knew he was capable. And she was constantly remembering how gorgeous he'd looked naked. *Ugh.*

She couldn't believe she'd opened up to him before, had started to tell him about her past as she felt all sorry for herself. Goddess, she needed to get it together. She sloughed off all thoughts of the past and mentally steeled herself as a vampire opened the plain white door to the three-story brick building for them. The male inhaled slightly, then simply nodded at them, scenting that they were all supernatural and let them in, easy as that.

She hated places like this. Crammed full of people, and the music was always too loud for her sensitive dragon ears—but this was part of the job. And she was good at it. But she'd much rather infiltrate a place in the dead of night when everything was still and quiet.

The entryway opened up into a small foyer and then stairs heading downward into a small hallway beckoned them. The walls along the stairs were brick-lined with black-and-white prints of people in various states of nudity and sexual acts.

At the end of the stairs, another door opened up into a huge space with purple lights overhead and a whole lot of supernatural beings. People were dancing, grinding on each other, drinking at the many bars. The same color lined the underside of the three bars —one for each wall. Because of her extrasensory abilities, she blinked at the flashing lights and attempted to mute out all the scents of sex and perfumes. The ceiling had been removed to combine the space with the floor above so it was wide-open and likely thirty feet up. No windows of course, but everything felt bigger than it likely was. Chains hung from the ceiling above, suspending giant gilded cages where males and females were dancing erotically.

To the left of them was a VIP area roped off and hidden by thick, heavy curtains. Ren headed in that direction—the male never had any problem charming anyone, into anything. The feline had a gift, and Juniper had no doubt he'd be invited into the VIP section in the next couple minutes.

Griffin split off from them as well, moving toward the bar on the far end of the room. He bled into the crowd immediately, almost disappearing from sight.

Zephyr made his way to the bar on the left, the one that backed up to the VIP room, but wasn't part of it. People made way for him whether they realized it or not.

Juniper headed for the bar on the right and murmured, "You'd love this place, Hyacinth."

"Ugh. Don't rub it in," Hyacinth grumbled through the earpiece.

Hyacinth was the lookout for this job. She was currently standing outside across the street, smoking a cigarette and pretending as if she was waiting for someone.

Juniper felt a little bad because Hyacinth hated cigarettes, but this was all part of their cover.

She made her way to the nearest bar, ignoring a couple of the inviting looks from a table of scantily clad female vampires.

Her target was a male and she had a good idea what he looked like —he had a tattoo on his neck that would hopefully be visible. Dark hair, dark eyes, likely a dark soul. And he apparently liked to wear gloves. Not much to go on, but it was something.

As she approached the bar, a male stepped up next to her, flashing his fangs at her.

"What's your poison?" the vampire behind the bar asked, his voice monotone, as if he wanted to be anywhere but here.

Yeah, you and me both, buddy. Juniper ignored the male next to her and answered the bartender. "Double vodka," she said, adopting a Russian accent. When they were undercover, they always took on roles—and occasionally they used magic to conceal their appearances if their covers had been blown. "Chilled," she added as she glanced in the mirror above the bar. It was surrounded by purple lights as well.

"I'm Jedediah," the male next to her said.

"And I'm not interested." She didn't bother to look at him as the bartender slid her a drink. But she noticed that the bartender's mouth curved up slightly in amusement.

"Thanks." She turned around without paying—they'd already been informed that no payment was expected here. This club was all about hedonism and they welcomed humans and shifters here for their blood—and other things.

"Is this your first time in here?" Jedediah asked, clearly not deterred by her rejection.

She took a sip of the vodka, savored the coldness.

Zephyr was at the opposite bar from her, smiling down at a petite female with blonde curly hair who looked ridiculously innocent. She had on a cream-colored bustier, dark jeans and looked...adorable. Like the kind of female who needed to be protected.

Juniper frowned. Did Zephyr like cute and adorable? Her dragon snarled, slashed at the idea that he was flirting with that female. She shoved her beast back down, annoyed that this was happening at all. She was always in control of her dragon and this…was a simple annoyance. That was all, she decided. She wasn't *jealous*. He was just doing his job, blending in.

As much as the giant sexy god *could* blend in.

"Are you originally from the territory?" The male vamp scooted a couple inches closer. She glanced at him, and her dragon must have been in her eyes because he took a step back and held his palms up. "Sorry, I'll leave you alone."

She simply looked away without responding. Taking another sip, she scanned the bar, looking for this elusive male. She saw a couple females with neck tattoos. But no males. She needed to actually walk some laps and get up close with people. *Blech.*

She couldn't see Griffin, but that was no surprise. The male was like a ghost. Ren had gotten into the VIP section so they were good there. And Zephyr wasn't talking to the female anymore. She hated that she was relieved by that.

Juniper was ready to grab another drink and then head into the crowd when a tall, slender female slid up to the bar. She recognized the female from a photograph in their file on the territory and decided to stay for the moment. This was Ingrid, a powerhouse in the territory.

"Another for me and another for my new friend." The gorgeous vampire's voice was silky smooth. "You're definitely new here," the vampire with long, caramel-colored hair said as she picked up what was definitely vodka and handed the other glass to Juniper.

She set her empty tumbler down and took the other one. "Thanks," she murmured, not bothering to look at the female. She knew this female was interested in her, could scent it even over all the other scents. And ignoring someone this powerful was sure to garner more interest.

"So what are you here for?" the vampire asked, leaning against the bar. She had on a dark green turtleneck, long black slacks and spiked heels. "Because I know it's not for sex."

Juniper shot a surprised glance at Ingrid, leader of the Cheval coven. Not the strongest vampire in the city, but she was still a power nonetheless. According to the file Juniper had on her, she was originally from Portugal, over two hundred years old, and could be ruthless. She was also a good coven leader, respected by her people.

Oddly enough, Juniper couldn't get a gauge on Ingrid's power level. Maybe the female was muting it. Because some supernatural beings of a certain age could do that, and it was a very handy trick when you didn't want someone to know how powerful you truly were.

Juniper tried to mute hers, but knew it leaked out anyway. It was one of those things that happened to dragons. It was like the energy and power simply couldn't be contained in their human forms. It was why she had to release her magical chains every so often even when she wasn't working. She'd never met another dragon like her, and unfortunately August had absolutely no idea what to do about those powers. He'd never heard of another dragon having the ability either.

"Just looking for a friend," Juniper murmured.

The female gave a soft snort. "A friend or foe?"

Juniper glanced at the female again, surprised at the bluntness. "Who are you?" She knew, but wanted to see how honest this female was.

"Ingrid. I run one of the covens here."

Juniper had contemplated asking King to reach out to the coven leaders in his territory about the vampire they were searching for, but she needed to keep knowledge of their presence in the city very limited. They weren't sure who the vampire they wanted worked for and she didn't want to risk anyone inadvertently mentioning them and spooking the guy.

"I recognize your name. I'm new in town and here with some friends. But if I'm being honest, I am looking for someone who owes me. He took something that doesn't belong to him." She mixed truth and lies because the vampire she was after *had* taken something that didn't belong to him. Juniper planned to find anyone he'd taken and save them. *If* they could be saved. She shoved her beast back at the thought of anyone imprisoned right now because of the vampire named Ryan and his companions. His name was so common as well that she wondered if it was even real. Maybe it was a cover too.

"Is he a vampire?" Ingrid asked, her voice butter smooth.

Before responding, Juniper spotted Zephyr giving her a chin nod across the bar.

She suddenly heard a commotion from behind the VIP curtained-off area.

Then, "Oh, shit, we've got a runner," came Hyacinth's voice over their comm line. "Escaping out the side door!"

"I've got to go," she said to Ingrid. "But it was lovely to meet you."

Juniper set down her mostly full tumbler and rushed into the melee of people. She wasn't sure what was on her face, but people moved out of the way as she raced across a bar area and dance floor. The music didn't pause, however, the party still raging on.

Zephyr had already disappeared into the VIP area, just clocking the guy by the ropes who'd tried to stop him. That vampire male was now passed out on the floor.

Juniper jumped over his supine body. Inside, she took in the scene in seconds. Two tables were overturned. And a booth had been ripped out of the wall. *Holy shit.*

Ren was kneeling next to…Grace? What the hell was she doing here!

"Go! After him!" Ren shouted. "You're the fastest. I've got her."

Zephyr was by an exit door, holding it open, all the muscles in his body tense. She wanted to ask what had happened but it didn't matter. So she didn't pause, just shoved past a trio of vampires and sprinted toward Zephyr.

"This way. The underlying cedar scent is him," he said, sprinting down the alleyway in a north direction.

She inhaled deeply and followed, her legs eating up the distance. "I'm going to shift, go camouflaged." They were nearing the Quarter and it would be impossible for her to shift without drawing attention there. It didn't matter if supernaturals were out to the world, she wasn't going to go around shifting in a crowd unless she could help it.

"I'll stay on foot," he said as they reached the end of the alleyway.

Juniper heard footsteps racing their way, saw Griffin. He didn't say anything, just nodded and raced past as she jumped up onto a nearby wall lining the long alley. Another big wall was on one side of her and a huge oak tree on another. This was going to be a very tight shift and the clock was ticking.

She tossed her earpiece to Zephyr and called on her shift, letting only her wings extend even as her camouflage fell into place.

She hated partially shifting like this. But it was the only way right now with limited room. She raced forward a couple steps to gather energy and dove off the wall. Using a massive amount of energy, she flapped hard, shooting straight up into the sky. Her right wing barely brushed the wall before she breached the building top.

As soon as she did, she let her dragon take over completely, extended her wings fully and banked a hard right. That cedar scent was in the air, and now that she had it she wouldn't lose it.

Below her, Zephyr was on foot, racing at top speed down a cobblestone street. There were no vehicles on the street, but unfortunately this was one of the nights King had opened up the nightlife in the city.

The streets were teeming with people. Laughter filtered up, and as the streets grew narrower she flew a little higher. There were no other dragons that she could see and she really hoped no one else was in camo mode like her.

There were too many people down below on the cobblestone streets, walking, some riding bikes or even bike-pulled rickshaws which were becoming popular.

Hyacinth darted out from a side street wearing all black, her heels pounding against the pavement as she fell into step with Zephyr. Griff had long since disappeared but Juniper wasn't worried.

As she banked right and flew over Jackson Square, a cluster of scents assaulted her senses at once. Food, perfumes, so many people and— Cedar teased the air, just on the edges of everything else.

She flew straight over the enclosed park toward Chartres Street and made a hard right. The crowd thinned out as she angled east and that was when she spotted him.

A dark-haired male sprinting down the sidewalk. He threw a quick glance over his shoulder, and from her angle she could actually scent his fear. Whatever had happened in the VIP room definitely had him spooked enough to run from them.

A woman on a bike yelped in alarm as he ran across the next street in front of her without stopping. She toppled over and shouted a curse but he kept sprinting at top speed. Too bad for him it wasn't enough to escape a dragon.

For a moment he disappeared from sight as he ran under an awning. But seconds later, he reappeared. He slowed at the next crosswalk for a fraction of a moment and she realized he was heading for the nearby hotel. Five stories with whitewashed brick, and other buildings on either side of it. Every bit of real estate was used down here.

Shit.

She was going to have to shift to her human form now. Angling downward, she drew her wings in tight to fit between the buildings, let her magic overtake her and shifted to human.

Her camouflage fell as she slammed into the middle of the road, her boots making a thud.

Unfortunately, the male heard her descent. From twenty yards away, he turned, made eye contact—and she got a good view of the spider tattoo on his neck. His fear spiked as he caught sight of her.

"Make it easy on yourself!" she shouted as she raced at him, avoiding two stunned-looking humans on the sidewalk.

"Fuck you!" The male raced up the short set of steps and through the revolving glass door of the hotel.

She was very aware of people in the lobby—well-dressed in sparkling dresses and tuxes, and some dudes were in kilts. *Oh hell.* There was some kind of party or event going on.

The vampire sprinted past a wolf who shouted in alarm. She recognized one of King's security. *Oh, double hell.* Zephyr had said something about allies from another territory visiting and she really, really hoped this wasn't where that was happening.

A couple shouts rose up behind her and she heard Zephyr's voice snapping at someone as she slammed open the door to the stairs, chasing the vampire.

"This isn't worth it!" she shouted even as she practically flew up the stairs after him. "You're outnumbered and the place is locked down." Okay, not true, but whatever.

She heard a door upstairs bang open, then slam shut. But...then she heard a soft whisper of noise. Oh, this guy was crafty. At the third floor, she eased around the platform and—jerked back.

Two bullets slammed into the wall feet from her head. *A gun, really?*

Oh, he was going to pay for that.

Footsteps pounded up the stairs again and she gave chase. As she reached the top floor, she called back to Hyacinth and Zephyr, who couldn't be far behind.

Down the hallway, the male shoved open a door, likely to a guest room. Oh goddess, she couldn't let him hurt someone.

Heart pounding, adrenaline surging, she practically flew after him. Inside the bedroom, he stood by the window, dark eyes wide, panic in every line of his face.

He lifted his gun and she reacted on instinct, releasing one of her magical chains. It slammed into his wrist and she felt the vibration of his bone breaking along her chain even before she heard the distinctive crack of it.

He screamed as the gun fell from his fingertips and...then he dove out the window.

Why did these guys always have to make life so damn difficult? Why couldn't one of them just surrender without running?

Gritting her teeth, she raced forward and dove after him. Immediately she realized her mistake even as she let her wings extend and unfurl. There was a huge pool below and a shit ton of string lights throughout the trees.

The vamp slammed through a bundle of them, screaming as he hit the hard brick courtyard—where a very fancy party was most definitely happening. Oh hell, there was King and his mate, Aurora. The Alpha couple of New Orleans.

So much for her having a low-key presence in their territory!

Shouts of alarm rose up as she descended, curling her wings to slow her descent.

But it was no use. One got caught in one of the sturdy string lights and she lost control, slammed into an oak hard before she landed right on the brick—and her arm snapped under the impact.

Pain lanced through her, but she fought it back as she shoved to her feet. *Fuuuck.* She couldn't even lift that arm.

"Stop!" King ordered some of his wolves as they started to move in on her and the vampire.

Juniper reacted on instinct as the vampire went to grab a dagger. It looked as if he was about to stab himself.

Oh, hell no. He wasn't getting away this easy. She snapped out her good arm, let her chain free and wrapped it around him three times before he could even move.

He screamed in agony as she tightened her grip, the chains squeezing his middle, the dagger falling from his grip.

"I told you to give up," she snarled, then winced at the pain hazing her vision, her broken arm hanging limply at her side.

Multiple voices raised in alarm among the shocked gasps, but King ordered everyone back as he and Aurora rushed up to them—and oh yeah, they were super fancy. He had on a tux and Aurora was all sparkles and light.

"I'm sorry," she wheezed out as another blast of pain surged through her. Maybe she'd broken her arm in two places? Yeah, she totally had. Upper and lower.

Aurora just stared at her, eyes wide as they dropped to her limp arm. "How can I help you?"

"I'm fine, this will heal in no time." She managed to keep her voice steady even as Zephyr dropped down from a tree only a few feet from her and Hyacinth made her way through a crowd of wolves and other supernatural beings. Griff hung back, clearly waiting for her order, nodding once at her.

"This is one of the people from your investigation, I take it?" King stood in front of her, his expression opaque even as he glanced at her limp arm.

"Yeah. We need to question him."

"You need a healer," Zephyr snarled, rage in his voice as he hovered next to her.

She couldn't look at him, couldn't focus on anything right now as another pulse of agony ripped through her. "I'm fine—"

"Ace, escort this vampire to holding," King snapped out without taking his eyes off Juniper. "He's on suicide watch."

Juniper loosened the chains, pulled them back in, and the relief at not having to expend so much magical energy eased some of the pain in her injured arm. "Look, I don't need a healer. This will heal and—"

"You're going to a healer—" Zephyr started.

"Stop it," Aurora snapped out, power in those two words. "You will go to a healer right now." She stepped closer, her eyes glowing a pale violet as she dropped her voice low. "Greer has some of my blood in storage and you may use it to heal yourself. I can see your bone," she hissed out.

Oh. Juniper didn't dare look down at it. Because the longer she stood there, a wave of nausea swept through her. So it had to be bad. She finally turned to Zephyr. "Go with the vampire—"

"I'm going with you." Muted rage and worry sparked in his gray eyes. "Hyacinth and Griff can go with the vamp."

"I have a vehicle on standby to take you," King said before he nodded at one of his wolves. "Greer will be expecting you. Once you're healed, you can see your captive."

"Thank you. And…I'm sorry about the mess." She winced slightly at the glass from the lights littering everything around them. Then she had to close her eyes because oh boy, she was going to puke.

Zephyr scooped her up from her good side, careful of her injured arm, before King could say a word. Under normal circumstances, she wouldn't have let anyone carry her.

But right now…oh goddess.

"I can't believe you jumped out that goddamn window," he snarled as he stepped out the front doors of the hotel and it was just the two of them. "Once you're healed, I'm going to shake some sense into you."

"Wait, you're mad at *me?*" She'd thought he was just pissed at the vampire. "I didn't know about the damn lights. I would've been able to make that jump without them." Hell, if there hadn't been so many people below, she could have just blasted them away with her fire. She hadn't wanted to risk that, however.

In response, his jaw tightened as a wolf drove up in a Jeep. He eased her into the front seat before he jumped into the back. "Be mindful of her injuries," Zephyr snapped at the wolf.

"I'll try to drive as slow as possible," the male driving said. He looked familiar but she couldn't place his name.

"Thanks," she murmured, clutching onto the side bar and breathing through the pain, the hand of her injured arm lying limp in her lap. Blood was starting to pool so...yeah, this was definitely a compound fracture.

The vampire was in custody, and even though she wasn't getting to question him right now, they had him.

It made the broken bones all worth it.

CHAPTER SEVEN

Starlena controlled her heartbeat so it remained steady as she approached the Alpha of New Orleans and his mate. She smiled politely at the couple, giving away none of her emotions.

Before she could speak, King said, "Apologies for the interruption."

"It is nothing. I'm not feeling well so I'm going to retire." She was ancient and was used to simply disappearing from gatherings when she felt like it. Her dragon clan was accustomed to her behavior, but she and her people had come here for a specific purpose. And that purpose had just revealed itself far more quickly than she had imagined.

"Of course. It's been a pleasure talking with you tonight." Aurora, the Alpha female of this territory, glowed as she spoke, her smile genuine.

Starlena found that she liked the young phoenix. "We will reach out tomorrow," she said before turning in the direction the large male dragon had carried the female with the broken arm.

"What do we do?" Cosmo asked the moment he and Starlena stepped out into the street.

She shot him a sharp look. Perhaps he had lost his mind. Anyone could overhear them.

"Right," he murmured.

Energy buzzed through Starlena even as they crossed the street away from the brick hotel with more character in it than much of the "modern" buildings she'd seen. The three others from their clan she had brought with them headed in a different direction, back to where they were staying. But Starlena would be tailing that female with the broken arm.

"We're following, yes?" Cosmo asked once they reached Jackson Square. She'd studied this place before they'd arrived, but the pictures could not give an accurate depiction of the scents and sounds.

The square was loud with people out partying, some putting on street shows. She ignored them all, her steps brisk. "Of course we are." The female's scent was a wild one and...one Starlena recognized. One she would know anywhere.

"Should I contact—"

Starlena shot him another look, this one darker. "Not until we know for sure." They could do *nothing* until they knew for certain that the girl was...who Starlena suspected.

A thought that was difficult to hope for, to even imagine after all these turns of the planet.

But those enchanted shackles the female had displayed...they were of Starlena's line. She just wished she'd been able to see her face, but the female had been turned away from them the whole time. "Did you get a picture?" she asked Cosmo finally as they moved onto a quiet street, leaving the melee of the Quarter behind.

"I did. And a short video. I did not want to be obvious, so it's not long."

Starlena sniffed once. *Good.* The male did have some uses. She was unused to human technology but many of the younger dragons of her clan had been crossing over to the human realm for ages. They learned as much as they could about this realm and brought back knowledge of it. Starlena could do without most of it, however.

It was easy to follow the other dragons' scents, even on foot. She and Cosmo moved at a fast pace but did not run—she didn't want to draw any unnecessary attention to themselves. Which was why she chose not to shift.

Twenty minutes later they found themselves outside a huge home she believed was Victorian-style. Though there was much she did not know about this realm, she recognized the style of the elegant manor. And considering the conversation she'd overheard between King and the injured female, this must be the healing center.

"Should we go inside?" Cosmo asked as they stopped across the street.

Starlena bit back a sigh as she questioned her choice of bringing Cosmo with her on this trip. He asked far too many questions. And, okay, he was young, inexperienced, and she was being cranky. She simply looked at him, raised an eyebrow. She wanted to send him away, but he knew too much about humans and this realm, and might be useful.

He grumbled and shoved his hands into his pants pockets. "I'm just trying to help."

"We wait," she said finally. "In silence." They would wait, then they would follow the female when she left.

Then...Starlena needed to figure out what to do. She needed to contact her daughter and tell her about the female, but it was far too soon for that.

Starlena had given up on hoping for impossible things long ago. She'd chosen Hibernation instead, only coming out of her long sleep a decade ago. Now...to be faced with the possibility of her long-ago lost granddaughter returning was almost too much.

No, Starlena would not give her daughter that hope if it wasn't true.

But if the girl with the broken arm was Starlena's granddaughter, then she was the long-missing princess of the Nova realm.

Which meant she was next in line to rule their people.

CHAPTER EIGHT

Zephyr was barely containing his protective instincts right now as he and Juniper left Greer's healing center.

"Are you sure she's okay?" Juniper asked into the phone.

Nope. Zephyr plucked it out of her hand as they walked out the front door of Greer's place. They'd been here for the last couple hours and Juniper was the worst patient. But her arm was as good as new and Greer had given her a sweater to borrow. Ignoring Juniper's protests, he held up the phone to his own ear. "Ren, it's me."

"Hey, Grace is fine. She's settled back at her house and Cas is going to be here all night." He paused. "I'm staying here too. How's Juniper?"

"Healed. Stubborn. Insane," he added, giving her a sharp look as she leaned against the column on the front porch. He leaned against the other column at the top of the short set of stairs and stared out into the yard and beyond. The street was quiet tonight, the few dogs barking in the distance the only real noise. "She jumped out of the fucking window. Five stories up." He knew Ren was already aware of what had happened, but he wanted to say it out loud. For Juniper's benefit. Because he was still pissed that she'd put herself in danger like that.

"Yeah, Griff told me. He's pissed. So's Hyacinth."

Zephyr gave Juniper a triumphant look. "See, it's not just me who's angry." She gave a haughty sniff and looked away from him, staring out at the well-lit, lush yard. "She has no sense of self-care."

"You're telling me," Ren grumbled. "I could tell you some of the situations she's run into headfirst without—"

"Hey," Juniper snapped, clearly hearing the other end of the conversation. "Tell Ren that's enough. If he's telling stories, so will I."

"Fine, fine," Ren said. "Just take care of her ass or her parents will have my head."

"I will." Because Zephyr cared for the female who apparently had a death wish. She'd broken her arm at the elbow joint and in two other places. The fact that she'd been talking and standing afterward was a testament to her strength. If she'd been human...well, she'd be dead. Or likely so after jumping out of the window. At that thought, his dragon saw red. He had to shove his beast back down.

Juniper grabbed her phone from him, hung up, then pulled up another screen. "I'm heading to meet Christian. You can come if you promise not to ride my ass about this."

The words "ride my ass" had him straightening to attention. He would love to ride her, love for her to ride him. Would love *so* many things with her. He stilled and he knew his dragon was in his gaze as he looked at her again.

She narrowed her bicolor eyes at him. "Goddess save me from males," she muttered before stalking down the short set of stairs. "What did Hyacinth say, because I know you talked to her too when I was in with Greer."

He fell in step with her, his anger at watching her dive right out that damn window into the unknown still buzzing through him. It mixed with an odd sense of fear. Something he was unused to experiencing. He knew Juniper was a dragon, could take care of herself. But the courtyard area with all the trees and the pool had been too small. She should have climbed down the building like he had done. "She's waiting outside the vamp's room, hoping he'll wake up."

"I can't believe that cowardly bastard took a poison pill." Juniper's expression was dark as they stepped out onto the sidewalk. "I should have been there, not at the healer's," she grumbled.

"Sure, because you would have been able to stop him from taking a poison pill hidden in one of his teeth."

She sniffed imperiously.

Most of the homes they passed were double and single shotgun-style homes, with the occasional cottage. And many houses had Irish flags hanging outside. Things he only knew because Avery had taken him on a tour of the city and she was always talking about construction and architecture styles. Greer's healing center was one of the few large homes in the area on a very wide lot.

As they headed down the street, he didn't think they were alone. Behind them he scented someone, but it was so faint, he wasn't sure if he was correct.

"Whoever he works for will be violent and sneaky," Zephyr murmured. The vampire would rather die than be questioned and face the wrath of his boss, Zephyr guessed. "He'll wake up." King had exceptional healers in his pack and they were working hard right now to make sure the vampire didn't slip into death. Which was way better than he deserved. He shouldn't get to just fade away. No, he needed to pay for his crimes.

Juniper simply grumbled a response, clearly still annoyed the vamp had gotten the best of them. She started to say something, but Zephyr caught her eye, touched his nose subtly once.

She blinked at him, then seemed to take a mental pause even as she kept walking, her strides even. She gave him a subtle nod that she smelled whoever was behind them as well. Pulling out her phone, she texted…*him*, Zephyr realized.

He pulled out his phone and read her message. *At the next crosswalk, you go left, I'll go right. We both shift and take to the air. Camo mode, fly to the lake, dive in. We wait half an hour. Then we head to Christian's.*

He nodded as he read—he'd been learning to read English since he'd escaped the Hell realm, and some things were still a struggle. Thankfully this was succinct. He'd have to hide his stuff in a cache and text one of his brothers to come get it but this was a good plan.

As soon as they reached the crosswalk, she sprinted right and then disappeared from sight. It was still strange to him how she could camouflage her entire being even with clothing. More than that, he hated being away from her, letting Juniper out of his sight at all. And he hated that he would miss getting to see her shift—she was as stunning in dragon form as she was in human. Her scales were a shimmering whitish gray that sparkled under the sunlight or moonlight.

Following her instructions, he raced to the left, stripping his clothes as he ran. If they were being followed, they would have to act fast and disappear quickly. After a text to his brother—and a catcall from an unknown source, likely at his nakedness—he raced into a quiet, darkened park and tucked his stuff away.

Then he shifted, called on his camouflage, and took to the air.

He needed to get to Juniper as soon as possible. It was clear that she didn't take good enough care of herself—so he would be there to have her back.

CHAPTER NINE

"Behave," Juniper muttered to Zephyr as they strode up to the back door of Christian's mansion. It had taken an hour overall before she was sure they'd lost their tail. Only then had she and Zephyr felt it was safe enough to come here. And she didn't want Zephyr acting like a possessive dragon in front of her friend.

Her friend who was still mourning his dead mate centuries later. It broke her heart that Christian hadn't moved on, couldn't seem to heal his fractured heart. She'd never known him "before," just the Christian he was now—a male who carried his loneliness around like a comfortable old coat he didn't want to part with.

"I'm not the one who jumps out of five-story windows." His tone was dry.

She flicked a glance at him, and her breath caught in her throat as his gaze met hers. She hated that every time they made eye contact she felt the awareness of him like a punch to her senses. It was those gray eyes, they simply ensnared her.

And okay, his cock was on full display right now because unlike her, he couldn't shift with clothing. He'd had to leave everything behind to be picked up later.

He had no problem strutting around all naked either. He let every glorious inch hang out. And goddess, all. Those. Inches. She kept her gaze on his face instead of trailing downward, but when she did that she started wondering how his beard would feel if he went down on her. Would it tease her inner thighs, add to the pleasure? Or be an annoyance? No, she would like it, she was certain. She was pretty sure she'd like anything he did.

As they reached the huge wraparound porch, Christian stepped out the back door, a bundle of clothing in his hands. "These aren't mine, but they should fit you," he said to Zephyr upon greeting.

Then he smiled at Juniper and gave her a hug, she was pretty sure just to piss off Zephyr.

Because the male started growling. And boy, she should not like it. But she found that she did.

Soooo much. It was messed up, but she was messed up, so there you go. Stepping back, she shot Zephyr an annoyed glance, even as desire coiled tight in her core. Damn it, she had to lock this down. They were here for a job.

Zephyr ignored her look and pulled on the sweatpants that just barely fit him. The dark blue jogging-style pants were small, showcasing all his muscles. He held out the matching hoodie and then shook his head, handed it back to Christian. "Thank you, but I think this might be too snug."

Her dragon might as well have done a mental fist pump in the air of pure joy that he was going to keep that chest on full display. He was all carved up with scars, a testament to his strength, endurance. This male was a prime fighting machine and her dragon half wanted to curl around him, drink him in, bite that gorgeous ass.

"No problem," Christian said, motioning for them to step inside.

The place was a mix of modern and antique. Just as she remembered it from a couple years ago. One wall was all bookshelves, and what she was certain was an actual Persian rug covered the wood floors. Little figurines from different periods were on the bookshelves as well as the hundreds or maybe thousands of books.

"This is all for you." Christian motioned to the too-thin black binder on a small, marble-topped table as he sat on the chesterfield by the electric fireplace that wasn't giving off any warmth, just ambience. He picked it up, handed it to her. "I've been working my contacts hard the last couple weeks. I don't frequent clubs or bars anymore so I had to ease myself back into that scene." He sounded exhausted as he said it. "Being around those children makes me feel about a thousand years old."

"Instead of the five hundred plus you are?" She snickered slightly.

But it made Christian laugh. Just as quickly, he straightened, looked between the two of them. "I've organized everything for you and added notes, but from what I've gathered, there's a vampire who's established a small territory right where the border between Tennessee and Arkansas used to be. There's supposedly a door to a Hell realm there." Christian paused, his eyes narrowing slightly. "You already know this?"

"It's what we've heard. But it's good that this is what you heard too. It means we're on the right track. I want to hear everything." She would read the file he'd created later, but wanted his account of who he'd talked to.

Because they didn't know who this leader was. And there were only whispers of where the alleged Hell realm gate was.

"The vampires who work for...whoever they work for, are stealing humans and weaker shifters and trafficking them through the Hell realm door. For labor or sex or both, I don't know," Christian said. "And I don't know the actual location, just an area, and that area is vast."

She didn't know either, but it was mostly females and males who were in their early twenties going missing, so she could imagine what they were being kidnapped for. None of it good. "How many of their people are in New Orleans?"

"At least three. And from what I heard, you took someone down earlier this evening?"

Damn it. If Christian had already heard about what happened only a couple hours ago, then word would have spread all over by now. "People are talking about me by name?"

"Not you specifically. Just that a tall, gorgeous dragon female jumped out of a hotel window chasing a vampire." He shook his head slightly, frowned at her. "But no names. Still, there was a buzz in one of the more hedonistic clubs. The vampires there don't care for humans. Which is ironic. And daft. Since most of them used to be human."

"Is anyone who's part of this territory helping to traffic people?"

"Not that I know of. But they're not stopping it or reaching out to King about what they know either."

"Which is just as bad," Zephyr growled.

The male had been so quiet, so still, that while she hadn't forgotten he was there—that was an impossibility—the rage popping off him rippled through the air and startled her. And she agreed with his words.

"Agreed," Christian said, mirroring her thoughts. "I need a shower after being there the last few hours." He shrugged once, as if sloughing off the memory. "They might not know who you are, but there's a description of you going around." He looked at Zephyr. "Of you too."

"What about my crew? You hear anything about them?" Juniper asked.

"Not specifically. But a human and a feline shifter were mentioned in passing as being part of a 'drama' at Club Vibe that sparked things off."

That would be Ren and Grace. "Word really spread fast," she murmured. "What do you think of Ingrid of the Cheval coven?" Because she had been at that club earlier in the evening.

Christian paused, as if weighing his words. "As a vampire coven leader, she's excellent. She keeps her people in line easily. Her coven respects her. She prefers females as bed partners, but occasionally takes a male as a lover. Her weakness is that she can have blind spots where her current lovers are concerned. To my knowledge, that has only happened twice, but she made foolish mistakes by listening to the wrong people—lovers who lied to her. And she paid the price for it."

"Could she be involved?"

"I want to say no. I believe no. But…it is impossible to truly say. To truly know someone."

Zephyr snorted softly.

Christian turned, narrowed dark eyes at him. "What?"

"You *can* truly know people. Their hearts. Even if you don't know everything about them." He looked over at Juniper as he finished and she felt that look deep.

Too deep. Keeping her expression neutral, she turned back to Christian. "So she might not be involved, but could be looking the other way?"

"Anything is possible. My instinct is no, however. I don't think she knows. And before you ask, no, Claudine of the Bonavich coven is not involved."

Juniper hadn't planned to ask him that. Everything she'd learned about Claudine said the female would never allow any innocents to be harmed. Period. Didn't matter the species. But it was good to have it confirmed. "Even if she's not involved, do you think she's heard anything about this?"

"No. I had to fish around for this information and it was only given once certain vampires were high on intoxicated humans' blood." He gave a look of distaste. "All their names and information are in there." He nodded to the binder. "None of them are part of a coven."

"Will it come back on you if I hunt them down, question them?"

"Maybe, maybe not. I don't care if it does." He flashed fangs and power rippled off him in a subtle wave.

"Good." Juniper nodded and stood.

Zephyr followed suit. "Thank you for allowing us into your home," he said politely to Christian, then looked down at himself. "May I—"

"You can keep them." Christian's mouth curved up slightly.

"Thanks." Zephyr paused, then glanced at Juniper who gave him "a look" she hoped he understood.

He nodded politely at Christian, then headed out back, so yeah, he understood that she wanted a moment of privacy with Christian.

Once alone, she turned back to her old friend. "You're sure you won't suffer any fallout from telling us this information? I will never use your name, but—"

"Juniper." His quiet voice cut through her words. "I'm an old vampire. I'm not worried. And these vampires need to be stopped. There's no room in the world for evil like this. Whatever you need from me, I'm here." He sighed slightly. "I've been getting too complacent anyway. If you want to put me to work, need me to go undercover, let me know."

His words surprised her—Christian truly loved his solitude—but she nodded. "I might. Thank you." She clutched the binder to her, planning to dive into it soon.

"So…" His mouth curved up then, and for a moment he looked more like a feline than a vampire. "You and the big one?" He gave a chin nod.

She simply rolled her eyes. "Since when did you start gossiping?"

"Darling, that one is worth gossiping about, wouldn't you agree? He was quite lovely to look at all shirtless."

"Keep your eyes to yourself," she snapped before she could control herself. Then groaned at the grin he gave her. "I think I hit my head when I fell out that window," she muttered.

"Whatever you need to tell yourself."

Rolling her eyes again, she kissed him on the cheek and headed out, meeting Zephyr on the back porch. And he had a smug sort of look about him, as if he'd heard her words.

Ugh. He probably had. Damn it, she simply needed to scratch this itch, to get naked with him, and to get him out of her system. That was it. She'd gone too long without sex.

That. Was. It.

"Want to go to Cynara's club for an hour?" Most of the levels at her club were loud and obnoxious, but the place had a rooftop bar that was supernaturals-only and she could review this file and drink. Maybe she could drink enough to forget this burning hunger she had for Zephyr.

One that was growing by the second. When he'd gone all caveman dragon and carried her out of the hotel, something inside her had shifted. And it scared the hell out of her. No one but her parents took care of her. That was it.

And even then, she kept them at an arm's length. Always had.

Zephyr scared her on a fundamental level. Because she had a feeling he could break her heart. Just completely shatter it if she let him in.

"Sure." His gray eyes flared with heat as he watched her with a primal intensity she felt all the way to her marrow.

And she had absolutely no doubt that if she asked him to get naked with her right then and there, he would.

CHAPTER TEN

"What's wrong?" Zephyr asked, watching Juniper intently across the high tabletop on the rooftop bar.

"What's *not* wrong?" She shut the binder she'd been poring over. Even as she'd read over everything, she still hadn't been able to tune out Zephyr's presence.

He was still wearing those ridiculous jogging pants but it didn't matter one bit. They'd been admitted to the supernaturals-only rooftop bar and he'd received more "come fuck me" looks than she wanted to think about. Her dragon side was *not* happy about that.

"If there's nothing we can use tonight, let's head out. We can regroup in a few hours." He leaned back slightly, rolled his shoulders once.

She realized it was already close to three in the morning. Yeah, they should head back to the house they were staying at as their base of operations.

They really, really should. But she was too keyed up, too edgy—wanted Zephyr too much. She needed to get him out of her system. Needed to get this weird hunger for him slaked and then she'd be okay. And given the hungry looks he'd been shooting her way, she had a feeling he wouldn't turn her down. "I heard this place has private rooms?"

He blinked those gorgeous gray eyes at her. "Uh, I think so. I've never been in one before."

"Want to grab one?" She couldn't hide the heat in her eyes and didn't want to. She'd seen the way he looked at her, witnessed all his scorching lust—it mirrored her own. And she wasn't going to fight this anymore. It was stupid to. They were both adults, both older dragons. They could just enjoy each other sexually and then maybe she could get her brain to work again.

He blinked again, then his dragon flared to life in his gaze. "Hold on." He slid off his stool and weaved his way through the other table-tops that were mostly empty now before he disappeared behind a steel door that led inside.

With him gone, everything seemed quieter, muted. Except the need in her body—heat coursed through her, a simmering desire that was growing with each second that passed. Especially now that he'd gone to get a room for them.

Even the street below had thinned out, with minimal noise filtering up. An icy breeze rolled over her, making some of the Edison lights and the striped umbrellas shift slightly with the wind. Nothing could cool her down though.

Not now, as anticipation buzzed through her.

Mere moments later, the door practically slammed open before he reached her table in the blink of an eye. "Got us a room."

She couldn't help the grin that spread across her face. "That was impressively fast."

"Nothing else about tonight will be fast." His words were a deep, sexy rumble as he grabbed her hand and tugged her with him.

And ooooh sweet goddess, everything inside her clenched. Tight. She couldn't find her voice in that moment, simply followed after him, hoping he made good on that promise. Normally she didn't like anyone to take over, but she didn't mind him taking the lead now, practically shoving people out of the way.

Juniper was vaguely aware of clubgoers around them as they

hurried through the open dance floor inside toward another steel door. Zephyr opened it as if he knew where he was going.

"You've never been in one of these?" she demanded as the door shut behind them. He said he hadn't, but he sure seemed to know his way around. For some reason, that bothered her.

It was just the two of them in a long hallway filled with closed doors. He glanced over his shoulder as he slid an old-fashioned key into a lock. "No, but Cynara gave me a key. She said tonight's on the house. I have used this hallway to exit before," he said as he pushed the door open. "Which is why I know my way around here."

Juniper stared at the plush room. Lots of lavenders and darker rich purples for the bedding and so many flickering candles on glass surfaces. Not to mention soft, relaxing music was being pumped in from somewhere.

She took it all in before her gaze landed on Zephyr, who'd already shut and locked the door behind them.

The plethora of candles on the tiered shelving behind the bed were a nice touch, and she was impressed they were there at all. Likely they'd been lit with magic. Not that she cared. No, she was only concerned with one thing.

Zephyr. Who was watching her with hungry gray eyes that seemed to see right through to all her wants and needs. The male was ridiculously ripped, his arms and chest cut from granite.

Her gaze dipped down to Zephyr's chest, drank in all his hard lines and muscles. "I've been wondering how your beard will feel between my legs." And how it would feel to rub her hands over his buzzed dark hair as he ate her out. And…how that tongue of his would feel teasing her clit, working her up, getting her off. She'd also wondered how he would taste, what it would be like to push him to the edge, to make him crazy.

"Fuck me," he growled, stalking forward. It was as if her words had unleashed something inside him. The way he walked was pure, lethal predator. A true warrior.

Which was what she wanted. She didn't want sweet or soft. She wanted all of Zephyr. Her entire body ached for him to claim her. For tonight only. This was simply about sex, getting this out of her system. She knew she needed to make that very clear between them, but he cupped her face as he backed her up against the bed.

And he crushed his mouth to hers, claiming it exactly as she'd fantasized about. Raw energy hummed through him, vibrating all around them as his tongue teased against hers.

She could almost swear she felt the earth rumbling far beneath them, but knew it was more likely she was just anticipating so. Many. Orgasms. She simply had to believe that Zephyr would be amazing in bed. The male was built for sex.

With her.

Only her.

Damn it, why was she getting all possessive when this was just tonight? Or maybe…it could be a couple nights. They could fuck until they couldn't walk and then she could get back to normal.

One moment they were kissing, then the next he had her on her back, the silky covers beneath her making a soft swishing sound under their bodies.

Her instinct was normally to take over, to take control—to *be* in control. But with him, she found she liked the weight of his body on her, the way he was pinning her to the bed, his scorching heat. The anticipation of what was to come.

She stroked her fingers up his chest, down it, lower, skating her fingers over his ripped abs. As he started to drop featherlight kisses along her jawline, she teased her fingers at the top of his pants. She wanted to stroke him, hold that heavy length in her fingers. But—

Zephyr moved quickly, grasping her wrist and drawing it back up as he looked down at her. "Not yet," he growled.

Her nipples tightened at his words, his tone. The way he was watching her, as if he could consume her.

"I want to see all of you." He reached for her bandana and paused.

She nodded and pushed up so she was sitting. "Okay." Moving quickly, because it would be a lot easier if she did it, she tugged the bandana off, then unwrapped the long ribbons of fabric around her braid. It took her ages to put them in, to cover her tresses, but it was worth it. Because people didn't stare when her hair was covered.

But she had this down to an art and had them unwrapped and tossed onto the bed in less than a minute.

Zephyr reached out, started threading his fingers through her shimmering silver strands of hair. Not white, not blonde, but an unnatural silver that basically glowed.

"This is—"

"Weird." Yeah, she knew.

His gaze snapped back to her, his beast in his eyes. "Magnificent," he breathed out.

Why did he always seem to say the right things? It was unnerving and making her question herself, get all caught up in her head. Because she couldn't deal with him watching her like this, staring at her as if she was wonderful and precious, she reached for the hem of her T-shirt.

This was about *sex*, she reminded herself. Scratching that itch. Not getting all caught up in *feelings*. She wasn't going to open up her heart to anyone. She moved lightning fast, tugged her shirt off.

And Zephyr sucked in a breath.

Confidence swelled inside her as his gaze traveled all over her breasts, her abs. She was scarred up like him, most of them faint slashes, long faded from fights to the death. Clearly, he liked what he saw.

Yeah, she'd chosen right with this warrior. She grabbed the back of his neck, brought his mouth to hers in a hungry grip, but he pulled back, gave her the most wicked grin.

"Slow," he murmured as he dipped a head to her breast.

Slow? Yeah, that sounded nice. So did hard and fast. And everything in between. More than that, she wanted that thick cock inside her. *Gah.* But slow would work for now.

He rolled his tongue around her nipple, torturously slow, flicking it over her already hard bud. As he did, one of her chains shot out of its own accord and—wrapped around his ankle.

He sat up slightly, looked down, then looked back up at her and grinned, completely unbothered.

She had no clue what was happening, and when she tried to order her chain back it didn't budge. He didn't seem to care so she— "Oh, goddess." She arched her back as he suddenly sucked on her nipple. His mouth was wicked, amazing, and she wanted it lower. Everywhere.

Then she wanted to taste him, to suck him deep into her mouth. But first…

"This is just casual, okay," she rasped out. "One night between us." Gah, she was such a liar. She wanted more than this.

She needed to say the words for herself. Because she knew this wouldn't last. Nothing did. So when he walked away later, that could be the balm on her battered heart—she'd said this was casual. Nothing more. This was the lie she was telling herself because even now she knew it would shred her up when he decided she wasn't good enough.

Zephyr sat up suddenly, staring down at her. "One night?" The words came out like an accusation.

"Or two." *Whatever.* Her voice came out unsteady as she stared up at him. Why was he being like this?

His jaw clenched tight as he stared right back, his dragon right in his gaze. "You are a warrior goddess, the most stunning being I've ever seen. In any realm. But I'm not going to simply fuck you as if this is casual. Because I will not do casual with you. Ever."

Panic punched through her. "What the hell is wrong with you?" she snarled, heat creeping up her neck and over her cheeks. She'd bared herself to him, let him see her hair. Let him see *her*. And he didn't want this? Her chain completely disappeared as suddenly as it had appeared.

"Nothing is wrong with me. And nothing is wrong with you." He stood back, shoved off the bed, and had the audacity to somehow look even more gorgeous as he stared down at her, fully aroused.

She shoved off the bed too, refusing to be lying down and half naked right now. "I didn't say anything was wrong with me!"

"But you must think there is if you're trying to label tonight as a one-off. As if you haven't been obsessing about me. Haven't been thinking about *us*. About how hard I can make you come." His words dripped with a ridiculous confidence.

A red haze descended on her vision for a moment because dammit, he was right. Before she could respond, he leaned down toward her slightly, all menacing predator.

She, who'd never backed down in her life to *anyone*, sidestepped him. Because this was too much. *He* was too much.

But he took another step and continued talking as he stalked toward her. "I know because I've been obsessing about you too. I think about you when I stroke myself off in the shower. At night when I do the same. I'm turned on all the time because of you. I'm a walking hard-on. For you. And I know you feel the same. So until you decide that you want more from me than casual, or one pathetic night, this isn't happening. You are worth far more than *casual*."

She blinked at his words but shoved at his chest when he took another step toward her. She needed space. Needed to get away from him. He was saying way too many things she couldn't deal with. Didn't want to deal with. "You think far too much of yourself! I could go out right now and screw someone else. Grab someone from this club, bring them up here and not think about you at all."

She didn't actually mean the words, wasn't going to go find someone else tonight. Or any night as long as he was around. But she was angry and lashed out. She wanted to hurt him, or at least dull the river of embarrassment flooding her veins. Goddess, he was full-on rejecting her right now. And she couldn't back down, take back what she'd said about this being casual. *Oh no. No way.* That would give him all the power between them and she simply wasn't giving up control like that. Because she knew he would still walk away in the end. And if she gave up control to him, that would hurt even worse.

But he moved lightning fast in response, pinning her up against the door without actually touching her. His arms caged her in, his big callused hands planted on the door by her head. And she knew she could move, but the look in his eyes? Oh no, she wasn't going anywhere. She was paralyzed. Unable to break eye contact with him.

Her dragon half stared at this wild beast and felt seen for the first time in…ever. Seen and terrified. Not that he'd hurt her. Not physically anyway. But that he'd rip her heart out. Her blood family had abandoned her—something that did not happen in dragon clans. But she'd been tossed aside like trash.

"If you go to another male tonight, I'll gut him." His words were a savage snarl, truth ringing in every one of them.

Her instinct was to scoff, but…she wasn't sure he was joking. He wasn't human, didn't play by the same rules. And the beast staring back at her now… A shiver of something primal rolled down her spine. She liked this far too much.

She ducked away from him and stalked to her discarded shirt. "Fine, you psycho! Let's go home—to the house!" *Gah.* It sure as hell wasn't their home.

He simply leaned against the door and watched her as she yanked her shirt over her head.

Her heart was a wild, erratic beat in her chest. He made her feel that way, weak and out of control, as if she could crawl right out of her own skin. She wanted to punch him and fuck him at the same time. It was beyond maddening.

Hands unsteady, she picked up all her fabric she'd tossed to the floor and shoved it into her jacket pockets. She wasn't going to take the time to cover her hair, not when he was just watching her, wanting her. Making her crazy.

She kept one of the strips out and pulled her hair back into a low ponytail. Then she shoved into her boots and stalked to the door.

Still watching her, he left the key on the table by the bed and followed. His dragon was in his gaze the whole time.

Almost as if he was daring her to change what she'd said, to give in to what she really wanted and agree to something more than casual.

But he never said a word as they left the room and headed down the hallway. Remained silent as they stepped outside into the icy night air. And still quiet as a damn wraith by the time they made it back to the house.

To her surprise Ren was on the front porch with the human,

Grace, talking. She didn't have the bandwidth to talk to either of them, so she ignored Ren's look of surprise—likely because her hair was down and visible for all to see—and stalked through the front door.

And like a toddler, slammed it in Zephyr's face.

CHAPTER ELEVEN

"Is everything okay?" Grace asked Zephyr, her wide eyes flicking to the door Juniper had just slammed shut, then back to his face.

Zephyr just grinned even as he scrubbed a hand over his face and beard. He'd gotten under Juniper's skin. Which was all part of his plan —though he had hoped to feast between her legs, to hear her moan out her pleasure tonight as she came against his face. Then his cock.

Until she'd tried to put bullshit rules on them, to claim that tonight would mean nothing to her. His grin fell and he shelved thoughts of earlier as he moved toward Ren and Grace who were sitting on a small bench close together. "I should be asking you that." He crouched down because she was smaller and would soon be one of his sisters-in-law—as soon as Cas and Jo officially mated. Which wouldn't be long now. "How are you? Are you okay?" The details of earlier were still fuzzy.

Her cheeks flushed in what he assumed was embarrassment given the tart scent that rolled off her. "Yeah, I'm fine. I just feel so stupid that I fell for that vampire's charm."

Ren reached out, clasped her hand gently. "You didn't do anything wrong."

"What happened exactly?" He'd seen the aftermath, the overturned tables and booth ripped out of the wall.

"He tried to drug me, and the only reason I noticed is because I saw him do it from the mirror behind our booth." She shook her head slightly, her auburn hair loose around her face. "Then..." She glanced at Ren before looking at Zephyr again. "Ren was there and things got kind of crazy."

"I attacked him and he tried to throw the booth at me. He missed." Ren's tone was dark, his jaguar in his gaze for a moment. "But it worked as a distraction because he was able to escape."

"Did you want me to call Cas—"

"No! I mean..." She cleared her throat. "No, please. I don't want to have to retell this story to Jo or Luna. Or my grandmother. And honestly, I don't want to hear Cas go all caveman dragon. He's taking his overprotective big brother role to a new level and it's only been a couple weeks since he moved in."

Zephyr frowned. "Is his behavior bothering you?"

Grace shook her head, a soft smile pulling at her mouth. "No. Not really. It's actually nice to have him in the house. He was always around anyway, but...dragons are really overprotective."

"So are jaguars," Ren said, his tone neutral. His expression was *not*.

Ooooh. Ren was into Grace. Like, really into her, Zephyr realized.

Grace shot him a confused look before she focused her attention on Zephyr. "Are you going to tell Cas about what happened?"

"I don't have to. But I won't lie to him, so if he finds out and asks about tonight, I'll be honest... Would you like me to escort you home tonight?"

"I'll take her when she decides to go," Ren said as he stood, a low rumble to his voice.

Zephyr blinked and stood as well. The male knew Zephyr wasn't interested in her, that she was soon to be his relative. It was only natural that he escort her home. But he wasn't going to get into that in front of her, not when she'd been traumatized. "Where's Hyacinth?" he asked, changing topics. Because she'd said she would pick up his cache of clothing.

The tension in Ren's shoulders eased and he jerked a thumb behind him toward the house.

Zephyr simply nodded and walked inside. He was tempted to head upstairs, where he knew Juniper had gone. Her scent was strong in that direction, but he wanted to talk to Griffin and Hyacinth first, see if they'd talked to King recently. Or anyone from King's pack.

They were both on the back porch, Griff with a beer and Hyacinth with red wine. "Hey," he said to them.

"Hey yourself," Hyacinth said. "Left your stuff on your bed. You guys find out anything interesting?"

"Yeah, a little." He recapped everything they'd learned from Christian and what Juniper had told him was in the binder.

Griff nodded, took a sip of his beer. "We might need to bring more people in on this. From King's pack."

Yeah, Zephyr had been thinking the same thing. "We'll need vampires more than anything. Especially if we want to infiltrate their tight-knit circles."

"That's where I come in." Hyacinth's grin was practically feral. "I've got plans for tomorrow night. Met a couple vampires outside the club. They told me about an underground party going on. Not in the city proper, but more on the outskirts."

"Are shifters welcome?"

"Yeah. They just don't want anyone from King's pack. No wolves. Sorry," she said, looking at Griff.

He simply shrugged. "I'm coming. I just won't shift. They won't know what I am."

Zephyr wasn't sure how that was possible, but guessed the wolf had a way to hide his scent.

"If we don't track down who these vampires are, who sent them..." Zephyr trailed off. This wasn't his crew; he wasn't in charge. But he knew what he wanted to do.

"What?" Hyacinth asked.

He shrugged, looked behind him up at the house. The light in Juniper's room was on. "I want to talk to Juniper about it. But," he added, looking back at them, "I want to go after that territory. Take out as many of those bastards as we can before they disperse. We can find that Hell realm gate and put a guard on it." Or maybe a witch could create a barrier or something. He wasn't really sure how that would work, but imagined there had to be a way to safeguard it and prevent any being from entering or leaving it. After they saved any humans who'd been sent to another realm—because he wouldn't rest until they'd done that.

Griff and Hyacinth shifted slightly in their seats and Griff finally nodded thoughtfully. "Those weren't our orders."

"August isn't my boss. So." He lifted a shoulder. And he wasn't going to ask for permission to take out some evil assholes.

"I'm in if you decide to go after that territory," Hyacinth said before finishing the rest of her drink. She stood, picked up her empty glass. "And I've got a couple things to take care of before I get some rest."

Zephyr took her seat across from Griffin at the round patio table and stretched his legs out, exhausted and keyed up at the same time. He knew that giving Juniper space right now was the smart thing, but it didn't make staying away any easier.

Especially now that he knew for certain that she was his mate. When they'd been kissing, he'd felt the earth rumble beneath them, knew his mating manifestation was kicking into gear. She hadn't seemed to notice at least. And...he was going to ignore the fact that there hadn't been a manifestation from her. When dragons recognized their mates, it manifested when they were sexually intimate in various ways. Most dragons put off waves of fire or something very visible. His clan had always exuded quakes in the earth. He wasn't sure what her manifestation was and wasn't going to ask.

"She won't be easy," Griffin said into the quiet.

Zephyr didn't need the male to specify who. "I know." He let his head roll back, stared up at the dark sky glittering with only a few stars tonight. But he didn't want easy. He wanted Juniper.

"She'll push you away."

"I know." She already had. He wasn't going anywhere.

"She'll test your patience."

He snorted. "She already tests it. She's worth it. She's worth everything."

Griffin popped open the cooler by his chair that Zephyr hadn't seen until then and pulled out a chilled beer, handed it to him with a nod.

Zephyr felt as if he'd passed some sort of test in that moment. While he didn't care what anyone but Juniper thought of him, he was still glad the crew seemed to accept him.

Because he didn't plan on going anywhere. Nope, he was going to claim Juniper's heart—and then her body.

But to keep her, he had to win her heart first, that much he knew.

CHAPTER TWELVE

Grace breathed in the night air deeply, savored the familiar scents. Even after The Fall and all the changes King had made to the city, it still smelled the same. There was a crisp energy in the air, and tonight she swore she could smell fried…bacon. And her stomach rumbled slightly, making the intriguing, gentle male next to her laugh.

"You want to get something to eat?" Ren asked, his hands casually shoved into his jeans. The dark-haired jaguar shifter was quiet and kind, had been there for her after the whole mess at that club. He was also a savage fighter; she'd gotten to see that firsthand.

Instead of scaring her, it made her feel safe right now when she kept replaying the way that vampire had ripped the booth out of the wall with his bare hands and thrown it as if it was as light as a basketball. "I should get home." It was already four thirty in the morning.

"You sure? Because I could eat if you want to grab something."

She laughed lightly. "Well, I'm hungry, but I know you're working with Zephyr on…something."

He lifted a shoulder. "We mainly work in the evenings. That's when stuff tends to happen. And right now I have no plans other than getting you home safely."

That was vague, but she found herself nodding. Because she really didn't want to go home yet. Her adrenaline had crashed but this male made her feel safe. She didn't want to give that up yet. "Okay, there's a place not too far from here. A little family restaurant right in the middle of a neighborhood." They usually opened early, at around five in the morning. She had a feeling they'd started cooking early and that was what she was smelling. "I feel so stupid," she found herself saying. It was just a repeat of what she'd said earlier, but she couldn't help but keep mentally beating herself up.

"You've got to stop with that," he murmured, his voice soothing her.

She wasn't sure what it was about Ren, but he had such a calming presence. She hadn't even noticed him before when they'd come over to her family's house for dinner, not really. But now she was wondering how she'd missed him. Because he seemed to take up all the space around them and demand her attention. "I can't."

"Yes, you can. You didn't do anything wrong. Except trust a monster."

She knew that, but still felt dumb. And...scared. So much had happened since The Fall, including the loss of her parents. She, her sisters and their Nana had lost so much, just like everyone left behind after rogue dragons had destroyed more than half the world. But she'd settled into a sense of normalcy, had felt relatively safe. There wasn't much crime now with King in charge of the territory. Or she hadn't thought there was.

Now...reality crashed back in on her. "My equilibrium of safety is just out of whack. I'm probably going to be dealing with this for a while." And yeah, mentally berating herself. She knew it was a negative thing to do, but she was always hard on herself.

"If it makes you feel better, the first female I fell for tried to carve my heart out. Literally. She used a very sharp blade to do it." His words were oddly light as he spoke.

She jerked to a stop on the sidewalk, stared up at him. "What? Seriously?"

He lifted a casual shoulder. "Yep."

"Are you…okay?" He was here, so obviously he was alive, but that was horrifying. "What happened?"

"I'm fine—now. A witch I thought I was in love with decided she needed my heart for an important sacrifice. So she tried to take it after drugging me. She didn't account for shifter metabolism and that drugs don't work on shifters like humans."

He started walking again. So Grace fell in step with him and linked her arm through his on instinct. He'd done so much for her tonight and she felt the need to comfort him. He didn't pull away, just tightened his arm slightly, tugging her closer. "I'm so sorry."

"It's okay. I didn't tell you to make you feel sorry for me. I'm just, I don't know, letting you know that you didn't do anything wrong. And I hate that he rattled your sense of safety. But what he did, that's not on you. You agreed to go on a date with someone, that's it." He sort of seemed to struggle with the word date.

And for some reason Grace liked that. He hadn't hit on her or anything and seemed to be acting in a protective manner because he'd happened to be at the club at the right time. So she wasn't going to read anything into it. But she realized that she might be developing a teeny bit of a crush on this quiet jaguar with kind eyes.

"Thank you," she murmured. "And I'm sorry you dealt with an actual crazy ex."

He snorted and rubbed at his chest almost absently. "Me too."

CHAPTER THIRTEEN

Juniper came downstairs, completely ready to ignore what had happened last night. They had shit to do today anyway. And the Alpha of the territory had just texted her, saying he'd be here in less than ten minutes. So she'd texted everyone and hurried to tug on clothes and pull her hair back into a braid—she wasn't going to bother covering it now because she didn't have time.

She put aside what had happened with Zephyr only hours before and steeled herself to see him. Normally she was up when the sun rose but it was now eight o'clock and she'd basically tossed and turned the last few hours. Mostly due to sexual frustration.

And anger. Soooo much anger. But mainly sexual frustration. She'd tried masturbating in the shower but it had been useless. She hadn't wanted to get herself off, she'd wanted his hands on her. His mouth between her legs. And she still didn't know if his beard would feel good against her thighs.

Her dragon half snarled, annoyed at everything that had gone down. Annoyed…at *her*.

Calm, she ordered herself! She had to be all relaxed when she saw Zephyr this morning. If she pretended that nothing had happened, then he would too. She seriously doubted he would want the crew to know they'd almost gotten naked together—until he'd decided to act like a jackass.

Ugh.

Cool. Calm. Collected. She chanted the words to herself as she reached the bottom of the stairs and headed to the kitchen because she heard everyone in there. Even Hyacinth, who normally preferred to sleep during the day despite being a day walker, was up and chatting.

Juniper kept her expression neutral as she stepped into the kitchen. Of course *he* was there, but she ignored him. Refused to look in his direction. She simply couldn't look at that gorgeous face.

"Hey boss, do you know why King is stopping by?" Ren asked, sipping coffee as he leaned on the countertop, looking wide-awake even though she knew he'd only gotten in a couple hours ago. He was going to get his heart broken with that human female, Juniper thought, then quickly shelved it.

"No, he just said we needed to meet here in ten minutes." Ignoring Zephyr's presence, she glanced at her phone. "Six now."

"Here, princess," Zephyr said, his voice liquid smooth as he handed her a mug of coffee. "I made this just for you."

The entire room went still.

Her gaze snapped to his. "What did you call me?"

"You don't like that nickname? I figured June bug was off the table, but princess might work."

What. The. Hell.

"Or I could just call you my queen." His gaze went to her mouth, his eyes flaring with heat and hunger. Sooo much hunger—and all for her.

"What. Is. Happening?" Hyacinth whispered loudly, open-mouthed as she looked between the two of them.

"Shut up," Ren murmured, and out of the corner of Juniper's eye she saw him nudge the vamp.

"Oh, didn't mean to say that out loud. But seriously, what's happening now?" Hyacinth whispered again.

Griff simply grinned, the bastard, and strode out of the kitchen, actually whistling to himself.

"Did you hit your head last night?" she growled at Zephyr, still holding the coffee mug he'd handed her—which smelled so amazing.

"Nope." Then he gave a chin nod toward the mug. "Try it. I made you a latte, just the way you like. And I think I'll call you princess until you officially become my queen." The look he gave her was positively challenging.

"Oh my Godddd," Hyacinth breathed out as Ren dragged her from the kitchen, mouth still wide-open.

"What the hell is wrong with you!" Juniper whisper-snarled even as she took a sip of the latte. And oh sweet goddess, he'd gotten it exactly right. How had he done that? The sneaky bastard. She couldn't just toss this out because it was too delicious. Well she *could*, but she wasn't going to deprive herself out of spite. She hadn't had a drink like this in months. How did he even know to make this for her? One of her crew must have told him. "Did you tell them about last night?"

"Hell no. What happens between us is our business only."

"Yet you felt the need to start calling me random pet names this morning in front of my crew." What the hell was he playing at?

"Not random. I thought on them long and hard last night." Those gray eyes fell to her mouth once again and he growled low, the sound primal, hot. "Since I didn't get to thrust inside you long and hard, I had to do something to pass the time."

Oooooh. Her entire being clenched at his words. And her brain fritzed. Just. Stopped. Working.

A sudden, sharp knock sounded from the front door and she nearly jumped out of her skin. Unable to be in the same room with him anymore, she swiveled and stomped out, feeling out of control in a way she'd never experienced.

This could not be happening. Was he...trying to court her? No. No way. He was just being a dick because of last night. Except...that didn't make sense.

Growling to herself, she yanked open the front door and found herself staring at King and Aurora. They both tensed and she realized that her dragon was in her gaze and she probably looked like a psycho right now. She certainly felt like one anyway.

Juniper smoothed out her expression. "Welcome, please come in." Goddess, this was the Alpha couple of the territory. She needed to keep it together before she got all of her crew kicked out.

"Thank you." King and Aurora stepped inside together, almost as a unit they moved so in sync. "I know this is last minute, so I appreciate you seeing us," King said.

"It's your territory. We appreciate you letting us stay here." Oh no, maybe he was angry about last night and he actually *was* coming to kick them out.

She tensed as he glanced at the others who'd congregated in the foyer, his expression opaque.

Finally he spoke. "May we sit and talk?"

Oh, right. Seriously, what was wrong with her? She tossed a quick glare over her shoulder at Zephyr because *he* was what was wrong with her. But when she looked back at the couple, she smiled sincerely. "Yes, of course. Apologies. Would you like coffee, tea? Snacks?"

Ren and Hyacinth snapped to attention, ready to grab an army of food and drinks.

"No, but thank you."

"Let's talk in here, then. It's comfortable." The living room was huge, with high ceilings, robin's-egg blue walls, creamy white molding, a marble mantel and a white plaster medallion around the chandelier. Zephyr's brothers and brother's mate had renovated the place and it was hard not to appreciate all the details.

Once everyone had sat—with Zephyr sitting right next to her, only inches separating them on the couch—King spoke.

And he didn't bother sitting. Both he and Aurora stood by the fireplace, their expressions slightly tense.

"The vampire from last night succumbed to the poison," he finally said, looking at all of them. "Our healers tried everything they could, but it invaded his blood fast. It's amazing they were able to keep him alive as long as they did. He was very determined to die." King's jaw tightened once before he continued. "After last night I want more of my people involved in this operation." By his tone it was clear that he wasn't asking.

"Of course," she said, even though the thought made her uneasy.

The faintest hint of amusement lit his ice-blue eyes. "I'm not taking over. But if this vampire was willing to kill himself rather than risk telling us anything, I want to know who he worked for. I want to know everything you do. And when we manage to drive away these traffickers from my territory—which we will—I want to stop this operation completely."

"Even if it's not a threat to your territory?" Juniper asked.

He paused a long moment, considering his response. "I certainly don't plan on policing the entire world. But the territory you told me about is close enough to mine that I can do something about it. So I will. Because evil is an insidious thing. I'm under no illusions—it will always exist in one form or another. But if I see it growing some-where, I'm going to stop it." His wolf peeked out at her a moment.

She felt exactly the same way. It was why she did what she did. Evil was everywhere, always slipping into the cracks, trying to take root, gain a footing. "Good. We'll tell you everything we know, everything we've learned. I will say, I think we need to keep this operation small. If the people we're after even have a hint that your wolves are involved..." She lifted a shoulder. "It'll make it harder to find out what we need to."

She quickly recapped what she and Zephyr had found out last night from Christian, including giving King his name. She wanted to be as transparent as possible and knew Christian wouldn't mind.

"He's offered to help us in any way he can," she finished. "I think we should take him up on it."

"A few of my packmates used to work for a secret branch of the government. When there was still a government," Aurora said, the first words she'd spoken since she and King had arrived. "I would like you to add one of them to your crew. His name is Axel. He's a lion shifter. And he knows your friend Christian. They'll work well together."

King shot his mate an inscrutable look before he turned back to Juniper.

Juniper realized she needed to respond and nodded. "Of course. That works for us."

"The lion can fight," Zephyr said, his voice a deep rumble she felt in places she absolutely didn't want to feel. "He'll be a great addition to the team."

The others nodded then—because apparently they now liked having Zephyr's stamp of approval. Or maybe she was just being a bitch.

"How are you feeling today?" Aurora asked, changing tracks in a smooth beat.

Juniper felt heat creep up her neck. "Well, thank you. And thank you for asking Greer to use your blood. I would have healed on my own but it would have been slower and more painful." Thanks to the phoenix's blood, Juniper had been up and ready to go in no time—with no lingering pain. "That was very kind."

Aurora smiled at her, her expression so warm and kind it was unnerving. "It was no problem at all."

Juniper was used to people trying to kill her. To only depending on her tight-knit crew. Not...so much kindness and warmth from so many random people. Unnerving was right. To top it off, Zephyr was completely under her skin and she was having a hard time just functioning this morning. Her whole world seemed to have shifted in days. She didn't like it.

"I'd like to ask you something else. Something random," King continued.

Everyone in the room stilled at his words. They were benign enough, but his tone had an undercurrent of something she couldn't quite define. "Okay."

"Last night, at the hotel." His expression turned dry for a moment. "When you crash-landed. There was a group of dragons there I'd only just been introduced to. They were watching you very intently after you fell."

"I'm sure a lot of people were." She winced inwardly at the spectacle she'd made. In hindsight, it had definitely not been the best move. But she'd been running on adrenaline and hyperfocused.

"This was different," Aurora said. "And I think one of them took a picture of you."

Everyone went preternaturally still now, except Zephyr, who stood, waves of power rolling off him. "Who?" he demanded.

King held up a hand, his expression one of patience as he motioned for Zephyr to sit back down. "They are dignitaries from another realm—the Nova realm. They reached out to me because my father…" He seemed to stumble on that word, cleared his throat. "My father is well acquainted with them, says they are trustworthy. They reached out a couple weeks ago wanting to talk allyship. Last night was the first night I've seen a spark of anything from any of them— and it was after your big show."

Ren rubbed the back of his neck, Hyacinth shifted nervously in her seat, but neither Griff or Zephyr moved.

"I've never heard of them," Juniper said.

"Well, I would like you to look at the file I have on them," King answered. "It includes pictures. I think they might have followed you last night after you left the hotel. And I don't like unknowns in my territory."

"Someone followed us last night after we left the healer's," Zephyr said.

King and Aurora exchanged a look, seemed to have a sort of silent conversation before they looked back at her. "I'm going to be keeping an eye on them," King said. "And now you know to do so as well."

After that, they more or less wrapped up, with Aurora giving her the male named Axel's information and Juniper promising to contact him immediately.

"We need to figure out who these people following you are," Ren said once King and Aurora had left, picking up the file and flipping it open.

"If we know where they're staying, we can tail them too," Zephyr said.

"That's a good idea," Juniper said. She stood behind Ren, glancing at the photos, but not recognizing anyone. "They could be enemies from a past job. Maybe I locked up one of their relatives or something." She scrubbed a hand over her face.

She'd been doing this job a long time and had countless enemies. Most of them didn't actually know her face, however, as she usually worked in the shadows. But she had revealed some of her magical powers last night. It would be a good way for someone looking to ID her, no matter how careful she'd been to keep her powers concealed over the years.

"We also need to get spells to cover our real faces tonight." Hyacinth said, leaning against the fireplace and crossing her arms over her chest. "Juniper and I can go to a place close to here. It's run by a human called the Magic Man."

"I know of him," Zephyr said. "My brother's mate Avery is friends with him. And Mikael likes him too for helping save Avery's life once."

Juniper made herself look over at him, and was immediately ensnared by his gray eyes. She pretended to be unaffected. "Can you find out what kind of payment he would like? Maybe something special we can bring him." She liked making allies everywhere they went and this guy sounded like a good contact to have. Magic was in his name.

He nodded and pulled out his phone, and she forced herself to tear her gaze away—to find Hyacinth staring at her, curiosity burning in her gaze.

Oh no. They were not having a conversation about Zephyr now. Or ever. Zephyr was finding information on the Magic Man and she knew Ren would pore over the file better than she could.

"I'll be back. Gonna go talk to that lion," she said even as she made her way to the front door. She needed to get out of the house. Alone.

She needed some space from the tall, deadly, sexy dragon for a few minutes. Just so she could breathe.

CHAPTER FOURTEEN

Juniper stood next to a burbling fountain, staring at the shocking pink flowers growing wildly around the base and curving up into the fountain itself. "I can't believe how well everything is growing here," she murmured to Hyacinth.

The *here* was the courtyard they were currently in—waiting on the human called the Magic Man. They'd already been met by two other humans who'd offered them refreshments.

"Well duh, this guy is the Magic Man," Hyacinth said, laughing slightly. "And I want to know what's going on with you and the tall, deadly dragon. Did you guys get together last night? Or 'hook up' as the kids say?"

Juniper simply rolled her eyes, turned away and strolled toward the surrounding walls of the courtyard, her gaze rolling over more pink flowers. This time oleanders. Beautiful and deadly.

"So, nothing to say, *princess?*" Hyacinth practically purred before falling into a cackle.

She'd turned, a sharp reply on the tip of her tongue, when a tall, handsome older human stepped out of the courtyard doorway. His eyes were as dark as his skin. It was the same human who'd been watching her at the party at Aurora's weeks ago, as if he'd been able to see her right down to her soul. He wore a three-piece suit with an antique-looking pocket watch tucked into a navy blue pin-striped vest.

"Apologies for the wait. I'm Thurman, but you may call me the Magic Man if you choose." Amusement lit his dark eyes as they rested on Juniper. "It's what the rest of the city seems to prefer."

"I'm Juniper, and this is Hyacinth."

"Ah," he said, looking between them, his face crinkling into a smile as it landed on Hyacinth. "Hyacinth, a beautiful but deadly flower."

"Just like me." Hyacinth grinned at the older human as she strutted toward the waiting mosaic table. Though Hyacinth looked to be in her thirties, the vampire was much older—older even than this human. "And I've brought gifts." The barest hint of her English accent peeked through. That only happened when she was in a mood about something. Good or bad, and right now an odd sort of energy was rolling off her.

Juniper wasn't sure what to make of it.

"Please sit, ladies." He indicated that they should sit first and Juniper knew this was a human custom of politeness so she did just that. "How do you feel about chai?" he asked Juniper. "And Earl Gray for you?"

Hyacinth gave the male an even wider grin as she sat, crossing her legs and scooting her chair closer to his as he sat. "That sounds perfect." Her words were practically a purr.

Oh goddess...was Hyacinth flirting with him? What was happening right now? Because this was not part of their plan. The male was handsome enough, looking maybe sixty to Juniper. It was so difficult to gauge humans' ages. But this male...his eyes held far too much knowledge for such a young age. It was unnerving.

"Chai is good for me. I remember you from the party for the Alpha couple some weeks ago," Juniper said suddenly. "You watched me as if you knew me." She'd decided to just play this straight and see if she got the answer she wanted from him. Because she wanted to know why he'd been looking at her so intently.

He looked up as a male who was a younger version of him walked up and poured two separate drinks for her and Hyacinth. "I apologize if I made you uncomfortable," he continued once they were alone. "I'm a seer. Sometimes I watch people and get lost in their auras. We've never met, but I found myself fascinated by what I saw underneath the surface."

"You can check out my aura anytime," Hyacinth said, picking up her teacup.

Oh sweet goddess. Ignoring her friend, Juniper simply gave the male a polite smile. "Is that how you knew what we wanted to drink? You see stuff like that?" She'd only met a seer once and hadn't cared for the experience. She didn't like anyone being able to see a part of her she wanted to keep hidden.

He nodded, a half-smile still in place. There was definitely a calming presence about the human, Juniper realized, now that they were all just sitting here with no outward distractions from a party.

"So you know what we are?" she pressed.

He paused, then nodded. "I do. And I know why you've come. And before you ask, I will definitely help you."

Juniper glanced around, wondered how many ears might be listening.

As if he'd read her train of thought—uh, maybe he had?—the Magic Man said, "This place is spelled. No one can overhear us. Not here." He indicated to the courtyard surrounding them and then the brick building behind it. "Or next door." Now he pointed at the brick building that was a mirror image of the one behind the courtyard. "That is my home." He shot Hyacinth a mischievous look and her friend simply grinned.

Juniper resisted the urge to rub her hand over her face. Clearly the world had gone mad. Hyacinth never flirted with anyone unless it was for work, so Juniper wasn't certain that was what was even happening. "We need spells that will essentially cover our faces, hide us in plain sight. We need five of them."

"Six," Hyacinth corrected.

Juniper frowned at Hyacinth.

"The lion. He's coming with us too."

Oh, right. "Maybe seven, then." Because she hadn't been thinking of Christian but she wanted him to have the option to use a spell in case he wanted to go incognito as well.

Thurman gave a nod that she could only describe as regal. "That won't be a problem."

"We've brought a variety of gifts for you as payment." She nodded once at Hyacinth, who started to pull up the bags to display the contents—vintage wines, gems, and an assortment of seeds for planting that they'd been told the human would like.

"I would also like a favor," he said, looking at Juniper in that eerie way of his. His eyes were so dark, so knowing.

Juniper resisted the urge to rub her arms—she was a *dragon*. She could burn this place to a crisp if she wanted to. But she didn't like the thought of anyone seeing to the heart of her. "What kind of favor?"

"I don't know yet. But I would like one to save for later."

"As long as it—"

"Doesn't hurt innocents, I know. I will ask for nothing that will harm another being."

"Okay. Deal."

"You don't want a favor from me?" Hyacinth's grin was back.

The look he gave her friend was... *Oh.* Very, very inviting. His gaze focused on Hyacinth's ruby-red lips, but he didn't respond. Instead, he turned back to Juniper. "We have a deal, then. Seven spells and I'll throw in a few other tricks and protection spells for you. Also, some free information." He flicked a look at Hyacinth. "Because I like *you.*" Then his gaze was on Juniper again, all business. "Darkness surrounds you. It's coming for you," he said abruptly.

She couldn't fight the shiver that rolled through her, but she didn't outwardly react. "What kind of darkness? Because I've got a lot of enemies."

"An old one... An ancient one."

"I'm not ancient."

"Not you. But the darkness after you is."

Oh. Well, shit.

"What is this darkness?" Hyacinth demanded, uncrossing her legs and leaning forward. Just a hint of her fangs showed now as she shifted to all-business mode.

"I don't know, unfortunately. But I can see it on the horizon, angry buzzing wasps. My gift doesn't show me everything clearly. But something is coming for you."

Juniper only nodded because what else could she do? She was hunting down scum of the earth traffickers, she had countless enemies from past jobs, and now some random dragons had been watching her at that party she'd inadvertently crashed. "Thank you for the information. I will keep it in mind."

He nodded and handed them a small package wrapped in simple brown paper. "Your spells."

"You already knew what we wanted..." Hyacinth grinned. "How far does this magic extend? Can you tell what your lover wants in the bedroom without them having to ask?"

"Maybe you will find out." The male's voice was now low, gravelly, and Juniper was seriously wondering what had happened to the fabric of her reality. "But only if I am lucky."

Hyacinth's expression turned almost predatory in the way of vampires who saw something they wanted. "Something tells me you're going to be."

Juniper cleared her throat and stood, taking the package he'd offered. They needed to get out of here. Mainly because she didn't like being around someone who could read her, no matter how nice they very likely were. And this sexual tension between the other two was making her uncomfortable. "Thank you for this."

"Anytime." He paused. "Be careful on your quest."

"I'll keep her safe." Hyacinth set a piece of paper on the table along with the bag. "My cell number in case you can't use your magic to guess it."

Wordlessly, he pocketed it and Juniper turned away, simply done with this whole day already.

Once they were out on the cobblestone street, she finally felt as if she could breathe again.

"Oh, I am going to show that male a very good time once this job is over." Hyacinth had an actual spring in her step as they made their way down the sidewalk.

"You are such a weirdo. He's human."

"So? He's got *style*, and goddess, he smells so good. I bet his blood tastes amazing."

Juniper didn't resist the urge now to scrub a hand over her face. "I don't even know what to say to that."

Hyacinth shrugged then tugged her crimson, off the shoulder sweater back up. "We've been working hard the last year. I need some playtime. And so do you," she added.

"I'm fine."

Hyacinth snorted. "No. You were close to burnout before The Fall and now you're pushing away a male who very clearly wants to worship you in bed. Why?"

"I'm not pushing him away," she snapped as they reached a crosswalk. And if all he wanted was to worship her in bed, there wouldn't be a problem. Then she forced herself to take a deep breath. "Sorry. I'm just—"

"Sexually frustrated?"

Laughing at Hyacinth's knowing tone, Juniper nudged her once with her hip. "Yes. We got a room at that club last night and everything was going great until…" She cleared her throat. "I told him that things between us would be casual and he didn't like that."

"What do you mean?"

"Essentially he said that things would never be casual between us." She wasn't going to go into detail because she didn't want to relive his words. Why did he have to get all serious about them? Why couldn't he have just enjoyed what would have no doubt been amazing sex? And lots of orgasms. They could both be sated right now.

"So? Do you really want casual? You just want to screw him once and then let him go? Toss him onto his next lover without any concern?"

Her dragon rose up at the thought of Zephyr being with anyone else, but she quickly shoved her beast back down. "I just…wasn't thinking of the future." *Lies, lies, lies.* "I didn't want to make a big deal about last night." She kept her voice low as they reached another crosswalk. There was a sort of outdoor area where people were selling and trading goods.

"Well, I like the male. He clearly doesn't care what anyone thinks. Not our crew anyway. Man, he just laid it all out in the open this morning, made himself completely vulnerable—and he made you coffee. Kinda hard not to like that kind of boldness."

"Then you sleep with him," she muttered, not meaning it. She'd burn Hyacinth to a crisp before allowing it.

Which just made Hyacinth cackle, as if she'd read her mind. "You're ridiculous. But I get it. You're taking the coward's way out—"

"Hey!" They were in the middle of the roped-off street now, making their way through various booths of food and clothing stuff. She ignored a surprised look of a nearby shopper and lowered her voice. "I'm not a coward."

"So says my sexually frustrated friend."

"You are so annoying when you're right."

Hyacinth's ruby-red grin widened. "I know."

CHAPTER FIFTEEN

Claudine sighed almost dramatically—for her anyway. Any expression of emotion might as well be considered theatrical for the old vampire.

"What?" King frowned, looking at her. It was just the two of them right now standing outside the greenhouse their mates were currently inside. Dusk had fallen an hour ago but the garden and connected greenhouse were lit up with enough solar lights to illuminate half the block.

"I'm afraid you and I will likely be allies forever at this point."

"What, why? Not that us being allies is a bad thing." He wasn't certain of her tone. Or the abrupt change in topic. He and Aurora had met Claudine and her mate Frederick at a local greenhouse to speak in a neutral area—and so Aurora and Frederick could spend time talking about hybrid fruits.

Claudine simply moved her chin in the direction of Aurora and Frederick. The two were standing by a long trough of soil, and if he had to guess, they were still discussing the best soil to use as if it was the most important thing in the universe.

Because King knew the two of them texted often now that they were friends—about art, books and how to create the best fruit hybridization.

"They're like twins," Claudine murmured, shaking her head slightly. "Frederick has always been eccentric, something I adore about him, but no one in my coven has ever been interested in botany the way he is."

King found himself snickering. "You're right, our mates will keep us allies forever." He knew that Aurora saw Frederick as a father figure. She adored the male who'd been turned around the age of fifty —over five hundred years ago.

"Or perhaps not twins, but more of a father/daughter relationship," Claudine continued.

"I think so," King said. "Aurora missed out on having a father. And…" He cleared his throat. "Aurora said that Frederick reminds her of her own father who was taken from the world too soon."

Claudine shot him another look, paused for a moment before she said, "Frederick lost his daughter before I changed him. Years before," she added. "He confessed that Aurora reminds him of who he lost too." There was a sadness in her voice when she looked back at them, but then she smiled. "I'm glad they're friends. I…thought I would experience jealousy at their growing closeness. But I find that it just makes me happy."

"Same." King only wanted Aurora content, and there was absolutely no underlying sexual element to her relationship with Frederick. It was a pure friendship, and he liked that she was establishing her own allies in the territory that had nothing to do with him. Not that Aurora would see it that way—she was simply making friends.

But his phoenix needed more ties, needed to cement herself in this territory as a part of its fabric, because if the day ever came that she was taken or targeted for who she was, her allies would not stand for it. King wanted her to have all the protection she could get.

"So tell me what you know about the Nova realm, the clan," King said abruptly, shifting subjects. He'd invited her here today specifically to discuss the Nova clan. And this way Aurora and Frederick got to talk more about soil.

He needed all the information he could gather on these unknown dragons. Because Starlena had been watching Juniper with an unnerving closeness. King had reached out to his father, Sorgin, but it could take days to hear back from him since he was in another realm. Sorgin had given his recommendation of the Nova clan, had said they would be good allies, but if the clan was a threat to Juniper—who worked for August and was therefore an ally of King's—it could be trouble. All these connections were complicated.

"Nothing." Claudine shook her head slightly. "And I do mean nothing. I've heard about them, yes, but that is quite literally it. From what little I've discovered, they shut themselves off from the world and have a few allies they keep in contact with, but a century or two ago, they just...stopped connecting with this realm. And even before then, they'd been mostly closed off. I only know this because I dug deep when you told me they'd be entering the territory for a possible alliance. But they might as well be ghosts of the supernatural world. Have you reached out to August about them?"

"He doesn't know much about them either. Shockingly little for a male who makes his living on secrets and intel." And that bothered King.

"What do you know of the dragon female, Juniper?" She smiled slightly as Frederick shoved his hands into one of the big pots and said something animated about the rich dirt in his hand to Aurora.

"Just that she works for August, has been into black ops work the last half century. And that August views her as a daughter. He didn't say it outright but he threatened our allyship if something were to happen to her. So Juniper *matters* to him."

Claudine shot King a look, raised one perfect eyebrow. "That is surprising. I always viewed him as sort of soulless."

King let out a bark of laughter before he could stop himself.

She shot him another look. "What?"

"Nothing." He cleared his throat, looked back into the greenhouse, saw Aurora watching him. She blew him a kiss before turning to a bunch of hanging plants and continuing talking to Frederick.

"I know people view me as soulless too," she said, clearly guessing what he'd been thinking. "So maybe I shouldn't have formed that opinion of August."

"How do you know him, anyway?"

She lifted a shoulder, snorted. "Probably from the same way you do. One of my people got tangled up in something that put him on August's radar. That put August on my radar. It was all a very bloody, messy affair that ended with me executing one of my coven members. I like August. I might not always agree with his methods, but I respect what he did—still does—for the supernatural world."

King nodded his agreement. August worked in the shadows, had been helping supernaturals across the world for centuries. King had a feeling they all owed the male one way or another.

"I'll keep my ear to the ground about them. And that other thing."

King had brought her into the fold regarding the trafficking of humans. Since vampires were involved and she was the most powerful vamp in the territory—and he trusted her—he'd gone with his instinct. He couldn't operate in a vacuum.

At that thought, his mate looked at him, and once again he was struck by the love in her gaze. Now that they were mated, they were connected on a whole other level and he could feel that love punching right through to his core. Goddess, he was a lucky male.

The luckiest.

And he would do everything in his power to stop these traffickers. Because that shit would not happen in his territory. Ever.

CHAPTER SIXTEEN

"Thank you for doing this," Juniper said to Christian and Axel—who'd turned out to be one of Aurora's roommates. So far she liked the lion. He seemed easygoing and Zephyr said that he was a good one to have around for a fight. She didn't need a hothead as part of this job, so he seemed to be the perfect addition.

"Of course." Christian gave a stiff nod and glanced across the street at the seemingly abandoned warehouse. He was almost a bit out of sorts, and she wasn't sure why—except he kept sneaking looks at the lion when the other male wasn't paying attention.

He'd assured them that this place was where he'd heard humans were being taken from—and it was the same address Hyacinth had been given when she'd been invited to a vampire party.

To get here they'd crossed Lake Pontchartrain—which didn't seem to be an actual lake by any accepted standards, human or otherwise. So now the plan was for her and her crew to infiltrate and look for humans. And if any humans left with vampires, willingly or otherwise, they would tail them.

Which meant they'd have to split up.

She glanced around at their surroundings. They were in a gravel parking lot of an abandoned strip of stores. Most of the windows were knocked out or boarded up but she couldn't scent anyone inside. Across the street, behind a wire fence and about a football field length of overgrown underbrush, was where they'd have to get inside. The warehouse itself was a simple box and had once been a storage place. Christian said it was now being used for "underground club nights." And since it was a couple hours till midnight things should be getting started.

"Everyone remember the pass phrase?" she asked.

Everyone nodded, though Griffin snorted, likely because the phrase to enter was "little red riding hood."

"Okay. Ren and I will head in now." There were absolutely no vehicles across the street, nothing to give away that this place was in use. Which was very likely how the operators managed to keep its existence a secret from the sentries of King's pack. Not to mention the surrounding area was one that his pack hadn't fixed up yet.

"Be careful," Zephyr said, and she knew his words were directed at her.

She should be annoyed with him but...ugh. Whatever. She just wanted to sit on his face more than anything. Freaking dragon.

"Always," Ren said in response when Juniper simply ignored him.

After she and Hyacinth had returned from the Magic Man's place, Zephyr had been needling her all day. Okay, not needling. But he'd been around her, just driving her mad with his huge, sexy presence. He'd basically staked a claim earlier that morning and she couldn't get his words out of her head.

Once they crossed the street and slipped through an opening in the big fence, Ren said, "Testing."

Everyone behind them answered in the affirmative that they could hear clearly through the comm line earpiece. Juniper immediately did the same with hers and got all affirmatives. So they were off to a good start.

All the Magic Man's spells were in place as well, masking their faces. She appeared to be a dark-haired female with bangs and dark eyes, and the shape of her face was rounder. Her body type was the same because it was hard to hide height with a spell, but at least she didn't look like the same female who'd jumped out of a hotel room window and crashed a party.

"How do I look?" Ren asked, doing a ridiculous head toss.

She grinned as they stalked across the underbrush. The closer they got to the warehouse, she could scent other beings and feel a pulse of music from somewhere. "Adorable." Under the spell, his hair was a pale blond and he had the "California surfer" look down—tan, cheeky grin, bright blue eyes. But she could still see the real him. It was weird, like looking at an overlay over him, but at least no one else would be able to see the spell in place. Not unless they were related through blood. She could barely see Zephyr's overlay—which was more blond hair and blue-eyed surfer. No, all she could see was *him*. Because that was all she wanted to.

The only one not in disguise was Christian. He'd said he wanted to go as himself so he'd be able to get information out of contacts if necessary.

"I feel ridiculous," she murmured as they neared the back of the warehouse. They'd been told that the door was on the west side and that they'd have to knock three times, then give the pass phrase to whoever opened it.

Ren glanced at her getup and grinned. "At least they'll know you're not hiding any weapons."

She had on a silver sparkly "top" that barely covered her breasts and was connected behind her back with two strips of fabric. Her skirt was the size of a headband and she had on ridiculous five-inch heels—which made her six and a half feet, and taller than almost everyone.

"Good thing I don't need them." She was a dragon.

As they rounded the side of the building, she spotted the door Christian had told them about. It was go time.

"She's incredible." Axel nodded at Juniper, who was dancing on one of the raised platforms. Ren was on another one nearby, also dancing.

The two of them had a dragon's-eye view of the club from their position. Even with the spell covering her real face, Juniper was a magnificent-looking female. Everything about her was larger than life. It was hard not to admire her moves.

Christian simply sniffed in that obnoxious way of his that Axel both loved and loathed. Goddess, he wanted to punch the male so much. But he also wanted to do other things. Hot, urgent things where neither of them were talking or had any clothing on.

"At least pretend you're having a good time with me," Axel muttered, turning back around to face the long, glossy bar. He had no idea how someone had managed to trick out this place so well but it was incredible.

There were multiple hardwood bars with incredible finishings, multiple dance floors, different levels with cages and platforms inter-mixed for dancing and other things. The space was huge and wild and clearly meant for partying.

"Hard to do that when you're checking out everyone with a pulse." Christian sniffed once and took a sip of his drink.

He was all proper and elegant too in his ridiculously hot custom-cut three-piece suit, and Axel just wanted to mess up his hair, get his suit wrinkled and kiss him until his mouth was swollen. Just to rile him up. *Not* to claim him or anything.

Axel cut a glare at Christian. "That's not what I'm doing." He was keeping an eye on the others inside the club. Zephyr was the only one not inside—his job was to keep an eye on any potential strange happenings outside. Since he was a dragon, he was able to do better recon than anyone, so Juniper had assigned him that role.

"Cut it out, you two." Juniper's subtle voice came over their connected comm line.

Right. Axel smiled smoothly at Christian and leaned closer to him and that spicy scent hit Axel hard. Damn it, this vampire made him crazy. "Do you need another drink, darling?" He laid it on thick, ignoring the flash of heat in Christian's eyes. Oh, did his vampire not like that? Too bad. And damn it, Christian was not *his* vampire. The male had made it very clear that he was too good for Axel. *Jackass.*

As if summoned, the young vampire bartender, who couldn't have been turned more than a decade ago, strolled up to them. Shirtless and wearing a sparkly gold thong—and matching beads around his neck—he grinned at Christian, checking him out in the most obnoxious way.

He and Axel might not be an actual couple, but it was clear they were together. Axel started to growl low in his throat, then cut it off. He'd never been the jealous type. And he couldn't start now that they were undercover.

The bartender turned to Axel then, his flirty grin still firmly in place. "What can I get for you two boys?"

Boys? Axel resisted the urge to grit his teeth at this child who'd likely been turned at the height of his frat boy days. He hated places like this: loud clubs with people just looking for hookups. He liked a good party, but everything about this club felt cold, impersonal. The parties he preferred involved friends and simply being around people he genuinely liked.

"Another Manhattan for me and a beer for my friend," Christian purred in the most fake way Axel had ever heard the male talk. Christian had a boyish quality to his face because of when he'd been turned, but that was just surface. Everything about him was polished, elegant, refined. "And maybe you can tell us where we can pick up some humans looking for fun." He winked and Axel's stomach tightened.

Yeah, he didn't like this. Many, many years ago he'd worked spec ops for a paranormal branch of the government, gathering intel and wreaking havoc. He, Harlow and Brielle had done a really good job of blowing shit up when they needed to. But he wasn't good at this kind of undercover stuff, even if Aurora had thought he'd be perfect for it. And he hated it more that he was forced to work with the male he couldn't stop fantasizing about.

At least the spelled cord around his neck changed his appearance.

"I can definitely hook you up." The bartender grinned as he started pouring a beer for Axel. "Or maybe I can get between the two of you later." There was a lot of hope in the male's voice and Axel turned away while Christian continued talking.

He should have told Aurora no to coming here tonight, because he wasn't in the right headspace. But she rarely asked for anything, and hell, she was his Alpha now. It wasn't in his nature to say no to his Alpha.

"You get anything?" he murmured, his question subvocal when the bartender moved off.

"Other than a phone number, no." Christian sighed, sounding defeated.

Axel knew Christian wanted to bring down this ring of traffickers and was stressed that they'd lost their lead the other night. Going on instinct, Axel reached out and squeezed the male's knee, but then withdrew it at the way Christian stiffened.

Goddess, Axel got it—Christian didn't want him. Didn't even seem to like him anymore.

It shouldn't cut so deep, but...it did. When they'd first met, there'd been a powerful spark between them. One that even Christian couldn't deny. But after a flirty conversation, a couple drinks, and some kisses, it was like this wall fell in place between them and Christian just...didn't want to be around him anymore.

"Hey," a male voice murmured so low Axel almost didn't hear it. He turned to find the bartender sliding a piece of paper to them. "If you're looking for fun with humans, try here later. I'll be off here in a couple hours and can meet you there."

Nodding, Axel forced himself to smile at the male, glanced at the paper then pocketed it. "It's an address." He read it off and kept his voice subvocal so only Christian and those on the comm line would be able to hear him.

Juniper did an erotic sort of twist on the platform before she slid down the attached pole to the main dance floor. "We'll check it out soon," she murmured, easily making her way through the crowd until she almost disappeared from sight among the throng of people. "I just saw some humans leaving with some vamps and they did not look sober enough to be walking on their own. You two stay here."

Axel knew she meant him and Christian. He bit back a sigh even as Christian said, "Of course."

Right about now he wished he was at home with his pack, far away from the male who made him want to crawl out of his skin. He slid off the barstool, held out his hand for Christian. "Want to dance?" At least then they could do a couple laps around the place, search for more humans who looked out of place.

Something wild flashed in Christian's eyes, and to Axel's surprise he took his hand, tugged him close.

And it was impossible to miss Christian's erection as he pressed his body to his. Goddess help him. Axel didn't want to want this vampire so desperately. This vampire who'd lost his mate and was determined to be a sad panda for the rest of his days, unwilling to let Axel in at all because he wanted to wallow in his misery.

But...Axel was weak apparently. Because when Christian looked at him with that spark of hunger, Axel wanted to throw caution to the wind and chase after a male who'd made it clear that he was unavailable.

So damn weak.

CHAPTER SEVENTEEN

"We've got company." Zephyr's voice suddenly came through the comm line, sounding slightly out of breath. "There are three dragons waiting in the shadows about two blocks from the warehouse. I saw them from the air." His voice was whisper quiet, but Juniper heard him as she and Ren slipped out of the club.

The vampires with the trio of human females were leading the humans across the overgrown lot. One glanced over his shoulder and tensed when he spotted Juniper and Ren.

So Juniper threw her arm around Ren's shoulders and started singing a silly sea shanty off-key. Ren joined in and the vampires quickly lost interest in them as she and Ren veered in another direction.

"They haven't moved but one of the individuals is the same dragon female from the other night," Zephyr continued. "The older one. I'm certain it's her. What are your orders?"

Even though Zephyr's mere presence was driving her insane, she loved that when it came to work, he didn't question her. Sure, he'd given her shit about jumping out of the window—and he'd been right. It had been rash and she should've known better. But there was never a question that she was in charge of this crew. Unfortunately she knew from experience that some supernaturals had fragile egos, especially males, and couldn't deal with a female giving orders. Those kind of supernaturals didn't last long in the black ops world.

Once she and Ren reached the opposite gate from the vampires and humans, she let their song trail off. "Keep an eye on them," she murmured to Zephyr. "I'm going to shift and go camouflage. I'll follow the targets."

"I'll head to the address Axel gave us," Ren said, though it came out more like a question.

She nodded. "Yes, follow the lead we got. Don't go inside until you connect with one of us. Zephyr, I want you to stay on the three unknowns. Griff, how's the club looking? Any more movement?"

"The vampire and lion have it under control," he said. "And you need backup."

Zephyr growled across the comm line, clearly agreeing.

Griffin was right. She was capable but her crew tended to work in pairs. "You need backup too," she said to Zephyr. But he could fly, which put the others at a disadvantage. And tonight was weird anyway—neither she nor Ren had a partner either.

Even though she didn't specify him by name, he snorted. "I'll be fine."

"Griffin and Hyacinth, you two team up for now. I'll contact you guys once I follow them to where they're going and give an update then. Everyone, keep me updated." She hated going after vampires in her ridiculous outfit but whatever. She could kick ass in stilettos just as easily as she could in boots. Though she'd likely end up ditching them, regardless.

"Let us know if you want us to follow," Axel said over the comm line quietly, though she could clearly hear the thump of music in the background.

"I want you two watching the club for now." They might be capable, but they weren't part of her core crew and hadn't signed up for this kind of work.

She moved away from Ren, giving herself plenty of space before she called on her beast. Magic rippled through her, her dragon emerging in moments. Feeling settled in a way she only did in this form, she immediately called on her camouflage and took to the air as quietly as possible.

The scent trail the vampires left behind might as well have been a little trail of candy. It was ridiculously easy to track and they didn't go far. Only about three miles on foot, and she watched as the trio eventually picked up the humans who'd passed out. Juniper was guessing they'd been drugged. Then they used their vampiric strength and speed to enter an abandoned apartment building four stories high.

Rising up to greet her in the air was the scent of humans. Too many of them. Fear and sweat battled each other for dominance. The humans were scared. In danger.

As she swooped lower, the overwhelming scents faded, which was odd. She wondered if there was a spell around the building. Because she'd only scented it when she'd been high above it with her dragon's-eye view.

She made a mental note of it, and oh so quietly landed in the middle of the street by the building. She let her magic overtake her once again and shifted back to human. She kept her camouflage in place, however, so she wouldn't be seen. She winced as her heels made clicking sounds on the pavement, so she immediately took them off.

Quietly placing them on the sidewalk, she hurried up the crumbling pathway toward the building's entrance. Maybe forty years ago this place had been nice but it had long since been abandoned, even before The Fall. And it was on the outskirts of King's core territory, which was likely why it wasn't high on his priority to renovate. She knew he was making his way around the territory cleaning everything up, but that took time and manpower. Clearly someone was taking advantage of that lapse for their own evil gain.

As she neared a set of glass doors, she saw a vampire leaning against the wall smoking a cigarette. She contemplated knocking him out but decided to distract him instead. She picked up a discarded soda can and threw it behind her.

He straightened in concern at the sound and hurried past her toward the sidewalk, never sensing her.

She waited until he was to the sidewalk, his back turned, and opened the entrance door easily. As soon as she did, the scent of humans and fear almost choked her.

"I'm inside." She gave a quick description of the building and wished she'd seen an address somewhere. There hadn't been anything visible out front.

"I think this is the same place I'm at," Ren said quietly. "Four-story brick building with blacked-out windows on the third and fourth floors. I'm on the east side. There's no address but there is one listed next door on that building. If the addresses are in order, then this is the place Axel and Christian told us about."

Well, hell. "Everyone else, report."

Silence.

"I'm in the lobby." She kept her voice whisper quiet, trying not to worry that no one else had responded.

"I'll scale the side, enter through the roof if possible." Ren's voice was just as low as hers had been.

Still no response from the others. She didn't like it, but knew that noncommunication could mean a lot of things, not all of them necessarily bad. Moving on silent feet, she passed a set of elevator doors and was surprised the power was on. She wondered if they were siphoning it from somewhere. Or maybe they had a generator—or were utilizing magic. She took the stairs instead and eased the steel door open. As she did, voices from somewhere above trailed down to her.

The fresh scent of blood assaulted her so she hurried, racing up a flight of stairs in seconds. At the next steel door, she quietly pulled it open and slipped into the hallway. Wincing in disgust as she stepped onto dingy brown carpet that was peeling away from the hallway walls, she focused on the scent of blood and headed toward it.

At a slight cry, she hastened down the hallway, her heart rate kicking up. An apartment door with strips of dark green paint peeling off it was slightly ajar.

Slap.

"I didn't do anything wrong," the female rasped out.

Slap.

Still in camo, Juniper stepped fully inside to see a male towering over a dark-haired woman on the floor. The human female was huddled in on herself and holding her nose as she looked up at the male. And that was when Juniper got a good look at the human's swollen black eye.

"I'm going to drain you dry," the male hissed. "You're freaking useless. You can't do anything right."

The girl simply sobbed. "I've done everything you asked."

The male laughed, the sound skittering over Juniper's skin. "Once I'm done with you, I'm going to go back for your sister. She's going to take your place."

"No!" The girl screamed and tried to attack him, but he shoved her in the chest, sending her flying back into a wall.

Juniper covered the distance between them in a millisecond, let her camouflage drop right as she wrapped her arm around his neck and broke it in a practiced move.

He dropped to the floor with a thud, his head at an odd angle. She wished he'd had to suffer more, but right now had to be about stealth. She still had the element of surprise and needed to keep it as long as possible.

The girl stared at her, eyes wide, and Juniper knew the human was going to scream.

Moving lightning fast she held a finger up to her own lips even as she pressed a hand to the girl's mouth. "Be quiet. I'm here to help. But I need to know how many vampires are here. And how many humans."

The girl let out a strangled sob but quickly sucked in a breath as she steadied herself. Juniper removed her hand to let her speak. "I don't know how many there are. Too many vampires come during the night. They take our blood. And other things." She looked away in shame as a tremble racked her too-thin body.

Juniper saw red, had to rein her dragon back in. She was going to burn this place to the ground. "Can you guess how many humans are here?"

"Too many," the girl whispered.

Oh goddess. Juniper's heart cracked in that moment. "Do you know who is in charge here?"

The female's gaze dropped to the male on the ground. "He sort of was."

She inwardly cursed because she'd needed the vampire in charge of this shithole. "Does he have a partner?"

"He works with a couple other vampires. There are three of them that seem to run the show. They tell everyone else what to do. And they work for someone else. Someone not here," the girl whispered even as she looked over Juniper's shoulder toward the door, fear in her gaze.

But Juniper had shut it and she hadn't heard it open. No one was there. "Who are the other two vampires who run the show?"

"A guy named Theodore and a woman named Holly."

"I have more questions, but I need you to hide somewhere and stay quiet. I'm going to clean this place out and save all the humans. I'm not alone. Backup is on the way, but until then I need you to stay as quiet as possible."

"Is this a trick?" the girl whispered shakily.

Juniper's heart ached in that moment that the human could possibly think this was some sort of trick. "I work with King. Do you know who he is?"

She nodded. "I've heard of him. I'm not from this territory. They picked me up and..." She swallowed hard and started shaking.

"I don't need the details now," Juniper murmured. "But we're going to stop every single one of these vampires. Can you hide for me?"

The girl nodded, nose still bleeding, and moved toward a little bedroom. "I'll hide under the bed."

Juniper nodded and stepped back out into the hallway. It would have to do for now. She wished she could take the girl out of here this instant, but there was still that vampire outside and she didn't know what else might be lurking around the building.

After sweeping the whole second floor and finding it eerily empty, she said to Ren, "One dead vampire on the second floor." The others were still quiet and she wondered if it was because they were out of range. She hoped that was all it was.

"Six tangos down on the fourth floor. I'm still moving." There was a bite of simmering rage in his tone. "I want to eviscerate all of them," he growled.

She did too. So desperately. "We only need two alive. If possible, let one escape." So they could follow, something Ren would understand without her explaining. "I'll keep one alive." Or she'd try to. Right now her beast was rattling against her cage, wanting to burn and burn until all these vampires were dead. "Moving to the third floor."

"Going silent," was his response.

As a burst of adrenaline punched through her, she heard a multitude of male voices when she reached the next floor.

Two vampires were right outside the stairwell door. "We need to move everyone tonight," one of them said. "Too many people know about this place."

"I think you're right," was a female's contemplative reply. "Brutus texted me, told me he invited people here tonight."

The male let out a low curse. "We haven't even vetted them."

"No shit. All right, I've got to meet up with another supplier. I'll be back later. Get the new girls ready."

Juniper eased back against the wall as the door opened.

A female vampire in tight black pants, a black sweater and booted heels hurried into the stairwell. She paused, looked around, but her gaze moved over Juniper, who was in camouflage. Juniper held her breath, not wanting to make a sound. After a long moment, the female turned and hurried down the rest of the stairs.

Juniper followed her, wanting to make sure the female didn't stop on the second floor, and was relieved when the vamp kept going to the lobby. She wanted to follow this female, wanted to see who the supplier was, but she had the female vampire's scent. If one of her crew didn't tail the woman, Juniper would trail after her soon enough.

Right now her priority was saving all the humans in this place.

It was going to be tricky, but she could handle a bunch of vampires alone. She'd never met one even close to her power level. Fire and vampires didn't mix well.

She eased the door open, heard a thud above her and winced. That was likely Ren, cleaning out the vampire trash. There were three vampires in this hallway, each leaning on a wall outside the doorway.

All of them straightened slightly and looked at each other. They either scented her or the thud upstairs was out of the ordinary. She moved with supernatural speed, racing down the hallway. As she passed the first vampire, she punched straight through his chest, ripped his heart out.

His blood dripped down her arm, and she dropped her camouflage because there was no point anymore. The second vampire barely had time to react as she reached him. With a quick burst of fire, she incinerated him.

Ashes burst everywhere as he exploded.

Wide-eyed, the third vampire turned in the other direction and sprinted toward the end of the hallway.

She'd started to chase after him when a door right next to her flew open.

A vampire with his pants unzipped stepped out. "What the he—"

She struck out fast, slammed her fist into his throat even though she knew she should just kill him right away. But he deserved a throat punch.

His fangs dropped and he slashed out at her with the deadly claws that vampires could grow.

She quickly dodged back, was aware of another door opening down the hallway as his claws almost grazed her stomach.

Footsteps pounded behind her. Without turning, she reached out lightning fast, ignoring the vamp's next would-be strike as she grabbed his head, snapped his neck like a rag doll.

She was aware of human females in the room he'd just come from, but had to block them out as another vampire ran through the doorway at her.

On a scream of rage, she released another burst of flames from her throat. She rarely breathed fire in this form—it was harder to do.

Even as she released a stream of fire, her chains released as well. She snapped one out as she sensed another vampire emerging from a connected room. Her chains wrapped around his neck, ripped his head off even as the vampire she'd killed moments before turned to ash.

Threat neutralized for now, she turned to the human females, caught their shell-shocked gazes. *Oh goddess, these poor humans.* "My crew and I are here to save you. Do you know how many vampires are on this floor?"

They just stared at her, clearly in shock.

She inwardly cursed, then said, "I'll be back," before she sprinted out the door. As she reached the hallway, three vampires turned almost as one as they attempted to escape her.

Her magical chains reacted even before she could consciously order them to. They lashed out, caught two of the vamps around the middle and squeezed tight.

More ash coated the floor as the vampires died under the magic of her chains. She let the third escape—he jumped out a window, shattering the glass and jumping down three stories. She'd hunt that one later too. Because this operation was bigger than just this little building, these disgusting vamps.

By the time Ren raced into the hallway, she'd killed another six vampires. "Are you clear?" she asked.

He nodded. "I shot one of them with one of my arrows. He's incapacitated now."

"Two got away earlier. I've got their scents." They wouldn't escape for long. And would hopefully lead them to more vampires.

Ren gave a sharp nod, then paused. "Good. I think I'm getting a signal now."

Her comm line crackled slightly then too. "Guys?"

Before anyone could respond, Zephyr and Hyacinth raced out of the stairwell into the hallway.

"Is everything okay?" She looked between them.

"More or less," Hyacinth said.

That would have to do for the moment. "There's still a human hiding on the second floor," she said. "We need to get the others outside now. I'm going to contact King." Because he would have the resources to help all these females. And they needed to get them to the healing center—and then they would need a lot of care. She knew of a couple places around the globe that specialized in this specific kind of care and was planning on contacting all of them to see if they could take any of these humans if King's territory couldn't handle the influx. Though many might prefer to go back to their families right away—if they had any.

But all that would have to wait right now. Step one was getting them out of this shithole.

"The dragons who were following you are outside the building. They want to talk to you," Zephyr said, his tone difficult to read. But there was a hint of frustration in his gray eyes, shining out. He scrubbed a hand over his face and dark beard. "They wouldn't take the bait and follow me. So I tailed them while they tailed you. I don't think they want to harm you."

"The ones King told us about?"

He nodded. "We tried contacting you, but something was wrong with our comms."

"I think this place is spelled. Or it was." Her comm line crackled again. "Are they threatening anyone?"

"No. But they won't leave. The oldest one is ancient. I can feel it. She's...powerful."

Zephyr himself was ancient and powerful. So whoever this female was, she was a force to be reckoned with.

"Fine. I'll deal with them now if they won't leave. My orders still stand." She looked at Ren and Hyacinth. "Start getting everyone outside." She wanted to ask where Griffin was, but already had an idea that he was downstairs keeping an eye on the dragons.

Zephyr tugged his T-shirt off, handed it to her, something in his gaze and scent she couldn't define—didn't want to. He...cared for her. Wanted to take care of her. The scars crossing his chest and abs stood out under the harsh fluorescent lighting so she focused on that.

She looked down at her blood-splattered self. The vampires might have turned to ash when she killed them, but she'd still gotten some of their nasty blood on her. *Ugh.* Her skirt was falling apart and the loose top was almost completely frayed at this point, the sequins having all been ripped off in her fighting.

"Thanks," she said as she slipped the shirt over her head. She loved that his scent was covering her now, but would never admit it. "Are you good?" She looked at the three of them. Because she needed to handle these damn dragons and get them out of here. She didn't have time for any extra shit right now.

Everyone nodded and she hurried back down the hallway. She only stopped on the second floor to coax out the first human she'd met from under the bed.

"We're going to get you medical care. I promise."

The female, whose name was Angela, simply wrapped her arms around herself as she followed Juniper to the door. "They're all dead?" she whispered.

"All except one or two. They're only alive because we will grill them for information." Grill seemed like a nicer word than torture.

"I'll tell you everything I ever heard any of them say," the female rasped out, her voice trembling with rage.

Juniper looked at her as they walked down the stairs. They were cool against her bare feet. "Thank you. We're going to do everything we can to completely shut down this ring."

Before they'd made it to the lobby floor, the door opened behind them in the stairwell.

Angela froze, the scent of her fear popping sharp and bitter.

Ren stepped out, his hands up in a calming gesture, clearly having scented it as well.

"He's with me," Juniper said. "And he's not a vampire. He's a jaguar shifter. We're working together."

"We've got everyone gathered on this floor," Ren said. "But I want to do a head count once we get outside. Then we'll do another couple sweeps."

Juniper nodded once then looked at Angela again. The human looked fragile, breakable, but her jaw was set tight and Juniper had a feeling she would be okay. "I need you to go with him. I have to take care of something first and make sure it's safe for everyone to come outside." She was going to get rid of those freaking dragons who'd apparently decided to follow her while she was on a mission.

Ren simply nodded. "Griff is still outside."

Juniper nodded and promised the human that she would be in good hands before she hurried to face these unknown dragons.

As she pushed open the door, she stepped over a pile of ashes—probably the vampire who'd been smoking a cigarette.

But her gaze was immediately drawn to the three tall dragon shifters in human form standing on the sidewalk. Juniper recognized them from the pictures King had given her.

The older female had a regal bearing, her hair a light gray—which said a lot for how old she must be. Shifters didn't age the same as humans and this dragon actually looked as if she would be in her fifties if she'd been human. Her hair was swept back into a coiled braid and she wore long pants and a thick-looking coat with fur at the collar.

Juniper glanced at the others, made mental notes on them, but her gaze went right back to the ancient female. Because she was clearly the one in charge.

"Who the hell are you guys and what do you want with me?" she snapped as she stalked forward. She could scent Griff in the shadows nearby, was glad for his presence. He was a deadly fighter, and if this went sideways, she knew he'd have her back.

They all simply stared at her, with the gray-haired female's gaze sweeping over Juniper's ragged, barefoot appearance.

Annoyance popped inside her as she took another few steps toward them, her beast prowling under the surface, ready to shift and lash out. "I just killed a shitload of trafficking vampires, so if you guys want to fight, you picked the wrong day to mess with me."

The female spoke calmly as she stepped forward. "My name is Starlena. We have been following you because we wish to speak to you." Her voice was lyrical, soft and lilting, but Juniper could practically hear the steel lining those words.

"As you can see, now is not a great time." Then she glanced to where Griffin was because she knew these dragons were aware of his presence. "Griff, contact King. We need healers here ASAP."

He'd probably already done it, but she wanted these dragons to know that King and his people were on the way.

She turned back to the dragons. "So what do you want?" Because she still had a couple vampires to hunt down.

"Perhaps we should have waited to approach you, but I simply could not stay away."

Um, okay. They weren't putting off threatening vibes, but this was beyond strange. And the power pulsing off them... Zephyr had been right. It was palpable, a ripple in the air wrapping around her. "I'm covered in dead vampire blood and ash right now, so can you please get to the point?"

"I believe you are my granddaughter," the female said bluntly.

Juniper blinked as surprise ricocheted through her. That had *not* been what she'd been expecting this female to say. Not that she'd been expecting anything specific, but still. Not even in the same ballpark. A snort escaped. "Okay, yeah sure."

The female lifted an imperious eyebrow and ran a hand over her pale gray hair. As she did, it rippled to a silver color just like Juniper's.

Her own wasn't covered now because of the spell— Wait! This female shouldn't even be able to see her true face because of the spelled charm she was wearing. Low-grade panic started to buzz inside her. *No, no, no.* "Cool magic trick," she said. Because that little show could be accomplished with magic.

The female's eyes narrowed slightly before she held her arms out to her side and two glowing chains emerged in a snap.

Ohhhhhhh. Shit.

"Oh shit, indeed," the older female said in that same imperious tone.

Juniper blinked; she hadn't realized she'd said that part out loud.

She turned at the sound of Zephyr and the others stepping outside. He'd taken charge, was leading everyone while Hyacinth brought up the back, carrying one unconscious female, Ren carrying another.

She turned back to the three strangers—one who might actually be her grandmother. The thought of that was too surreal for her to wrap her mind around, however. "I don't have time to deal with any of this right now." She didn't know these people—who hadn't cared enough to find her before now.

"How can we help?" the female asked, seemingly unconcerned by Juniper's dismissal.

"You can leave. Tell me where you're staying and I'll contact you. But we've got too much going on tonight. And I just can't deal with..." She gestured at them. *Nope.* This was not happening right now. These people just showed up when she was clearly working? Where had they been her whole life? *Screw all of them.*

Before the female could respond, a tall male—definitely a dragon—appeared out of the shadows, dragging the vampire female she'd let escape earlier.

He stalked up to them and tossed the sobbing, begging vampire onto the sidewalk in front of Juniper.

"A gift," Starlena said, her mouth curving up in a pleased expression. "This one escaped your wrath."

Sighing, Juniper had started to respond when Starlena blasted the vampire with her chains, wrapping them around the female so quickly that Juniper could barely track the speed of them with her eyes. "Crap, no—"

The vampire's cry of agony was cut off before Juniper could finish her own protest.

"Damn it," she cursed. "I *let* her get away. I wanted to follow her."

The older dragon's eyes widened slightly. "Oh. Ah, apologies," she murmured as she called her chains back in. They disappeared completely from sight as the ash of the now deceased vampire blew down the sidewalk with a gust of wind.

Welp, her potential grandmother had the same impulses that Juniper did apparently. Kill first, ask questions later. *Fuuuuck.* She held a sigh in and turned as Griffin quietly approached.

"King's people are about sixty seconds out," Griffin said, watching the dragons warily.

She simply nodded and turned back to the newcomers because they were very, very dangerous. The power rippling off them as a group was immense, almost pulsing in the air. Or maybe it was all from the elder female. It was too hard to tell when they were standing so close to each other.

Zephyr also stepped up beside her so that he was in her line of sight. She knew what he and Griff were doing—presenting a united front. And she appreciated it.

The female gave her a long, searching look. "King knows where we are staying. Please call on us when you're done here." For some reason, her words sounded like an order.

"Maybe I will. Maybe I won't." Juniper might have a whole lot of questions, and yeah, she wanted to know who these people were. Especially the female who said she was her grandmother. But she wasn't going to do what this female said without question. And Starlena had better realize that right now.

Starlena paused, her mouth curving up slightly in what might have been approval as she nodded once. Then she motioned to the others and they turned, sweeping down the street before they suddenly shifted to dragon without taking off their clothing.

They just...*poof*, shifted in mere moments, the same way she did, and took to the skies in a shimmer of light. And it was impossible to miss that Starlena had the same shimmery white marble coloring that Juniper did.

Oh. No.

CHAPTER EIGHTEEN

Juniper resisted the urge to pace in front of the bound, captive vampire that Ren had captured earlier.

They'd checked the male for poison pills and weapons and had him fully secured to a chair with spelled bindings while they waited for Everleigh, a witch with truthsense capabilities. King had given them use of a nearby warehouse while he and his pack helped get all the humans transported to various healing centers. There was so much responsibility his pack was taking on right now and she was glad for it. Saving the humans wasn't enough. They needed help getting home or starting a new home here.

Juniper didn't want to wait for the witch to arrive, though it hadn't actually been that long. Every second that stretched out felt like a year of her life wasting away. She wanted to get the information they needed and then hunt down the rest of these vampires. But she'd promised King that they would work with his people on this. And she respected him, his pack.

Griff had left before King arrived to chase after the other male she'd let escape out the window. So at least he was out there and not stuck in this warehouse, waiting, waiting, waiting.

And...obsessing about the fact that a woman who had eerie abilities similar to her own claimed she was her grandmother. This was not supposed to happen. Her family had *abandoned* her, left her to die in the wilds of what was now Russia. They were dead to her.

"You've wanted to meet your family forever. Your *biological* family," Ren said, breaking the silence in the warehouse. "Because *we* are your real family. Always will be."

She lifted a shoulder. But yeah, her crew was her family. End of story.

"Shut up," Hyacinth murmured to Ren.

Ren did not. "So what are you going to do?" he continued. "After we deal with this piece of shit. Are you going to meet them? Do you want us to go with you?"

Juniper rubbed her hands over her face, turned on her heel and stalked out of the warehouse. Where the hell was that witch?

As she stepped outside into the icy air, she sucked in a deep breath that wasn't tinged with the stench of ash and vampire. At least someone had given her jeans, a sweater and sneakers to wear instead of the ridiculously skimpy outfit she'd worn earlier, but she still needed a shower to get the vampire stench and gore off her.

Savoring the silence, she leaned against the exterior of the warehouse and wasn't surprised when Zephyr stepped outside with her. He hadn't said much since the arrival of those dragons, or their departure. But he'd been a shadow, barely a few feet away from her at any given moment. It should annoy her but…she liked it. He had a sort of soothing presence. Not that she'd tell him that.

"Are you going to insist that I need to meet my family?" she asked, staring up at the stars.

He leaned against the metal wall next to her. "Nope."

"Really?" She glanced at him, drank in the casual way he leaned against the warehouse—and still looked like a lethal predator. A shiver slid down her spine as her gaze skated over his pecs and abs. He'd left his shirt off, was just fully showing off his honed-to-perfection body. And she clearly wasn't above staring. The male called to her on every level, whether she wanted it or not.

"Of course not. You have to make the choice for yourself. And you're probably feeling a whole lot of emotions right now. And all of them are valid, so don't let Ren, however well meaning, push you into doing something you don't want to do." He let out a little snort. "Not that I think you would let anyone push you into doing anything."

Being so close to Zephyr, being near his wild forest scent, had her feeling off-kilter. And him being all logical certainly wasn't helping. She needed… She needed to fight with something right now. Killing those vampires had barely taken off the edge. "I want to kill something right now."

"Those feelings are also valid."

Goddess, his whole calm demeanor was driving her insane. Was he…doing this to make her crazy? *Gah.* She felt like a bit of a psycho for even thinking that. But the energy humming through her was too much. Her supposed family had just shown up tonight and thrown a bomb at her. Just like that!

Juniper turned and slammed her fist into the warehouse exterior. The metal crunched under her fist and the only thing she got for her efforts were bleeding knuckles and a shot of pain up her arm. At least the brief pain grounded her. She stared at her hand, watching as her torn knuckles already started knitting back together.

"Feel better, princess?" Zephyr's tone was dry as he eyed her.

"I'd feel better if I could punch your face," she snapped. Why was he even out here? Other than to torment her, make her want things she couldn't have.

He simply grinned at her. "Pretty sure you'd feel better if you sat on my face."

Her mouth dropped open as she stared at him. Before he'd changed all the rules on her, demanded something serious, she would have taken him up on that offer.

How could she even respond to that? And oh, sweet goddess, heat rushed between her thighs as mental images flooded her mind, as she imagined *exactly* what it would be like to do just that. To feel his tongue flicking against her folds, then focusing on her clit, his beard grazing her inner thighs. Gritting her teeth, she turned away from him and stalked back inside.

The low chuckle he let out was too much, reverberating through her. She shut everything down. Or tried to.

She was even more off-kilter now. Once she was back in the warehouse, it was clear that the others had heard Zephyr's words because her entire crew studiously ignored her. Which was good because she still didn't have the bandwidth to deal with anything other than the mission.

She knew they were on the right track, that they'd managed to save an apartment building of humans. And that *mattered*. But she still couldn't get the images from tonight out of her mind.

The dirty rooms the women—and some men—had been forced to stay in, the broken bones of some of the humans, the scents of pain and agony filling that whole building, the shell-shocked stares of half the prisoners. She pressed her palms to her eyes for a moment but it didn't help, didn't banish anything.

Those vampires hadn't deserved such a quick death.

When an attractive female stepped into the warehouse with Zephyr, she straightened. She had choppy brown hair, olive skin and wore a loose multicolored tunic over jeans. Her earrings jangled slightly as she moved. This must be Everleigh.

Juniper shelved all thoughts of her potential biological family, Zephyr, everything, and put on her game face.

It was time to get answers. Then they would all go hunting.

CHAPTER NINETEEN

King steeled himself as he stepped into Greer's healing center. They'd taken about half of the rescued humans to her place, and a quarter each to two other locations that had enough social workers and therapists in the territory to help.

But he wanted his packmates involved in all of this. After what they'd just discovered, he wasn't trusting anyone he hadn't worked with personally to help these humans. Because this never should have happened.

Greer met him in the entryway, her smile tinged with sadness as he shut the front door behind him. "I'm getting everyone settled," she said. "Your wolves were wonderful in helping get the place ready. They moved in here like a tornado setting up more beds."

He nodded once because he had expected nothing less from his pack. "What else do you need from me?"

"Nothing now, but there is a place in Finn's territory that will be able to help all of these women on a longer-term mental health basis, if they so choose. So far the women with me aren't from this territory. They were taken from other places and imported here."

"I believe only the few taken tonight and a handful of others are from my territory." He rolled his shoulders, still unable to believe that this had been going on right under his pack's patrolling. His wolf flared to the surface, but he shoved his beast back down.

"You can't blame yourself," Greer said softly, as if she'd read his mind.

"I'm the Alpha. It is my fault." Everything came down to how well he ran his territory. This was on him. He'd missed something. These humans had paid the price.

She gave a sharp shake of her head, her copper-colored ponytail swishing slightly. "You've created a safe haven here. But sometimes evil finds a way. And I know you're not going to let this move any farther in our territory."

"Anyone involved will die." Right now he was keeping things as quiet as possible, but once he had everyone captured, had their leader's identity, he would definitely make an example of them.

"I heard Juniper made quite the example of those vampires."

"Oh, she's not done," he growled softly.

"Good." Greer's voice was sharp, the tone out of the ordinary for the normally very calm, gentle healer.

"I'd like to have one of my people or Juniper talk to the women. I trust you to do your job but we need as many details as possible on who these vampires are. I know many of the humans are still in a state of shock and some are still detoxing off drugs. But once you think they're able, we need to question anyone who can talk. We need to know if there are more victims out there."

"Of course. I'm already in contact with the other housing centers. We'll tag team with each other and keep you updated with everything. I want them all to get some sleep at least for the night—day, I guess," she said.

It was three in the morning, so yeah, day.

"Most of them are crashing hard right now," she continued. "And I've put some of them in a healing sleep. But I'll be monitoring all of them the next few hours."

"Do you want me to call Reaper back in from the field?" he asked. The male, her mate, was out on patrols, keeping the border secure.

"No. I've already talked to him. He's so big and can be intimidating without trying. I think it's necessary that I only have females here for at least the next twenty-four hours."

King reached out on impulse and squeezed her forearm gently. "Thank you. For what you're doing." He knew he was lucky to have such a powerful healer in his territory, one who was so giving of herself and her time.

She reached over with her other hand and squeezed his. "Thank you for being an Alpha worth following."

Right about now he didn't feel worthy. But he'd do everything he could to clean up this mess. To help everyone affected.

CHAPTER TWENTY

"We've got all we need," Juniper said as she stood, moving away from Everleigh and the vampire who'd broken so easily under their questioning that it was pathetic.

They now had the names of anyone in the territory who'd abused the humans at the abandoned apartment complex, including the bartender who'd given Axel and Christian the address. So Juniper was leaning toward believing that at least some of the names the vampire had given them were legitimate, since they lined up with what her people knew already. Everleigh had been able to suss out truths versus lies and it had been impressive to watch.

"We need to grab the remaining vampires before they realize something is up and disappear." Juniper looked over at the vampire who'd passed out and was slumped over in his chair. Blood trickled down the side of his face. She had no pity for him.

"I'll do a finding spell," Everleigh said, standing as well. Her face looked drawn now, not rosy and full of life like when she'd arrived hours ago. "The locations won't be exact, but I can send you in the right direction."

Juniper nodded. "Thank you. I'm guessing you need time to recover first?" She didn't know everything about witches, but they didn't have unlimited power. They had reserves of magic they basically stored, but even so, Everleigh would likely need to recharge.

The witch gave her a faint smile. "I will. Give me a couple hours to sleep and eat. I'll recharge, then work together with a couple other witches to do the finding spell. We know we've got a couple days at least." She glanced over at the vampire. "What are you going to do with him?"

"I'll take care of him." Zephyr's voice was sharp, pointed.

Juniper hadn't forgotten he was in the warehouse—that was impossible—but he had a way of blending into the shadows, being silent when he needed to be. It was a handy trick. "Unfortunately we need to keep him alive for now." Because her boss wanted to question him as well. She glanced at Ren. "Did you get a hold of August?"

He nodded. "He wants him transported to Montana. Vega and Gabriel are in the area, said they would happily transport him for us."

Juniper hadn't seen the mated couple in a while but had worked with them before and really liked the two of them. "When will they be here?" Because she wanted to get the hell out of here, to shower, eat, recharge and then get back to business. They knew where there would be a drop-off in a couple days—someone from the Tennessee territory was supposed to be picking up a bunch of humans. Juniper and her crew would be there to stop them. Before that, however, she planned to round up every single vampire in this territory who had hurt any of those humans.

"They're already on the way," Ren said. "They were at her father's so they're not too far."

Vega's father, Finn Stavros, ran the southeast territory of what had once been Mississippi.

"Sounds good. If you'll excuse me, I need to call King," she said, pulling her cell phone out and heading for the exit of the warehouse. "He said he'd spare us whatever and whoever we need." And they needed people they could trust to round up these criminals.

"You want me to ask my brothers to help?" Zephyr said before she could make it outside.

"Maybe. Let me see what King says."

He simply nodded, but watched her with intense gray eyes she had to force herself to turn away from. Right now was about the job. Not anything else. Certainly not her wants or needs. She didn't get that luxury right now. No matter how much she wanted a certain dragon shifter.

～

AN HOUR later Juniper stepped out of her bathroom and collapsed on the bed for a long minute. She was still waiting on Everleigh to get them potential locations and...she wasn't even sure what time it was at this point. She also still needed to eat. And maybe fit in an hour nap.

But first she probably needed to put clothes on—and not obsess about sneaking down the hallway to Zephyr's room and propositioning him. Because he'd just tell her that he didn't want casual. *Ugh.* Why did he have to be all noble or whatever he thought he was doing? They could both be getting amazing orgasms right now—and she knew they would be amazing.

After throwing on jeans and a sweater, she'd started to braid her damp hair when she heard a knock from downstairs. She paused, wondering if someone else had gotten the door.

Then she heard another knock.

So no, then. As she finished her braid, she hurried out of her bedroom to find Zephyr stepping out of his room as well.

The look he gave her was heated; he wasn't even trying to hide his lust for her. Which was both exhilarating and maddening. Because he wouldn't give her what she wanted—uncomplicated orgasms. "Are we expecting anyone?" he murmured.

She shook her head and they both hurried down the stairs. Everleigh had already said she'd call her with details when she had them, so Juniper couldn't imagine who this was. But even before she opened the door, familiar scents greeted her. She smiled, opening the door to both Vega and Gabriel waiting on the doorstep. Juniper pulled Vega into a hug immediately.

Vega Marius Stavros—hybrid daughter of Alpha wolf Finn Stavros and Lyra, bloodborn royal vampire—was one of the rarest of hybrids. Wolves and vampires didn't tend to mix, much less procreate. Her jet-black hair was pulled up into a ponytail and she had on her standard jeans, heavy boots, a black T-shirt and a leather jacket. Gabriel basically dressed the same, which made Juniper smile as she stepped back.

"Are you guys starting to dress alike now?" she asked as she fist-bumped Gabriel.

"I can't help it if he likes to copy me," Vega said with a grin. She was relatively young but she held her power well, embraced who and what she was. It was like she'd been born for black ops work.

Gabriel just shrugged, a grin playing at his mouth. He was about six foot two, an inch or so taller than Juniper, with pale green eyes, and he moved more like a feline than the wolf he was.

"Not that I'm not happy to see you both again, but what are you doing here?" She'd seen them an hour ago when they'd picked up that vampire. They should be on their way to Montana to drop him off now.

Vega grinned. "I asked a demigod friend to transport him for us. Only took a few seconds," she said, laughing. "We want to help with this thing, and August said we're cleared to team up if you need it."

"I actually might." She stepped back, motioning them both to come inside. They'd already met Zephyr back at the warehouse, and he nodded politely at them as he shut the door behind them. "Are you guys hungry or anything?" she asked.

"We're good. Unless you were about to eat. I don't want to stop you," Vega said.

Juniper was about to say they were fine too, but Zephyr said, "I'll whip something up for us. You guys can talk about things while I cook."

She was surprised by the offer, but probably shouldn't be. Zephyr had already proven he wanted to help out any way he could. And her dragon side really, really liked the idea of him feeding her, taking care of her. She wasn't even sure why, but she swore she could feel her chains practically tingling right now, ready to unleash and latch around him again.

Gah!

"I'll hang out in the kitchen with Zephyr," Gabriel said as they reached the back door that led to the porch and patio.

Juniper simply nodded and stepped outside as Vega gave her mate a quick kiss on the mouth.

She wasn't jealous of the couple, but a pang hit her square in the chest at the sight of their happiness. She was so damn afraid to want that for herself, to reach for it. Her entire life she'd never fit in—a dragon shifter with strange magical capabilities living with a bunch of wolves, half of whom were scared of her. And while she loved her parents, she'd always felt lacking. They were so calm, always looking for the peaceful solution whereas her first instinct was to burn things that pissed her off. She wondered if her...if those other dragons were like her. Or if she was like them, rather. She didn't want to care about them, didn't want to worry about getting to know them. But she did care.

"I feel like I work more now than I did before The Fall," Vega said as she sat down and stretched her long legs out in front of her.

Juniper snorted softly as she sat across from her on the iron patio chair. "No kidding." She glanced at the back door, wondering when Gabriel and Zephyr would come outside. Mainly she just wanted to see Zephyr. Because she had this growing obsession with the male that she couldn't deny to herself. She might deny it to her crew, but not to herself. Not anymore anyway.

"So is he part of your crew now?" Vega asked.

"He's working with us on this job. But I don't know about anything past it." She lifted a shoulder and hoped it came off as casual. Juniper didn't even want to think about what would happen after this mission. She'd be sent off on another one and Zephyr would...probably stay here with his brothers. His family.

Ask him to come with you, her dragon half purred. Juniper ignored her.

Vega crossed her legs and glanced around the plush backyard. "I hear you. We brought on some new people the last couple months, though I'm sure August has already told you."

"He did." Juniper had been working with August for decades, and Vega was young, had only been with them for a few years. She was good though, a skilled warrior Juniper was happy to have on her side.

"So what do you want from me and Gabriel? I was serious—put us to work."

"You sure?" She knew that Vega hadn't seen her family in a while and that she loved visiting, especially because she got to spend time with her little brother.

"I'm sure. Once we kick ass, I'll head back home. I think I was driving my dad a little crazy anyway. I tend to let my brother do what he wants and…" She shrugged, a grin playing on her features, her expression mischievous. "My dad doesn't like it."

Juniper shook her head slightly. "How many vampires do you want to hunt down?"

Vega shrugged. "You just tell me."

Juniper grinned. "Fine. How about five? King's people are involved too so I'm splitting up all the names with my crew, his people, and now you guys." She just hoped this stayed as quiet as King thought it would. She knew that her crew could be trusted, and right now all the humans were at healing centers and not talking to anyone. And King had guards stationed stealthily near that apartment site across the street. Anyone who went inside was getting picked up.

"That works," Vega said as Gabriel and Zephyr stepped outside.

Like always, Juniper's gaze was immediately drawn to Zephyr. The male was walking, talking sex. A huge, sexy dragon shifter with gray eyes that held wicked promises. She worried that she would never get him out of her system—and she hadn't even gotten a taste of him yet.

Still, she couldn't stop herself from obsessing about him, wondering what he would be like in bed. Up against the wall. On the floor. Anywhere. Everywhere. Sitting on his face. Damn him for putting that thought in her mind.

After a brief conversation with Vega and Gabriel, the two of them headed out to go see some of their own contacts, and Juniper and

Zephyr scarfed down the sandwiches he'd made for them. Since she still hadn't heard from Everleigh, she decided to get one thing out of the way while she had the time.

So she called King and told him she was going to talk to the Nova dragons—her grandmother apparently—and he assured her that he had two wolves watching their location. Which did make her feel better. She trusted her skills but these were unknowns and it never hurt for someone to have your back. Though she never counted on it —except with her own people. They'd always had her back. And she'd always had theirs. And now Zephyr was included in that equation. The thought should terrify her, and it did a little, but...she liked that he was part of her crew. Even if temporarily.

"Want me to go with you?" Zephyr asked as she ended her call with King, sliding her phone into her pocket.

"You don't have to do that." Though she really didn't want to go alone. Or at all. But she knew that she needed to at least talk to the strangers who claimed they were her family. Or they'd just show up again unannounced.

Griffin was upstairs sleeping, Ren was with Grace right now—he'd wanted to stop by and see the human while he could—and Hyacinth had gone to visit the Magic Man. Juniper wasn't even going to think about what was going on with those two.

"I know I don't have to. I want to. You shouldn't go by yourself." He held up a hand when she started to make a defensive remark. "Not because you're not capable. You are the most capable being I've ever met. But this is a lot to deal with, and they're essentially strangers. It doesn't hurt to show up with another badass dragon at your side."

Her lips quirked up. "Badass?"

"I *am* a very skilled fighter." There was no smugness, just raw confidence in his tone.

And he wasn't wrong. It warmed her from the inside out that he wanted to go with her so she nodded and stood, picking up her empty plate as he picked up his own.

"Okay, let's get this over with," she muttered. Still, she was glad to have the sexy dragon by her side.

CHAPTER TWENTY-ONE

The energy rolling off Juniper as they walked down the sunlit street was palpable. And when she looked at her phone's screen for the third time, Zephyr said, "Any news?" He hadn't heard her phone buzz.

She gave him a sheepish look and tucked her phone away. "No."

She hadn't covered her hair today. Instead she'd braided it, then coiled it at her neck. She'd tugged a wool knit cap over her head so most of the silver was covered. It didn't do much to hide how magnificent she was though. She was a tall, lithe predator. A sexy powerhouse.

"So you're just obsessively checking in the hopes that there *is* news so you don't have to go see your potential biological family?"

She lifted a shoulder, her mouth curving up slightly in admission. "Pretty much. I've never been so nervous in my life. I shouldn't even care what they think about me. I don't *know* these people. They abandoned me," she snapped out, her smile fading.

"If they abandoned you, then why does your grandmother want to see you now?" Zephyr sure as hell didn't trust them, but he'd seen the way that older dragon had watched Juniper last night. There'd been a lot of pain rippling under the surface. The female didn't mean Juniper harm—if she did, she'd already be dead. By his hand.

"We don't know that she is my grandmother." She shoved her hands in her pockets as they reached a crosswalk.

He wished he had the right to hold her hand, to touch her, to claim her. Sighing, he scanned the surrounding areas automatically. There weren't many kids out right now, either because they were in school or it was too cold out. But there were a few joggers and other adult humans walking little dogs.

"Fine, there is a probability that we are related," she murmured when he didn't respond. *"Maybe."* And she sounded positively sulky about it.

But there was no maybe about it. The similarities with their unique silver hair coloring and the magical chains... They were at least from the same clan. "I told you that I was stuck in a Hell realm for a long time," he started.

She seemed surprised by the change in subject but nodded as they crossed the street. "Yeah."

A park was to their left and he smiled to see wolves running around it while a female was teaching art to a class of young humans. "It felt like I was only there for forty years by earth standards, but in reality I was there thousands of years. I lost so much time. By the time I finally escaped, I discovered that most of our family was gone." Except his three younger brothers who were basically strangers to him now. "It's...*good* to have family. And I know you already have family that is not biological, but there is no harm in adding more people to your circle." He wanted Juniper to have more people to love her, to support her, to hopefully somehow convince her that she was worthy of being loved. Because he was starting to realize that was her real issue, why she was keeping him at a distance. She didn't want to let anyone in.

"I know. I've just been living this reality for over a hundred years. I guess I'm having a hard time processing that I might actually have biological relatives and that they might want to know me." She frowned to herself as they sidestepped two human females jogging.

"Do you remember anything from before you met your parents and Ren and Griff?" Zephyr only knew the basics, but he wanted to know all of it. Wanted to know everything about Juniper.

She shook her head and then rubbed her temple. "It's weird. Anytime I even try to *think* about my past before them, I get massive headaches. My mom thinks it could be a PTSD-induced reaction. She's used her healing magic on me in the past when I'd get nose-bleeds. I eventually stopped trying to think about the past."

Zephyr frowned, not liking what she described at all. "Did you ever look into—"

"Spellwork? As in, did someone create a trap in my mind?" She shoved out a sigh. "Yes. That was actually the first thing my mom thought it might be, but she probed using her magic and couldn't find anything."

"Your mother is a wolf, not a dragon."

She blinked. "What does that have to do with anything?"

"Maybe nothing, but you might want to have Greer take a look at your mind, see if she can find something." Greer was not only a dragon, she was a powerful healer.

Juniper made a noncommittal sound and slowed her steps.

He nudged her once. "If you don't want to do this—"

"I do." She picked up her pace again. "I'll just get this over with and then be done with them."

He doubted she would just "be done with them," especially if she got a chance to get to know them and they turned out to be decent, but he kept that to himself. She was processing a lot right now on top of having a high-pressure mission. And he didn't want to be an extra problem for her—but that didn't mean he was going to let her go. No, he was going to keep showing her that he would be there for her.

"What was it like in the Hell realm you were trapped in?"

He was surprised by the question, but answered. Because he wanted this female to know everything about him too, and he liked that she was asking. It meant she cared. "Deadly. Dangerous. Sort of what humans would consider prehistoric times. I stayed in my dragon form most of the time until..." He cleared his throat. "I met some humans, became friends with them." Then one day he'd lost *all* his friends to violence, something he was still dealing with. Before that time, he'd lost people, of course—he'd been part of a warrior dragon clan after all. But being stuck in that realm with so many humans, actually befriending them, it had changed him on a fundamental level.

"And?"

"And…they died. One human in particular, Circe, was a small, scrappy thing, but she was tough. For a human. She fell into the Hell realm because of a freak accident. We became friends." It was odd to think he'd become so close to a human. After Circe, he'd befriended more of them and had started to view them differently. Not as weak and useless. They'd been fearless, determined to survive and thrive against all the odds. And they'd been so open and welcomed him into their circle.

"Did you love her?" There was an odd note to Juniper's voice.

He looked at her in surprise. "Yes. But not the way you're asking, I think. I loved her like a sister. But I couldn't protect her. Couldn't protect the family I'd made there. I'd been away because of a threat, and while I was gone taking care of it…another group of dragons swooped in and killed them all. It was a massacre. Killing for the sake of killing. They didn't take anything, they just killed everyone." He still saw their bodies, the blood, the ashes, when he closed his eyes sometimes. It had gotten to the point where he didn't all the time, but it would sneak up on him when he was exhausted.

Juniper took his hand in her own, squeezed once.

He squeezed back and didn't let go—and she didn't pull away. He was surprised, but didn't let on—he didn't want to spook her into dragging her hand back. "I didn't make friends after that. I was looking for a way to escape anyway." He'd been hunting a treacherous vampire-mage who'd trapped Zephyr there—and himself inadvertently. He'd been hunting the male because he'd known that was how he would eventually escape. It had taken what felt like forty years.

"I'm glad you escaped. And I'm sorry about your friends."

"Thank you." Their deaths had been long ago, but sometimes it felt like yesterday and the guilt would never leave completely. At least he'd killed every single dragon who'd killed his friends. He paused with her, stood on the sidewalk outside the huge place.

It was clear King had housed the new dragons here as a show of respect given the location and size of the house. It was surrounded by a lush yard and large enough for a group of dragons to feel comfortable. "You ready?"

"As I'll ever be."

∽

Juniper was glad Zephyr was with her as they stood uncomfortably in the oversized sitting room of the double shotgun house. The place must have been gutted and everything opened up because this room was large—with enough space for all the damn dragons inside.

Staring at her and Zephyr. But mainly her. They'd been shown into the sitting room and over the last ten minutes six dragons had arrived, all smiling politely at them.

A chandelier glittered prettily overhead and a small fire was crackling in the fireplace. Tea candles were placed strategically around the room, throw blankets were artfully draped over the pristine white couches. This room was all whites and creams and boring. It was like something out of *Architectural Digest*, if that had still existed post-The Fall.

All the dragons were tall, elegant, and dressed in clothing that reminded her of Gucci. Thanks to years of doing black ops and having to infiltrate various events, she knew her fashion. She didn't think it was actually Gucci, but the cuts of the jackets were similar. It was like they all went to the same tailor.

Meanwhile she and Zephyr were dressed like bikers. *Ugh. Whatever.*

If Starlena didn't show up soon, Juniper was out of here.

The front door suddenly flung open and Starlena hurried in, her expression tense. "Apologies for keeping you waiting. I had a meeting with King and didn't expect you. But…that's not important. I'm sorry you had to wait. That was not my intention."

Juniper had been wondering if this had been some sort of weird power play, but it was clear that it hadn't been. The tension in her shoulders loosened as she nodded at Starlena. "It's fine, I should have called sooner. I just didn't know what my schedule would look like and I have a small window right now. So here I am." She shrugged.

"Of course." Starlena looked over at the others. "Did no one offer you refreshments?" There was a bite of censure in her words that wound its way throughout the entire room and had everyone stiffening. Oh, Starlena was definitely the one in charge.

Juniper hadn't actually doubted that, but the way everyone practically jumped just solidified it. "They did," she said quickly. "But we said no. Everyone has been very gracious," she tacked on. Even if they had more or less just stared at Juniper awkwardly, they hadn't been rude or anything. More like...curious and unsure how to act.

Perhaps unconvinced, Starlena still frowned and flicked her wrist. "Everyone go."

As one, they all stood—it was kind of creepy—and moved out of the room as if they'd practiced it.

Zephyr shot her a look that said he thought it was creepy too, which just made her smile.

Starlena motioned to one of the comfortable-looking chairs near the fireplace, a cream-colored leather chair with a wide seat and fuzzy blanket tossed over the back. "Please sit, we have much to discuss." She looked at Zephyr. "You can join the others if you'd like." Her words once again came out like an order.

Before Juniper could respond—in annoyance—Zephyr turned to her.

"What do you wish me to do?" he asked, all his focus on her.

She absolutely loved that he'd done that. But she bit back her smile. "You don't have to stay."

"Do you want me to stay?" he asked, instead of just going.

And hell, she wanted him to stay. Maybe even needed him to. She wasn't going to analyze that too much. Instead, she nodded. "Yes."

Starlena moved efficiently then, gathering up another chair and placing it in front of the fireplace so that the three of them would be facing each other. Then she turned slightly toward the foyer. "Someone bring us a tray of snacks and tea." No one was visible, but Juniper had no doubt that the others had all heard.

Because she didn't think they'd gone far. No, she had a feeling they were all eavesdropping close by. Which, she couldn't really blame them.

"So...I'm here," Juniper said once they all sat. "Are you in the territory because of me or did you come here for an allyship with King?" After what King had told her, this was a test. She wanted to know how honest Starlena would be.

The older dragon was silent as a female with silvery hair similar to theirs and pale green eyes rolled in a cart of little cookies and tea. Not much food for a dragon.

Once the female was gone, Starlena spoke. "Weeks ago I received a message from King Sorgin of the Latore realm. He'd discovered that the son he thought dead was still alive." She paused, cleared her throat as she seemed to gather herself. "And while at a party, he saw you. He said for a moment he thought he was looking at Soleil...your mother. So he contacted me immediately."

Juniper couldn't stop the wild beat of her heart. *Soleil.* That was the name of the woman who'd given birth to her. Maybe. She couldn't imagine why this female would lie to her. And...she could hear the ring of truth in Starlena's words.

"We look alike?"

Starlena nodded. "You have the same eyes, same hair, same walk, same attitude." Her lips curved up slightly at that. "She is the current queen of our realm."

Wait...what?

Starlena continued as if she hadn't just blown apart Juniper's world. "Which makes you the next in line to rule. Our princess."

Juniper sat there, unable to move as she tried to digest this stranger's words. Simultaneously she willed her stupid phone to alert her with an incoming call or text. She needed to leave, to simply not be here right now.

"As such, I would like to ask you to return home with us."

Zephyr shifted slightly in his seat, tension buzzing off him.

Juniper snorted because she couldn't help herself. "No thanks. My 'mother' couldn't even be bothered to come here to meet me, so fuck her. And fuck you. And fuck all of this!" She couldn't handle this. Nope. Not today. Not ever. Goddess, she shouldn't have come here!

Shaking now, she stood and shoved the chair back with more force than she'd intended. She was out the front door in seconds, sucking in a bucketful of crisp air as she stepped onto the front lawn.

"Please." Suddenly Starlena was in front of her, moving with a speed that Juniper couldn't even process at the moment.

She could scent Zephyr behind her, could see him out of the corner of her eye, but he gave them space. She wasn't sure if that was good or bad. "I don't have time to deal with any of this."

"Soleil's heart broke when you died—when we thought you died. She nearly went mad searching for you. I didn't tell her about you, about this meeting! I only told her that I was coming here to meet Sorgin's long-lost son, to see if he was worthy of an allyship. I knew that if it wasn't true, that if you weren't Seren, that it would break her. I was worried she'd finish what those mad dragons did and destroy the rest of your world in her grief. And that I'd have to kill my own daughter, my child, to stop her destruction."

Seren? Juniper's throat tightened with emotion as she digested everything. So her mother hadn't known about her being in New Orleans. That was something at least. "My name was Seren?" It sounded familiar, and when she tried to think of it, pain pulsed through her skull. Goddess, it hurt too much.

Zephyr was there suddenly, handing her a red and white cloth, and she realized her nose was bleeding.

"Yes, your name is Seren. And what is happening? Do we need a healer?"

"No, it's...nothing." She glanced around the yard, nodded at the bench that was positioned by a cluster of bushes and a small fountain with an angel pouring water out of a jug. "Would you like to sit out here?"

Starlena nodded briefly, and to her surprise, Zephyr kissed

Juniper's forehead once. "I'm going inside for now. Call out if you need me."

"I will." As they sat, she said, "I've heard that dragons have...sort of connections to their clans." But she'd never felt one. Ever. She only knew what she'd gathered through research, and she'd had more information at her fingertips than most, since she worked black ops.

"We do. And the connection we all had with you snapped one hundred and twenty-six years ago." Starlena's voice cracked slightly as she said the words. "Still, Soleil refused to believe you were gone. She wouldn't believe until she saw a body."

"What happened... Did I just disappear or..." She didn't know what questions to ask, or where to start.

"You don't remember anything?"

She shook her head. "There's a big blank in my mind. When I was a teenager I woke up in a cold, wild place naked and bleeding. I was found by wolves."

Starlena's eyebrows rose slightly. "Did they hurt you?"

"No. I..." She wasn't sure how much to share exactly. She wouldn't tell them her parents' names just yet, she decided. "I was taken in by two wolves. They're both healers. They adopted me and they've given me a good life. The pack that we were originally part of weren't so welcoming so they relocated us to a new territory. They're incredible parents." And she knew how lucky she was.

"That is a blessing at least," Starlena rasped out, then seemed to collect herself.

An icy breeze rolled over them, the trees around them rustling with it.

"There was a war in our realm. With another clan. You were young, a teenager, and we kept you and all the other younglings protected in the west wing of our castle. But someone must have infiltrated it because when your mother and I returned from battle we found your room wrecked. There was blood everywhere, three of your cousins had been killed in the nursery, one of your..." She paused once, watching Juniper carefully.

"One of what?"

157

"I'm debating how much to tell you," Starlena said bluntly.

"Everything. I don't want any lies or half-truths. Tell me all of it."

"One of your sisters had been killed as well. She was so young, just a baby." Starlena's voice cracked then and she looked away, composing herself.

"One of?" Juniper finally asked. Did she have more siblings?

"You have another sister. She's two years younger than you."

Oh. Juniper blinked. "Is she here?"

"No. I didn't tell her about you. She would have told Soleil—and insisted on coming."

"This is a lot to process." The biggest understatement of her life.

Starlena looked at her with understanding in her pale blue eyes. "I can only imagine what you are going through. And I will answer any questions that you have."

"You never mentioned my father."

Her gaze shuttered for a moment. "He went into Hibernation a couple decades ago. He was never the same after…"

Juniper looked away, stared out at the quiet street. It was like everything and everyone had disappeared. She couldn't even hear anyone inside. Just the breeze rolling over her, the sound of nature and birds around them. "I don't know if I'll go to your realm."

"It is your realm too," Starlena said quietly.

That remained to be seen. She couldn't make a decision so huge right now. It was simply too much.

"So the male with you—"

"Is not up for discussion." Zephyr was…well, she wasn't sure what he was, but he sure as hell wasn't anyone else's business.

Her grandmother nodded her head slightly, her silver hair glittering under the sunlight. "Fair enough. For now."

How about forever? "How did you…" She cleared her throat, almost embarrassed. "How did you hide your hair? I know it's with magic. Is it a spell or…" She hadn't even known about her chains until adulthood. They'd just snapped out one day and she'd been horrified. But clearly it was a familial trait.

"Nova magic," she said simply.

"So…"

"Oh, you can do it as well." She frowned then, and looked around. "When we are alone, you and I will discuss more on this. Yes?"

Juniper nodded, understanding. Or at least she thought she did—Starlena wanted more privacy. "I think I need time to wrap my head around this, and I have a job to do anyway." Mainly, she needed space from Starlena, from all the dragons inside. From this new reality.

"What is this job you've been doing?" Starlena stood with her. "Because I know you don't live here, but King has given you free rein. And we saw you capture that vampire—and I know you killed many of them. Are you a bounty hunter or tracker?"

"Of sorts. It's complicated." She couldn't tell this virtual stranger that she worked black ops.

Starlena simply made an agreeable sound, looking regal and elegant. "I will not leave this territory until you agree to come with us. And I will send word to Soleil that you are here."

"Please don't tell her just yet." Juniper was having a hard time processing that she had a biological mother out there, one who cared. Maybe. She didn't scent any lies coming from the other female—her grandmother—but she wasn't going to take Starlena's word for every-thing. She needed to tell August about this, see if he could dig up any information on them.

The female hesitated, then nodded. "I won't say anything for now. But…she might find out, regardless."

"I know you are in charge of everyone inside. They're all scared of you."

This amused the older woman for some reason. "They would be foolish not to be." Her tone was tinged with a kind of confidence that was pure dragon. "I'm not speaking of them. They would never betray me. But people have seen you in this territory and they've seen us. Sorgin saw you and told me. Anyone could tell Soleil as well. But I will not say anything for right now."

Juniper rubbed her hands over her face. "Okay, thank you. Also, I'm working today and for the foreseeable future. Don't ambush me again. It could jeopardize people's lives." She would leave it at that.

The female nodded once, and before Juniper could say anything the front door opened and Zephyr strode out. He'd clearly been listening and knew she was ready to go. He gave a brief, respectful nod to her grandmother then strode down the walkway with her. He didn't touch her, but she was aware of his presence and grateful for it. He was silent as they walked, with neither of them speaking for the next three blocks.

Only then did she shove out a long breath. "I don't think they followed us."

"I don't think they did either. Though she knows where you live. Or where you're staying," he amended. "And I'm pretty certain she's telling the truth."

She lifted a jerky shoulder. "I guess."

"You can do a simple enough test. You can just ask Greer to use her healer's magic and—"

"I know," she snapped, then winced. "Sorry, I didn't mean to snap at you. I'm just stressed out." She pulled her cell out and texted Everleigh, hoping for a response. She needed to get busy, to do something. Kill something. "I don't know what to do," she muttered more to herself than him.

"Luckily you don't have to decide right now. You don't have to go with them. Maybe you can talk to your clan about meeting you here or with your pack and parents. Maybe that would make it easier."

She groaned as they reached their home base, a house she was quickly coming to think of as more than a home base. An actual home. "Nothing will make this easier. I don't even know how I'm going to *tell* my parents."

"With what you told me of them, I think they will be happy that you have more family."

"They will. They have so much love to give it's a little intimidating. I never felt like I measured up to them."

"Because they made you feel that way?" he asked, but in a tone that said he already knew the answer.

No. This dragon was too insightful. Too annoying. Too sexy.

"Of course not." Annoyed with herself for being so damn attracted to him, she yanked the front door open.

When they stepped inside, she knew the others were there, could hear them on the back porch. Everyone was here and ready, just waiting on word from Everleigh.

She stalked up the stairs, not bothering to say anything else to Zephyr. By the time she made it to her bedroom door, she realized he'd followed. It said a lot for her state of mind that she hadn't realized he was on the stairs behind her.

He barged into her bedroom with her and shut the door behind them.

"What are you doing?" she demanded with more shock than anything else.

He surprised her by cupping her face in his hands. The look in his gray eyes was raw and possessive as he stared down at her. *Ooooh, goddess.* The way he was watching her—as if she was the only thing that existed, had *ever* existed. He made her feel crazy and treasured at the same time. She wasn't even sure how that was possible, but he'd staked a claim on her, and the more time she spent with him the less it scared her.

As he looked down at her, she realized he was giving her time to tell him no or push him away. Her gaze fell to his mouth and she clutched onto the front of his shirt in case he got the idea to pull back. She *needed* him right now.

He crushed his mouth to hers.

Energy buzzed through both of them, their scents mixing together in the room until all she could smell was their pheromones, wild and out of control.

Her fingers were still clutching his shirt and she couldn't order them to move as he teased his tongue against hers. His kiss was demanding as he backed her up against the nearest wall with a thump.

She couldn't believe he was kissing her like this after his speech about not accepting casual between them. Casual was all she could give him, especially now. At least that was what she kept trying to tell herself.

She knew she should push him away, have some dignity, but all her muscles were pulled bowstring tight. Her nerves were completely frayed and her dragon was riding right under the surface.

She'd never felt out of control like this, not since she was a teenager. She'd long since learned to control her impulses, her urges, but right now she was on a tightrope as Zephyr pressed his body into hers. He was raw male strength and all hers. For the moment.

She arched her back, pressing into him, her nipples already beaded tight just from his kisses. Because every time he flicked his tongue against hers, she imagined what it would feel like if he did the same against her nipple or clit. And each time she had *that* visual, another rush of heat punched through her, flooding her senses.

She slid her hands under his shirt, grabbed onto his back tight. Goddess, he was hard everywhere. He growled low in his throat as she raked her fingernails up his back then down again. She wanted to trace her fingers everywhere, to learn every inch of his body with her fingers and mouth.

Taking her by surprise, he suddenly reached between their bodies and flipped open the button of her jeans.

Realizing what he intended, wild heat flooded between her legs.

He didn't ask, didn't say a word, but she knew that if she told him to stop, he would immediately. That was the kind of male he was.

It was like he was on a mission, going straight for her core. He slid his big hand down over her abdomen, then straight down the front of her underwear. Her brain short-circuited at his bold move, and when he slid his middle finger right over her pulsing clit she rolled her hips against him.

She'd never been so turned on in her life. Not like this. And all they'd done was kiss—and now he was cupping her sex, dipping a finger into her wetness as if he had every right to.

Ooooh, goddess.

As he slid a finger inside her, her inner walls clenched around him tight. She hated that her pants were still on, that her movements were restricted. But there was something about this whole situation that was also insanely hot. She could barely move her legs apart as he slowly, slowly withdrew his finger and began to rub circles around her clit.

Suddenly one of her chains snapped out and latched onto his ankle, just as it had done before.

Seriously, what the hell? It was like her magic had gone haywire around him.

He didn't stop kissing her, didn't stop stroking her. Instead he shifted his palm slightly and slid two fingers inside her. Then he used his palm to rub against her clit with an intensity she could barely take. She hadn't expected any of this today—hadn't expected him at all.

But he'd barreled into her life and was renting space in her head. And he wouldn't leave. Right now, she didn't want him to.

He slid his free hand up her shirt, tugged her bra cup down and cupped one of her breasts, rolling her hard nipple between his thumb and forefinger. There was something so erotic about the fact that they were both mostly dressed as he teased her, pushed her to the edge.

She continued kissing him, unable to get enough of this male who'd started pulling down all the walls she so desperately tried to keep up. And when he nipped her bottom lip, it set something inside her off.

She dug her fingernails into his back, held him hard. Her orgasm started small and he increased the pressure of his palm, even as he added a third finger. The moment he did, pleasure slammed into her, releasing the balled-up tension inside her.

Her chain tightened around his leg as her climax crested, soothing all her frayed edges as her entire body relaxed. She practically turned to jelly against him, little pulses of pleasure still going off inside her. If he could do just that with his fingers, she really, really wanted to feel his thick length inside her. She was at least going to touch him, stroke him off.

With trembling fingers, she reached between their bodies, ready to shove his pants off—or incinerate them—but he stopped her, pulled his head back slightly.

His dragon watched her carefully. "I won't be something you regret. I kissed you because I couldn't *not* kiss you. I made you come because I was desperate to taste your pleasure." Then he slowly withdrew his hand and actually licked his fingers in front of her. And the expression he made... If he hadn't been holding her up against the wall with his body, she'd have slipped right down it.

Her lips parted and another rush of heat punched through her. *Holy shit.*

"But I cannot be casual with you," he continued. "When you're ready for something real, I'll be there. Hell, I'll be there for you no matter what. I'm not walking away from us. You are amazing, Juniper. But you've got to be all in if we take this next step. Princess."

Then he stepped back, opened her bedroom door, and quietly shut it behind him.

She stared after him, her breathing ragged, her body still lax from an intense orgasm—and her stupid phone started buzzing.

Of course.

CHAPTER TWENTY-TWO

Axel laughed as Enzo jumped down from the oak tree a couple feet from his head, the expression on his little face one of triumph.

"Did I surprise you?" the seven-year-old boy asked. As a rare phoenix, he stayed in his human form unless they were deep in the woods outside New Orleans, or inside their house.

"You're almost there," Axel said. "But I'm a lion. It's hard to surprise felines."

"I don't know about that," a familiar British voice said. One that got his blood pumping and made him think of hot, sweaty nights spent together under the moonlight. Stretched out on the grass, Axel tilted his head back to see an upside-down Christian walking toward him.

Of course he was in one of those sexy three-piece suits. It was like a trademark with the male. Tonight's was a dark navy with a pale pink shirt underneath. And his suit was slim-fitting, showing off a long, lean-muscled body. The floral tie should have looked stupid, but it picked up the hues of his shirt and *oh my God, stop*, he ordered himself.

Enzo simply stared up at Christian with curiosity so Axel shoved up from the grass. "Why don't you go tell Legend that it's almost time for dinner."

Legend was hiding in a tree about thirty yards away and doing a pretty good job of it. But the kids still had a long way to go in learning how to sneak up on people. As well as how to hide from potential predators. It was why Axel was out here with them—he wanted to teach them to be able to keep themselves safe when he or their pack weren't around.

"What are you doing here?" Axel asked bluntly when they were alone. Because Christian had made it pretty clear that he didn't want anything to do with Axel. They'd danced at that club and he'd been hot for him, but then it was like Christian had shut that switch off. Just snapped it down and left once Juniper told them it was okay to go. Axel knew he was a flirt, but Jesus, he still had feelings. Too many of them.

Christian casually slipped his hands into his pants pockets and looked around the well-lit yard. "I was just wondering if you'd heard from Juniper."

Axel lifted an eyebrow. That warranted a text, not a visit. "I haven't. But I do know that they got all of the humans into different healing centers. It's going to be a long road for some of them, but hopefully they'll all make it." Axel knew that wasn't always the case. He'd done enough recon and rescue-type work in the military, saving human civilians in a couple different wars, and the aftermath was often harder. Because sometimes people couldn't live with what had been done to them.

Or what they'd had to do to survive.

Axel still couldn't understand how completely horrific other humans could be to their fellow man. Not that supernaturals were above it. They were just as brutal. What those vampires had done to all those innocent humans was a case in point.

"I hate that I haven't heard anything." Christian looked around the yard again, anywhere but at Axel, his body language tense and uncomfortable.

Axel realized he likely wasn't here because of the job. And even though he knew he should tell Christian to get lost, he simply couldn't. Not when the male had a lonely look in his eyes. Goddess, he was such a sucker. "You hungry?" he asked. He knew Christian didn't have to eat, but he still could. He was an older vampire and food was not a necessity for him.

"Or maybe he wants to stay and play games with us!" Enzo said as he jumped down from the nearest tree, Legend right behind him.

Axel turned and caught one, then the other in his arms, laughing as the two of them giggled. "You're both getting better. I almost didn't hear you this time."

Enzo pumped his fist into the air and Legend simply grinned as he set them on the ground.

"My name is Enzo," the kid said, sticking his hand out politely.

Christian grinned at him and crouched down so they were more eye level. "I am Christian."

Legend moved closer to Axel and grabbed his hand—and squeezed Axel's heart right along with it. They'd moved into the house recently with their older sister, Phoebe. Aurora had made the decision to take the three siblings in since they were orphaned, and Axel already loved all of them.

"I like your accent. What are you?" Enzo asked bluntly.

Axel cleared his throat.

"Right, I know I'm not supposed to ask." He hit his forehead with his palm overdramatically and threw his head back. "Don't tell my sister!"

Axel had learned quickly that Enzo was definitely the talker out of the twins. Legend was happy to sit back and watch everyone around him but Enzo liked being in the thick of things. Even in the few weeks he'd been here he'd come out of his shell, and sometimes Axel couldn't get him to stop talking. It was like he went full force all day before he crashed at night. Then he repeated it the next day.

"So did you want to stay and play with us?" Enzo demanded.

"I'm sure Christian has somewhere else he'd rather be," Axel said almost stiffly. Being around the other male had his hackles up. Even if the lonely look in Christian's eyes tugged at Axel, he was second-guessing his decision to ask him to stay for dinner.

"I have nowhere to be," Christian said, surprising him. Then he took off his jacket and rolled up his sleeves—showing off his roped forearms. "Is this an indoor game or an outdoor game?" he asked all properly in that delicious upper-crust British accent.

"Outdoor. We like to play hide-and-seek. But not the kind that little kids play," Enzo said conspiratorially.

Christian shot Axel a look, eyebrows raised.

Axel lifted a shoulder. "I'm teaching them to sneak up on prey." They needed to learn how to hunt as well as how to hide. It was all part of the survival skills of shifters, and Axel never wanted them to be vulnerable again.

Christian nodded approvingly and for some reason Axel liked that way too much.

Goddess, he was in trouble where this vampire was concerned. So. Much. Trouble.

CHAPTER TWENTY-THREE

Two days later

It had taken two days to round up all of the vampires from the list the captured vampire had given them. Once Everleigh had given them locations using her gift, Juniper's crew, King's people, Gabriel and Vega, and Zephyr's brothers had all worked in tandem, infiltrating places at the same time so no one would have a chance to escape. It had been coordinated and effective. And the vampire coven leader Ingrid had discovered two of her people had been involved and turned them over to King, so she wasn't involved. For some reason Juniper was glad. She'd liked the female.

So Juniper kept her word and had given that treacherous male who'd snitched a quick death. Now, as she stared at the shackled vampires in front of her, all thirty-three of them, a dark part of her was glad that their deaths would not be quick. That they would suffer as the humans had.

She looked down the line of them, the scared ones, the defiant ones, the apathetic ones. "You deserve everything that will happen to you," she said simply. "And you will be held up as an example for future vampires who decide to cross King and those in his territory." She felt no pity for them. None.

Her crew was waiting by the door of the warehouse where they'd been imprisoning these vampires the last couple hours—after they had interrogated them.

Now she and her people were about to head out and bring down the rest of this disgusting operation based on the information they'd extracted. But she couldn't resist reminding them exactly what was going to happen to them. And why they deserved it.

"You won't live out the week," one of the females snarled, tugging futilely at her chains. She was the only one who hadn't given them any information. Too brainwashed to have even a shred of empathy for others.

"I'm so freaking scared." Juniper kept her tone dry as she stepped in front of the vampire, stared down into dark eyes in a pale face.

"You should be," the female hissed, her fangs dropping.

"Pretty bold talk for a female who's going to lose her fangs in the next hour."

Fear bled into the vampire's gaze, but Juniper didn't care. Not after what had been done to those innocent humans. Losing fangs was a cruelty to vampires. This bitch deserved it.

"That's enough of that," Claudine Bonavich said as she stepped into the warehouse, clapping her hands once. "I will take them from here," the ancient vampire said, her expression grim as she nodded once at Juniper.

Juniper knew the female wouldn't take pleasure in punishing these vampires. But it was necessary. They were going to be a cautionary tale for all vampires around the globe. So the punishment would have to be harsh. And it would have to be very long by supernatural standards.

"If you learn anything else, you have my contact information," Juniper said to her.

Claudine nodded once, then her eyes flashed to a glowing amber as she took in the shackled vampires. "You've all cast shame on our kind."

"Fuck you!" the female snapped. "We are—"

Her words were cut off as Claudine lifted her right hand.

Juniper realized the powerful vampire was somehow keeping the female from talking, because it was as if an invisible fist had clenched around the female's throat.

Juniper turned away, strode toward her waiting crew. Now that this was taken care of—sanctioned by King—it was time to go.

"I just got a call from my friend Nyx," Vega said as Juniper stepped out into the cool night air to greet the others. "She said if we want to be transported to my dad's territory, she can do it for us. No charge."

Juniper looked at the others, who'd remained outside once Claudine arrived, her gaze staying on Zephyr's longer than necessary.

She didn't mind being transported by a demigod. It would save them a bit of time. And now that they knew where the next drop-off point for trafficked humans would be, they needed to save all the time they could.

"That would be great, thanks," she said only when her crew nodded.

There was a rustle in the air and she paused, looking around. Claudine's people were in the shadows around the warehouse, but this was a quiet area of King's territory. One not populated by people. They'd only just started renovating it and... There.

Starlena suddenly strode out of the darkness from across the street wearing long flowing pants and a tunic, with two short blades strapped across her chest. Juniper wasn't sure if the blades were for show or what, because the female didn't need weapons. She was a dragon. With magical chains.

Juniper moved away from her people, her boots thudding against the street as she met Starlena in the middle of it. "What are you doing here?" Because she'd flat-out told Starlena not to ambush her or bother her while she was working.

"I'm going with you." Her smile was practically feral.

"No—"

"I'm Ren." Her annoying friend stepped forward, a grin on his face.

"We didn't get to officially meet the other night. I think you would be a great addition to our team."

"It's nice to meet you." Starlena nodded regally at him.

Juniper resisted the urge to scrub her hand over her face as the others stepped forward.

"I'm going to kill him," she muttered to Zephyr who'd moved up next to her as quiet as a wraith. He hadn't left her side for the last two days basically.

She didn't hate it. And she couldn't stop remembering how he'd played her body perfectly. Now she wanted more, craved it with an embarrassing desperation she couldn't seem to put a cap on. Her need for him kept spilling out, no matter how much she tried to ignore it.

"It was hot when you threatened those vampires."

She shot him a surprised look. What the hell was wrong with him? They were on a mission. And her grandmother had shown up against Juniper's wishes and apparently thought she was going with them.

"Also, in case I didn't tell you, you look magnificent today," he said with an approving nod, his gaze sweeping over her all-black attire.

She stared up at him, her stupid heart fluttering. "I think you hit your head again."

He leaned down and inhaled, not hiding the fact that he was drinking in her scent. "Nope. I just want you to know how absolutely amazing you are. Because you deserve to be told that at least a dozen times a day." He was stone-cold serious too. No smug expression, no obnoxious smirking, just...dead serious.

She blinked, then glanced away from him because she couldn't deal with this right now. It was like the world truly had gone mad in the last couple days.

She found Hyacinth grinning as she looked between the two of them, her eyes wide.

Vega and Gabriel were just staring, Vega's mouth parted slightly in a grin.

She stalked away from Zephyr and back toward Starlena. "Look, it's nice that you want help, but you don't know anything about what we're doing or—"

"I'm a skilled fighter. I'm older than all of you—combined. The other night you said you killed traffickers. That is something I understand and would like to help with. And it would be foolish for you to turn down backup simply because of your personal issues."

Personal issues? What the f—

"If you tell me not to come with you, I will anyway. So decide now if you want to be stubborn and foolish or if you would like to have another skilled fighter on your side who has killed more beings in her lifetime than you can possibly imagine."

Dammit. She felt like she was being scolded like a child right now. Juniper took a breath. "Does King know—"

"Of course he knows, child."

She bristled slightly at the use of the word child, but quickly realized it wasn't an insult. Starlena had said it almost offhandedly. And… compared to this ancient, she was a child.

The older female continued, her expression softening slightly. "I've already lost you once. I won't do so again. You are part of my clan. It is my duty and honor to fight with you."

Oh. Juniper blinked, her throat tightening with a sudden blast of emotion.

Before she could respond there was a rush of wind and then suddenly thirty yards away from them on the street a female and male were standing there. Juniper was glad for the distraction, as she had no clue what to say to Starlena anyway.

The newcomer female's long black hair was windblown around her delicate face. She was slender and petite with ocean blue eyes, peaches and cream skin and…she tripped into the male with darker skin and amber eyes next to her, but didn't lose her grin. "Your transportation has arrived!" she said to Vega and Gabriel, holding her hands up like a showman.

The male next to her didn't smile or say anything except nod at Vega and Gabriel and warily watch the others. So, this was Bo and Nyx.

Juniper could sense that Bo was Nyx's mate right away. Not from their scents, but by his obvious body language. He hovered next to the smaller female protectively, giving the impression that he'd kill or maim anyone who looked at her wrong.

And when Juniper glanced over at Zephyr, she realized he was watching her with a similar intensity.

Her throat tightened again as unwanted emotions bubbled up.

Clearing her throat, she turned away from him and focused on the newcomers. "Thank you for agreeing to transport us. We really appreciate the help."

She wanted to save all the countless humans, but she also wanted to finish this mission because she maybe wanted to explore something with the sexy, exasperating male who wouldn't give her a moment's peace.

CHAPTER TWENTY-FOUR

Zephyr watched as Juniper talked quietly with Ren near the boarded-up window of what had very likely once been a clothing store in a small beach town. He knew she was annoyed at Ren for so easily welcoming Starlena to their group. Though she didn't seem to be talking to Ren about Starlena at the moment, but their upcoming infiltration.

They'd arrived on the coast of what had once been called Mississippi nearly an hour ago and were in waiting mode. The drop-off time for the trafficked humans was soon and they would be heading out to capture anyone involved as soon as Juniper gave the order.

He still didn't know what to think of Starlena joining them, but he was certain that she cared for Juniper. So he didn't mind her being part of this mission as long as her intentions were good.

When he felt eyes on him, he glanced over and found Starlena staring at him. Hard.

He frowned.

When she gave him an abrupt chin nod, his frown deepened but he stalked across the open space.

The building they were using as a base of sorts was in good shape on the outside; the two-story brick facade had fared well. Most of the downtown area had fared well, and he knew it was because the Alpha of the territory had made sure to preserve all of it. It just wasn't in use right now. Most of the people in his territory lived very close to his pack about thirty minutes away. But this territory was still under his purview and he had his wolves keeping track of everything. Much like King did for his territory.

Except tonight, the Alpha had ordered his wolves away for tactical reasons. They needed as few scents around this drop-off area as possible.

Zephyr followed Starlena up a set of stairs to the second floor. Empty racks that had once held clothing stood abandoned. A few hangers shifted slightly as he brushed past them. "What is it?" he asked as she turned to face him, her expression opaque.

"You wish to mate with my granddaughter." Her tone was just as neutral.

"I do." He wanted to mate with her more than anything.

"How do I know you are good enough for her?"

"I'm probably not good enough for her. But if she'll have me, I'll spend the rest of my life making her happy." Because he wanted more of her smiles. Wanted Juniper happy, secure in the world.

The older female's gaze narrowed slightly. "Though she might not remember, she is from a matriarchal clan."

"Is there a question in there?" he asked when Starlena simply paused and stared at him.

"Not all dragons are able to follow females."

He snorted, unable to stop himself. "Those dragons are fools, then. Female dragons are deadlier than any force on earth." And he had no problem following Juniper's lead. She was a born leader and a deadly warrior. He wanted to fight by her side until the day they died. Though he hoped that was millennia from now.

She blinked, clearly surprised. "You truly believe that."

"I *know* that." His mother had been a fierce warrior, just as his father had been. They'd been equals, but his mother... Female dragons were not like female humans. Or any other female species. There was an edge to them. Not that they were a monolith, no species was, but in his experience the warrior subset of female dragons were definitely more lethal than anyone else.

Starlena sniffed imperiously in a way that reminded him so much of Juniper. "It's good that you have some brains in that head of yours."

He snorted again.

"We're bringing her into our clan. She is one of our own. Whether you will be welcomed or not—"

He stepped forward. "Juniper will go where she wants, when she wants. Whether she wants to be part of your clan isn't decided. And whatever she decides, I'll have her back. Because she makes all the decisions about her life. You might be her blood relative, but you don't own her and you don't make decisions for her. And you'll do well to remember that." And Zephyr didn't want to shackle her to him, he simply wanted to be with her, to create something real together.

Growling softly, Starlena stepped toward him, her dragon in her gaze. It was clear she was spoiling for a fight. "I never said I owned her."

"No. But you're talking about her as if you have a say in her decisions. She'll do what she wants when she's ready. And if you're stupid enough to pressure her—"

The female snarled, smoke coming out of her nose.

Zephyr knew his dragon was in his gaze as well and he didn't back down. "Back in New Orleans, you said you wanted to help with this mission. I seriously doubt it will do Juniper's mission any good to start a fight with me now. Because it's clear you want one. Maybe to see if I'm capable or whatever. I don't care what the reason is. I will not fight with you now." Because when dragons fought, it was not quiet. They would end up blowing off the roof to this building and causing havoc and destruction—and giving away their location.

Starlena suddenly grinned, her expression changing quickly. The abrupt change should have surprised him, but with dragon females, nothing could.

She reached out and patted him once on the shoulder. Hard. "Maybe you will fit in with us after all. Time will tell." Then she stalked past him and down the stairs.

Shaking his head, Zephyr wondered if he'd passed some sort of test as he followed behind her—only to find Juniper standing at the bottom of the stairs, as if she'd been about to come up after them. She looked between them, gaze narrowed.

"Are you two done?" Juniper's bicolor eyes sparked with temper.

Perhaps she had overheard them?

"Yes. What's up?" He moved closer to her, unable to stop himself from inhaling her wild scent. His dragon rumbled under the surface, ready to go into battle alongside her. Though he wanted more than that. He wanted a lifetime of shared orgasms with this dragon who owned his heart. His real-life princess.

"We're going to go over everything one more time," Juniper finally said after a long pause. Then she shot a sharp look at her grandmother. "I need to know that you will do what I say. I can't worry that you'll question my orders."

"I would never risk this operation. Because it would alienate you and I want you to be part of our clan," Starlena answered.

Zephyr was surprised by her bluntness but probably shouldn't be. The older dragon had laid it all on the line—she wanted Juniper in her life, wanted to bring her into the fold.

Because of course she did—Juniper was amazing, a bright star they would be lucky to have as family.

Juniper blinked once then pivoted away from the two of them before striding to the middle of the mostly empty room.

There was a fold-up table in the middle and she'd created a replica of what they were going into using little Lego pieces. He had no idea where they'd come from, but the pieces made a great visual of the unused boat storage facility they'd be infiltrating. There was a huge warehouse and a big yard of boats that had been left unclaimed and unused since The Fall. Made sense since they were by the coast.

It was a good place to make a dirty deal, though Zephyr was surprised at the location of the territory. It seemed risky to do this in a powerful Alpha's territory. Then again, they'd been trafficking humans in King's territory too.

"The three of us will be moving in aerially," Juniper said,

motioning to herself, Zephyr and Starlena. "Griffin and Hyacinth, you two will take up the west side and remain where you are until we have a visual of the humans. There's more than enough places for you two to hide undetected and we need eyes on the humans before we do anything." Her jaw clenched once and he felt the ripple of energy punch through the room. "I want to make sure they don't get caught in any crossfire."

Yeah, Zephyr was worried about that too—that the vampires would use the humans as shields. Or that they'd end up as collateral damage. Because when supernaturals battled, things got violent and bloody.

"Ren, you'll be positioned here." It was southeast of the center area of the boatyard, and because of the way the steel storage rows were set up, it had a good visual of where they suspected the actual handoff would be.

"And Gabriel and I will be covering the entrance," Vega said with a grin as she crossed her arms over her chest. "Covertly, of course."

Juniper gave her a small smile and nodded. "Everyone needs to be alert. We don't know what to expect other than trafficking. Taking down the vampires in New Orleans was easy enough but it's clear they've been operating for a while. And we know they have a boss, someone up north. Our main goal is to save all the humans and stop the vampires from alerting their boss that we've halted this part of their operation. But saving the humans is the main goal."

Everyone nodded in agreement. After this step was complete, they would all go north and cut off the head of the operation. But they had to stop this shipment first. Because if they didn't, it was very likely all these humans would disappear and never be found again.

"We're ready for this," Hyacinth said. She was dressed in all black, as the majority of them were.

Except Juniper's grandmother, who'd changed into some sort of bodysuit that blended with her surroundings. He'd never seen anything like it, guessed it had been created in her realm. Likely with her clan's magic.

"My dad is here," Vega said suddenly. "With my mom."

Zephyr couldn't scent the Alpha couple, but from the way Vega paused, it was as if she was having a telepathic conversation. Maybe she was.

The door opened moments later and they all turned to find Finn, the Alpha of Biloxi, and his powerful vampire mate Lyra striding inside. Finn was a broad wolf with midnight black hair cropped short, ice-blue eyes with the faintest glow, and an olive skin tone. His mate had long blonde hair, grayish-violet eyes, and sharp cheekbones that should have made her resting expression harsh. But the smattering of freckles across her nose and cheeks made her seem younger than Zephyr guessed she was.

Vega was a combination of both her parents, but she favored her father in height, skin tone and hair.

And when Zephyr looked at Juniper and Starlena there was no doubt in his mind they were related. At this point it was a given, but the more Starlena spent time with Juniper, the more he could see it in their facial expressions.

Finn paused at the entrance, his gaze landing on Starlena. His eyebrows raised just a fraction. "It's been a long time," he said quietly as his mate shut the door behind them.

The elegant, ancient female nodded once. "It has. And I was pleased to hear that you killed your uncle."

Zephyr knew the story, that Finn had killed his brutal uncle decades ago and taken over his pack, expanded his territory into what it was today.

"I only wish I had done it sooner. Why are you here? Not that your presence is not welcome," he added in a very respectful manner. "I'm just surprised."

Which told Zephyr a whole lot in that moment. If an Alpha with Finn's power level held respect for this dragon female, it spoke volumes. Because King had welcomed Starlena and her clanmates into his territory based on his father's recommendation. But King did not know them. Not really.

Zephyr watched as Juniper shot a quick glance at Vega, who simply shrugged. Okay, so it was clear that she hadn't known her father knew Starlena either. Which made sense. Vega was incredibly young, maybe in her mid-twenties or early thirties. He wasn't sure.

"I'm here helping my granddaughter," Starlena said simply, nodding once at Juniper. "Not that she needs my help. But we are family and it is always a pleasure to help kill those who need it."

Finn flicked a glance at Juniper as if seeing her for the first time, then looked back at Starlena, his eyes widening ever so slightly. But he didn't say more, just nodded his acceptance.

Juniper took a small step forward. "Thank you for allowing us into your territory."

"Of course." Then Finn made introductions between his mate Lyra and Starlena before turning back to them and getting straight to business. "My wolves have created a grid two miles out from the location. No one will see my people. I don't want any of these vampires escaping." It was clear from his tone that he wasn't asking for permission.

Juniper nodded. "Yes, of course. We're happy for the help. The only thing that matters is making sure all the humans survive."

Hell yeah. Zephyr loved seeing Juniper in charge. His female—and he was thinking of her as his—was a powerhouse.

Finn seemed surprised for a fraction of a moment, then gave a brief smile. Perhaps he'd been preparing for pushback. Then he continued, "Okay, then. If you need anything, communicate it to Vega. She can communicate with Lyra telepathically."

Juniper nodded and Zephyr rolled his shoulders once, ready to get out of there and hunt vampires.

"The scheduled drop-off is in two hours. I want to get there now." Juniper said to the crew. "So unless we need to go over anything else..." She trailed off and everyone shook their heads.

They were just as ready to kick ass as she was. Zephyr certainly was. The sooner this job was done, the sooner he could continue his courtship of Juniper.

CHAPTER TWENTY-FIVE

Zephyr swooped around the boatyard below, using his dragon's-eye view to look for any vampires that might be hiding. Salt tinged the air, making it difficult to pinpoint scents, but so far he'd spotted three vamps among the languishing boat hulls. Hyacinth and Griff had already incapacitated them so things were quiet on the ground.

Now he and the others were waiting for the rest of the vampires to show up with a cargo of humans. According to the intel they'd gained, the vampires should have shown up by now.

He could hear the faint rustle of Juniper's wings above him—they'd each carved out an area to fly so they wouldn't crash into each other while camouflaged. Starlena was north of them, closer to the entrance of the boatyard, which was massive.

At the sound of an engine in the distance, he angled back toward the direction of the Gulf waters. And that was when he saw a huge cargo boat in the distance.

It was heading straight for the boatyard. Since The Fall much of normal travel had stopped or was heavily monitored by whatever Alpha ran a particular region. And boat travel wasn't a common sight —at least not at this level of transport.

This…was how the humans were being transported. *Oh, shit.*

The vampire Juniper had interrogated hadn't known how they'd arrive, but they'd all assumed it would be by trucks or vans. If Finn didn't have people out monitoring the waterways, a ship would be the perfect way to infiltrate his territory, make a drop-off and escape.

Making a quick decision, he swooped down to a space in the boatyard where he could land without being seen from the water. Then he dropped his camouflage and raced toward his waiting cache to grab his comm line.

"There's a huge cargo boat coming this way," he said over the line, right as Juniper landed and dropped her camo as well.

Unlike him, she could shift with her clothing. Despite being on a mission, he was still disappointed not to get to see her in all her naked glory.

"Everyone report," Juniper demanded immediately. "Have there been any sightings of cargo vehicles inland?"

"Yes," Vega said after a moment. "Just now. A couple of my father's wolves have spotted two huge semis taking an unused back road toward the coast. They seem to be avoiding the highways."

"Griff and Hyacinth, did you get anything from the vamps before you incapacitated them?"

"No," they both said simultaneously.

Juniper looked at him, her expression tight. "We need to get closer to the boat."

"Agreed."

"Guys," Ren said suddenly, his tone urgent. "The boat is slowing down. Looks like it's turning around."

They must have been tipped off or they'd had scouts who'd seen some of them hiding.

"Oh hell no," Juniper snapped out. "Vega, let Starlena know that Zephyr and I are going in hot toward the boat." She focused on him, her bicolor eyes filled with determination. "We hold our camo and shift to human form once we're able, infiltrate that way. We use the element of surprise as much as possible, and we save the humans at all cost."

He nodded. He'd do whatever it took.

"Take at least two of us with you," Hyacinth said. "We can ride in on you and stay low enough to not be seen, then drop onto the water and climb up the side, or you can drop us on the boat if possible. And we'll be able to comm back to the others, keep communication open."

"Griff and Hyacinth, you're with me," Juniper said without pause. "Ren, stay here and keep in contact with the others."

Though Zephyr hated the idea of a male riding on Juniper—he didn't care if it was barbaric of him—he knew it was for the best. Juniper had been working with them for decades. They'd have utilized this kind of move before. But it didn't stop his dragon half from going all grumpy as he shifted back to his beast form.

He called on his camo before taking to the air and waited until he saw the others climb onto Juniper. He resisted the urge to fry Griffin, a male he actually liked.

Above him, he heard a rush of wings—Starlena was apparently coming with them too instead of waiting here.

As he took to the air, his wings expanding wide, he saw the boat had almost fully turned around now.

But that crew wasn't going to escape that easily. All the vampires on that boat were dead—they just didn't know it yet.

JUNIPER FLEW DIRECTLY above the cargo ship looking for a clear place to drop Griff and Hyacinth. Four huge storage containers covered the middle deck—and she didn't have to guess at what was inside.

She could scent the humans.

Luckily the moon was mostly obscured by dense cloud cover, giving them enough concealment. Because while her camouflage did exactly what it was supposed to, it didn't completely make her invisible. If someone was looking right at her, they might see a glimmer of light or something on the edge of their vision that they couldn't quite make out, but knew was there. That was how other supernaturals could spot dragons if they tried hard enough.

Decision made, she tucked her wings back and made a quick drop toward the stern of the ship. There was a big enough space for her to get in low enough so her crew could drop down.

They'd worked together for so long that Griff and Hyacinth weren't surprised by the sudden shift. She could feel them each moving down her back, toward her tail.

She straightened it as she went lower, lower— They jumped at the same time.

Even with her supernatural senses, she barely heard them hit the back deck.

No alarm sounded so they were still in the clear. For now. But she knew that wouldn't last.

There was a soft murmur of voices coming from the front deck. She angled that way, keeping her wing movements limited so she simply glided around. When it was time, she shifted to her human form midair, keeping her camo in place as she dropped onto the top of one of the storage containers.

Her feet touched down on one of the back containers nearly soundlessly. Adrenaline surging, she remained low, taking in her surroundings. Looking up at the bridge she could just make out a couple shadows moving behind the tinted glass.

"We should just dump the humans," a male voice said quietly from somewhere below. "This isn't worth the risk. The wolves have our trucks now."

So that was why they'd decided to turn around. Someone had seen Finn's wolves stopping the trucks.

"Or we could simply take on the wolves of this territory," another grumbled, their footsteps sounding as petulant as their tone.

"Those aren't our orders," a third voice said. This male's tone was more proper. "And if you want to question the boss, I can make sure you're reassigned elsewhere."

Reassigned sounded more like "executed."

"We're not questioning orders," the first voice said. "We're just wondering why we had to change course last minute. I don't like being on the water."

There was a short pause, then a sigh. "Because we were ordered to. Kelly spotted something odd from the air."

From the air? *Oh shit.* Did these vamps have a dragon or other winged creature working with them? *Well, hell.* That changed things slightly, but it didn't change the endgame.

"I—" The male's voice was cut off, followed by a gurgling sound.

Juniper crept to the edge of the container and peered over.

Hyacinth stood over three piles of ash. Fangs descended, she looked up, clearly ready to fight, but Juniper slid over the side, let her camo fall as her feet touched the deck.

"Griff's headed to the nav bridge," Hyacinth said quietly.

"There might be dragons with these vamps." Juniper kept her voice subvocal so that only Hyacinth and Griff and hopefully Zephyr could hear. She wasn't sure if he'd shifted to his human form yet or if he was still flying.

A sudden blast of fire lit up the sky.

Juniper's eyes widened as a dragon with unfamiliar pale yellow scales blasted fire at a dragon with shimmering white-gray scales —Starlena!

Her instinct was to shift, to dive right into the fight, but a dozen vampires jumped down from the top of one of the storage containers to surround her and Hyacinth.

Releasing her chains, Juniper lashed out, took off three vampires' heads in one sweep.

"Oh shit!" A female vamp sprinted away, ducking out of sight as two vampires raced at her.

Juniper blasted fire in a controlled arc, incinerating them right as they reached her, claws and fangs out.

Zephyr landed suddenly, his camouflage dropping as he shifted to human form on an upper deck and started taking out vamps.

She lost sight of him as she attacked the vampires. Ash exploded everywhere, coating the deck as she raced along the edge of the storage container, Hyacinth right behind her.

"We've gotta turn the boat around." The words were barely out of her mouth before there was a sharp shift underneath her feet.

The boat rumbled as it wildly swung left. That had to be Griff.

"Get to the bridge, help Griff!" she ordered when she saw Zephyr disappear through a door on an upper level about fifty yards away. He was shirtless but had managed to pull pants on. The relief she experienced at seeing him was so staggering she felt it like a physical blow. He hadn't responded to anything on the comm line and she'd been worried for him.

Above her, Starlena blasted out a stream of brilliant white fire, slicing off the tip of the yellow dragon's tail. *Holy shit balls.* She clearly had things under control.

Juniper raced after Zephyr, sticking to the shadows. Her heart skipped a beat when she saw four vampires disappear through the same door Zephyr had. He could handle himself but—

Fire erupted in front of her suddenly, the heated blast sending her flying backward. Another dragon was attacking! Her dragon's natural ability to repel fire saved her from getting burned to a crisp but the door Zephyr had gone through was completely destroyed.

And...the scent of accelerant hit her nose even as she shifted to her dragon form, took to the air to battle the newcomer dragon with pale yellow scales glittering under the fire they'd just unleashed.

Below her, fire spread. *Shit, the humans.* They were trapped in the containers. Would be burned alive unless she and her crew could get them free and off the boat in time.

But she couldn't do that until she'd stopped this dragon.

The enraged screeches of her grandmother and the other dragon filled the air as they continued to battle. Juniper shot downward straight for the water, diving deep and going underneath the ship. She called on her camouflage as she did and when she burst out the other side, she spotted the enemy dragon blasting fire at the spot she'd just dived into.

The fool thought she was running?

She arrowed straight through the flames on the boat like a rocket and instead of blasting fire at the dragon, she landed on its back, dug her claws into its wing joints and ripped.

Hard.

The agonized screams of the dragon rent the air as she broke its wings right at the joints. It blasted out fire wildly as it reared its head back.

Juniper opened her jaws and tore at its neck as she flapped hard enough to keep them both in the air. The screams stopped as she ripped through bones and tendons.

She let go then, barely watching as the dead beast plummeted to the water below. As she turned, she saw the dragon her grandmother had been fighting falling to the ocean in a lifeless heap.

Juniper turned back toward the boat, her heart racing. She needed to get to Zephyr. Saving the humans might be a priority, but Zephyr? Oh goddess, he was her priority. Zephyr and her people were. Always would be.

She wasn't sure when the frustratingly wonderful dragon had gotten so deep under her skin, but he might as well live there now. He was in her blood, her marrow. And she had to get to him.

An explosion of metal and fire burst into the sky and she lost a century of her life until she saw a dragon with scales the color of diamonds emerge from a jagged hole in a blast of fury.

Zephyr!

He'd come up from the cargo holds, just tearing through the metal to escape. The big cargo boat tipped dangerously, the containers starting to slide on the deck, and she knew what they had to do. There was no other way to get the humans out of here before the boat sank.

She arrowed low, sunk her claws deep into the center of the closest storage container and flapped hard, lifting the container off the boat with a loud creak.

Zephyr and Starlena followed suit, each lifting one of the containers up into the air.

"Get them out of here!" Hyacinth screamed from below. "We'll use the lifeboats to get the other humans out!"

Juniper couldn't see her friend through the smoke and fire, but had no doubt Hyacinth and Griffin would do exactly as she said.

Her wings strained under the weight of carrying the container and she tried her best to stay steady—and ignore the cries of alarm from below. She'd created two holes with her talons, ripping straight through the metal to get a grip, and the humans could see her giant winged body above them. They wouldn't know she was a friend and not a foe and the stench of their fear was overwhelming.

Goddess, these poor humans.

She flew as steady as possible, scanning for more threats as she went. Starlena moved in next to her, with Zephyr doing the same on the other side. She was so relieved he was all right. Wouldn't have been able to handle it if anything had happened to him. He'd just barreled into her life. She didn't want to lose him before they got the chance at something real.

As they flew toward shore, she tensed when she spotted a small figure flying toward them—until she realized it was Lyra. Only powerful vamps could fly, and usually only if they were ancient. At least she'd be able to help with the humans.

An icy wind rolled over Juniper as they flew, but she barely felt it as they descended toward the boatyard. Dozens of wolves, plus Ren, Vega and Gabriel were waiting. She eased her container down first, then shifted to human and jumped to the ground as Zephyr did the same with his container.

She busted the lock off the doors with her bare hands as Starlena was setting hers down. She turned as Vega and half a dozen wolves approached.

"I'm guessing we need lots of healers." There was a good chance that the humans inside would be dehydrated at the very least. And definitely terrified. "I've got to get back to the boat. There are more humans." Not to mention the rest of her crew. And she wasn't sure if there were enough lifeboats.

Vega nodded and started barking out orders.

Juniper didn't have to say a word to either Starlena or Zephyr, they all raced away from the containers and crowd and found an area big enough to shift.

As they flew back toward the sinking boat, flames from the mortally wounded ship licked into the sky.

Cries of alarm greeted them as they swooped in toward six

lifeboats, but they quickly died down—likely because Hyacinth, Griffin and Lyra had told the humans they were the good guys.

Juniper shifted near one of the boats and dropped into the icy waters. It was a shock to her system, but her heat quickly absorbed it as she swam toward Hyacinth's boat.

"Did you get everyone?" she called out.

"We think so but we couldn't check the lower cargo holds." Hyacinth stood at the front of one of the Zodiac-type boats, covered in ash and soot. "It was too hot."

Griff gave her a quick wave from his boat. He was bringing up the rear with Lyra guiding another boat, and some of the humans were steering the other boats.

"We'll double-check before it sinks," she said, glancing up at Zephyr and Starlena, who were circling the boat. "Did the humans say how many dragons were working with the vampires?"

"Just two, it seems." Hyacinth looked back at a human who'd tugged gently on her shirt. Then she looked at Juniper. "Or two that they saw. But they can't say for sure."

"Stay alert!" she ordered before she shifted. It was a pain in the ass to shift in the water, but she shook off the heaviness and took to the air, adrenaline riding her hard.

Moments later she shifted once again to her human form, landing on the deck with a thud. She'd used up too much energy reserves and couldn't bother to use magic to clothe herself. Fire bathed the deck and now bridge, but she didn't feel the flames, just a bit of the heat.

Zephyr and Starlena were behind her. Flames danced all around them, lighting up the night sky in an inferno.

"We've got to do a quick search of the cargo hold below."

"No human would survive this fire." Starlena looked around at the flames and destruction.

"I don't care. We search anyway." Because one thing she'd learned in her long life was that humans were surprisingly resilient for such fragile creatures.

"Fine." Starlena raced in the opposite direction toward a burned-out opening and disappeared inside it.

Zephyr simply jumped down into a hole that had been ripped open with fire.

He was so damn sexy and capable, just doing what needed to be done. She'd never contemplated mating, had never thought it was in the cards for her, but he made her want a different future.

Juniper followed and realized there was still a smaller container down in the big, nearly empty hold. Not small by human standards but about a quarter of the size of the ones the other humans had been in. It had slammed into one of the walls and was stuck.

And it had a padlock on the front of it.

She raced at it, Zephyr by her side. She reached it first and ripped the lock off with her hands.

As she tossed it to the floor, the boat shifted suddenly and she slammed into him.

He placed a steadying hand on her hip and they both grabbed the door, wrenched it open.

"What the hell…" Zephyr's eyes widened as he fully opened the door and held it open when it wanted to slam back shut again.

"Dragon eggs," she breathed out at the same time. Three precious dragon eggs. Nothing else could be that big.

The container was tilted at an angle so she had to step up and over the edge. "Keep the door open," she said just as the boat creaked and shifted, throwing her against the wall of the container.

She grunted at the impact but scrambled to the back of the container, gently picked up one of the cracked eggs. Hairline fractures spidered out all around the one in her arms. She just hoped they could save the eggs. Oval and smooth save for the fracture lines, this one was about the size of a medium or large dog.

"Throw it to me!" Starlena called out suddenly. "The rest of the place is empty. We need to get out of here before it sinks!"

Dragons were powerful and could withstand a lot of things. But these not yet born dragonlings were much weaker, wouldn't be able to handle being submerged under water for very long.

Zephyr's arm muscles flexed as he fully ripped the door off instead of continuing to hold it open. "She's right. Throw it!"

Using all her strength, Juniper tossed it upward, breathed a sigh of relief when Starlena caught it. She tossed the next one to Zephyr, then grabbed the third before racing up the uneven edge using her supernatural strength and speed.

"We need to get these someplace quiet and warm," Starlena said as they all emerged onto the deck. She narrowed her gaze because of the thick smoke. "It's too soon for them to hatch." She said it with the kind of matter-of-fact tone that left no doubt she knew what she was talking about.

"We all shift and carry one. Starlena, you shift first. Zephyr, you're next." The platform was too small for them to shift at the same time.

And the smoke was smothering everything now, the boat creaking loudly as it took on more water. She could barely see the others next to her. The only reason they weren't dead was because smoke didn't affect dragons either. Not the same way it affected other supernaturals and humans.

Starlena looked as if she wanted to argue, but then shifted and plucked up her egg. Zephyr definitely wanted to argue with her, but to her surprise he simply crushed his mouth to hers for one millisecond before he stepped back and shifted to his dragon form.

Surprise ricocheted through her, a cascade of emotions threatening to overtake her, but her training kicked in and she shifted, and clasped the egg in one of her talons as more fire exploded all around them. Metal fragments shot into the sky, pieces of the ship becoming projectile weapons.

The debris shot upward, narrowly missing them, urging her to fly harder, faster, higher.

As she did, Zephyr swooped up behind her, protecting her back.

Her male had her back. Belatedly she realized she'd thought of him as hers. And deep down, she had a feeling that he would always have her back.

CHAPTER TWENTY-SIX

"From what we've gathered, all these humans have been taken from Florida," Finn said as he looked between Juniper and Zephyr from across his desk.

For this meeting, she'd decided to keep it tight, just bringing Zephyr with her. Now the three of them were in the Alpha's office in his mansion in the middle of a historic Biloxi neighborhood. The last few hours had been a whirlwind of activity, getting all the humans safely transported to waiting healing centers in Finn's territory. "That state did not fare well," she murmured. Meaning, during The Fall.

Finn nodded once, his expression tight. His mate wasn't with him because she was helping get the humans settled. "Scavengers is all these vampires are."

True enough. "I'd like permission to question the vampires my people incapacitated." They should be waking up soon. And while she didn't technically need permission from the Alpha, she was in his territory. And he'd been very helpful.

"That's fine. I want to be kept apprised of everything you do when you leave here."

She lifted an eyebrow at his commanding—ahem, demanding —tone.

He didn't blink, didn't back down. Just gave her what she thought of as the standard Alpha stare. "They tried to traffic people through my territory. I want updates."

Juniper sort of figured that he could just ask his daughter, but maybe that was off-limits for him. She knew Vega liked her independence and might bristle at being questioned by her father. Either way, she nodded. "Of course. Once we cut the head off this snake, I'll let you know. I imagine we'll be leaving in the next couple hours."

"Is Vega going with you?" Ooh, this wasn't the Alpha asking, but Vega's father right now.

"If she wants to." Which was basically yes.

His jaw ticked once, the action subtle. But he nodded as if he'd expected it.

"I'll...keep you updated in general," she said. "Throughout our trip." She wasn't going to update him on Vega's actions moment by moment, but goddess, a parent who cared about their offspring was very clearly her weak point.

"Thank you."

"What are you going to do with the semitrucks you confiscated?" She needed to get a few logistics out of the way now. This was one of them.

"Reuse them any way my pack can for the territory."

Zephyr cleared his throat once, then gave her a look.

Yeah, she was on the same page as him. Or she thought she was.

Juniper looked back at Finn, who was watching the two of them carefully. "We'd like use of the trucks. Whoever tasked those vampires with picking up all the humans had planned to use the trucks to transport them somewhere. I want to find out where, and if they didn't get a chance to alert anyone they were under attack, I want to drive these to wherever they're supposed to be going. Trojan horse the bastards."

Finn paused, his expression thoughtful. "Can you use more firepower?"

"Meaning your wolves or packmates? Yeah, definitely. It could get bloody though." It most likely would.

"I have a large pack and many of my wolves are tired of patrols. This will be good for them."

"Do any of them have problems taking orders from a female?" Vega had told her a story about how her mother had literally punched through a packmate's chest and squeezed their beating heart to make a point so she was pretty sure of the answer. And Lyra was a vampire so she suspected the pack wouldn't have a problem with Juniper as a dragon. But she wanted to double-check.

He snorted, his expression one of raw amusement. "You've met my mate. So, no."

"Good, then. I'll gladly take help."

He stood and they followed suit. "I'll take you to the vampires. You can question the two drivers who survived as well as the ones your people captured. It's about a twenty-minute drive."

"Thank you."

They followed him through the mansion until they were outside. The layout of the property felt similar to one of King's properties in New Orleans. Lots of grassy areas, huge oak trees, and a big wall surrounding the property. Lights were strung up in many of the trees and there were wolves lounging around, some relaxing and many others she was sure she couldn't see on patrol.

Hyacinth and the others were all waiting in the long driveway, including Starlena, who had a tight expression. She had not been happy that Juniper had left her out of this meeting with Finn. The former queen and ancient was clearly used to being in charge.

Normally she'd have taken Ren to any meeting, because he had a way of keeping people calm, but...she'd wanted Zephyr with her tonight. *Whatever. Ugh.* Zephyr made her feel safe, on a deeper level. One she so didn't want to analyze, but couldn't stop doing just that.

They piled into two SUVs, with her crew in one and Vega and Gabriel ahead of them with Finn and another wolf.

"So what's the deal?" Ren asked from the back seat.

Juniper glanced at him in the rearview mirror. "We're going to question the vampires, then go from there."

"But you have a plan."

"Of course she does," Zephyr murmured, staring out the passenger-side window.

"Well, what is it?" Ren demanded, clearly antsy.

She didn't blame him. Rolling her shoulders she said, "Depending on what information we gather from these vamps, I'm thinking we take their trucks and pretend as if we're delivering their goods. Infiltrate that way." Of course, to do that they'd have to get good intel.

Which could be tricky.

"I love that idea." Hyacinth's tone was practically giddy.

"I would like to question one or more of the vampires," Starlena said.

Juniper was surprised she hadn't wanted to stay with the dragon eggs, but she'd gotten them wrapped up in blankets and was assured that one of the healer wolves was keeping an eye on them. They weren't dragon shifters, and if raised with kindness once hatched, they would be kind and loyal to their owners. Knowing the eggs were being kept safe seemed to be enough for Starlena, who'd been hovering over the eggs with a sort of adorable obsessiveness until that point. "I assure you we're capable of interrogating them."

"I can do it faster and with more accuracy." There was no smugness in her tone, just truth. And a hint of something else.

Juniper glanced in the rearview mirror, looking past Ren to Starlena who'd chosen the third row instead of the front—and Zephyr had offered her the front. Her gray eyes were currently storm clouds. "Is there something we need to talk about?" Juniper asked instead.

"No." She sniffed once, looked out the window. "But I can do this for you. I would like to."

Zephyr gave a small nod and mouthed *Let her do it.*

Juniper frowned at him, then shrugged as she took another turn. "That would be great, thanks."

Starlena gave a stiff nod and Juniper wondered what the hell was going on. They were on a mission; she didn't have time to manage anyone's feelings. Especially an ancient with whom she already had a complicated relationship.

The next few minutes were silent—the streets here were as quiet as they were in New Orleans. People didn't drive like they used to, and traffic, especially at three in the morning, was nonexistent.

It didn't take long to pull off the two-lane highway onto a quiet side road lined with big-box warehouses. Then Finn pulled through the open gates of a huge chain-link fence into a wide-open parking lot of sorts. The place seemed to be in the middle of nowhere, but she saw a couple RVs and motorhomes off to one side and figured this place had once been a sales location for campers.

He drove across the parking lot and they followed to a small warehouse tucked back off the road.

"The vampires are inside," he said once they were out of the SUV. "My wolves know you're going to be questioning the vampires. And I need to take this," he said, looking at his phone screen with a frown.

"You ready to do this?" Juniper asked Starlena.

Starlena had worn what seemed to be standard clothing for her—loose, flowing pants and an embellished tunic. She looked elegant and gorgeous as usual, but her predator was in her eyes as she said, "Most definitely."

Juniper almost felt bad for the vampires who were about to meet Starlena. Almost.

"Can we watch?" Hyacinth slid up beside Juniper, her eyes bright.

"Feeling bloodthirsty today, are we?"

"Kind of." Her expression darkened then, her amber eyes going bright. "Those humans were lucky, relatively speaking. But there were so many of them. I just…keep thinking what would have happened if we hadn't saved them all. None of them deserved to be taken, but some of them are…too young."

Zephyr growled low in his throat at that, clearly agreeing. When Juniper looked back at him, his dragon was in his eyes.

"I will make them pay for their crimes," Starlena said simply as they reached two double doors.

"We just need information from them," Juniper said quickly as a wolf shifter opened the door for them, nodding once at Vega.

"We'll get that too. But we will get their pain as well."

Juniper immediately took in the interior—it was a prison. Had very recently been created as a holding place of sorts. There were six individual cages in the middle of the warehouse, each one glowing with definite magic. She wasn't sure what kind it was, but it was very old, very powerful. Each cage softly glowed blue, and inside, each vampire had been shackled with glowing blue chains.

Blinking, Juniper looked at Zephyr. "Do you know what kind of magic this is?"

He nodded once, took a step closer to her, skimming his fingers down her arm in a gesture she wasn't quite sure how to interpret. But she liked it. "Demon magic."

Oooh. Okay, then.

Starlena walked up to the first cage and…it opened for her.

Suddenly Starlena's chains shot out and one shoved straight through the chest of the male vampire in the cage.

There were four wolves in the place, and they'd all been giving Juniper's crew a fairly wide berth—clearly they hadn't been worried about anyone escaping the cages. They all shifted nervously, but didn't try to stop Starlena.

Juniper stepped forward, ready to tell her grandmother that they needed a couple of these vampires alive. If she'd wanted to kill them, she could have easily done it herself.

"You will tell me everything I wish to know. Where you've come from, what you were here to do, where you planned to go—who used to command you. Because I own you now." Starlena's words were whisper quiet as she used her chain to lift the male off the ground.

He stared down at Starlena, fear pulsing in his eyes. He wasn't dead. She must not have punctured his heart. Clearly on purpose. Starlena knew exactly what she was doing.

"I will tell you everything you wish to know," the vampire repeated, his eyes glowing now, the same bright white as Starlena's chains. In fact, his whole body seemed to glow, as if he had a light bulb inside him. "I'm yours to command."

Juniper shot a glance at Zephyr, whose eyes had widened slightly. Okay, so she wasn't the only one who'd never seen anything like this.

And she'd been working black ops for decades. She'd seen a whoooole hell of a lot. But this…was creepy.

And kinda cool.

But mainly creepy.

Juniper wondered if she had the ability to do it as well.

CHAPTER TWENTY-SEVEN

Juniper jumped into the front seat of the semi, shut the door behind her. It had been a long time since she'd driven one of these things and she didn't care for it.

But they needed to get on the road if they wanted to make it to the delivery point at the designated time. According to the vampire Starlena had "questioned" they had two days to make it to the drop-off point.

"Look what I got!" Ren jumped into the passenger seat, a big grin on his face as he pulled out a bag of gummy worms from a small cooler.

"Gross." She made a barfing sound. "Do you have any tuna fish sandwiches in there while you're at it? How about some Fritos?"

"As a matter of fact…" He pulled out a jumbo bag of Fritos.

"How did you even get those?" They weren't being made anymore and they tasted like feet. Or they smelled like them anyway.

"Traded one of the wolves for it."

Of course he had. "Just don't open it while I'm driving."

"Whatever. You know I'm the best partner for a road trip."

She snorted. She'd wanted Zephyr to ride with her, but when Ren had said he was, Zephyr hadn't spoken up. And…it bothered her. What, did he want to ride with a bunch of wolves instead?

Ren glanced out the window. "Be right back."

"Ren! We're getting out of here in two minutes. I *will* leave you."

"Just hold on." He was out the passenger door before she could respond, slamming it behind him.

She let her head fall back. What the hell was wrong with her crew? Normally they were so organized but they'd spent a couple hours with Finn's wolves prepping to leave and it was like they'd all devolved into manic children.

When the passenger door flew open again, Zephyr jumped inside. He opened the cooler in the seat without a word, made a grunting sound, jumped back down and left, taking all the offending food with him.

Um…okay. She covered her face with her hands, then nearly jumped when her own door was wrenched open.

Starlena looked up at her from the ground, her expression contrite. "I apologize for being…snippy earlier."

Snippy didn't sound like a word Starlena normally used, but Juniper nodded. "It's fine. Seriously. You're ol—" She cleared her throat. "As an ancient, I know you're used to being in charge." And she hadn't really been snippy. Maybe just moody.

Starlena sighed slightly. "It is not that. I care nothing about that. Okay, maybe I do a bit. But I was out of sorts because I'd just received word that… Ah, it seems…Soleil is on her way to New Orleans."

"Wait…" Sound filtered out for a long moment and all she heard was her heartbeat pounding in her ears. "My…ah, your daughter is on the way to King's territory?" It felt too weird to say *my mother* just yet. Maybe ever. Oh goddess, why did she have to deal with this now?

"Yes. She is quite upset with me. Understandably, of course."

"I… Did you tell her that I wasn't there?"

"No."

"What do you mean no?"

"I didn't talk to her at all. Cosmo has informed me that someone told Soleil about you. I don't know who. She hates modern communication but has been trying to contact me. She's left me some very angry messages."

"Why are you telling me this?"

"Because I believe in being transparent with you. I told you I would not lie to you. According to one of her messages, she wishes to join us but—"

"No!" No way in hell could that happen. She absolutely could not meet her biological mother for the first time during a mission.

"I know that. I told Cosmo that we would return soon and to have everything ready for you."

"Ready?"

"It means he'd better have the house ready for a princess. For you, dear girl. I will not push you, but when we return to New Orleans, Soleil will want to meet you. And she is not a patient female. She can be quite the pushy dragon—she is a queen of the Nova realm after all. And whether you have accepted it or not, you are her missing daughter."

Juniper decided not to point out that Starlena had ambushed her during a mission. Patience clearly wasn't her strong suit either. Instead she closed her eyes and counted to five. "Okay, when we get to New Orleans I will obviously meet her. I...would like to. But I can't deal with anything else until we handle this."

"Of course, dear." She patted one of Juniper's hands gently. "We will destroy these vampires, then have a celebration. I know this is a lot to handle, but you are a strong Nova female."

Juniper nodded once. "Are you sure you don't want to ride with us?" There was plenty of room for her to join them and Ren could ride in the back seat.

"I need to stretch my wings a bit. Expending all that magic has made my dragon edgy."

"That was impressive, what you did back there." It had only been a couple hours ago but felt like an eternity had passed. Since getting all the information they needed from that vampire—and the others—they'd been packing up and planning out their route.

"You can do that too, you know."

"Do what?"

"Order people to tell you the truth and use your enchanted shackles to do it. You're part of the Nova matriarchal line." She said it as if it explained everything.

Juniper really wanted to know how to do it but figured that was a conversation for later.

"I will teach you—or more likely your mother will. We both will," she finally said. "There's so much to teach you about your heritage."

Juniper simply nodded, made a humming sound because she didn't know how to respond.

Starlena sighed. "I know this is a lot. I promise I'm not trying to overwhelm you. I'm doing that anyway though, aren't I?"

"Not you specifically." She glanced over her shoulder, wondered where the hell Ren was and what was taking him so long. And she wanted to know what had happened to Zephyr. There were some gorgeous wolves riding in one of the other trucks and she could admit that she did not like that at all. Jealousy did not feel good. "Just all of this in general."

"Of course." She patted Juniper's hand once again and stepped back as the passenger door opened. "I'll be flying above you for a while."

She nodded and shut the door before turning to find Zephyr, not Ren, getting into the passenger seat. And Zephyr had a different cooler with him. "What are you doing?"

"How do you feel about Nutella-covered croissants and a fruit platter?" he asked instead of answering.

Her mouth watered in response. "That's amazing. You got Nutella?"

"Yep. The tiny wolf healer made me a cooler of food."

"She made it for you?" Juniper's dragon prowled beneath the surface, annoyed that another female had made him food. Even if that female was happily mated to a grouchy wolf.

"Oh, not for me. I told her it was for you—that I was courting you. She took pity on me and gave me some of their best stuff. Her mate threatened to cut my face off anyway. I respect that."

Despite everything, a laugh burst free. "I don't even know what to say to that." Though…she liked that he was courting her. Goddess, she really, really did.

Before he could respond, the door flew open and Ren stood next to Zephyr. "What the hell are you doing? That's my seat."

"You snooze you lose, cat," Zephyr said, shoving him back and shutting the door. Then he locked it.

Juniper started the semi, not bothering to fight the grin spreading across her face. Ren and his smelly food could ride with the wolves in the last truck.

She wanted to spend time alone with Zephyr anyway, and could finally admit it to herself. The adrenaline from earlier had long since worn off and all she could think about was that kiss from the boatyard.

Yes, he'd brought her to orgasm back in New Orleans, and she wanted a replay, but there had been something about that kiss. It had been so…honest and raw. And goddess, she was obsessed with the male. Just absolutely obsessed.

"Whatever you're thinking about right now, I'd love to know." Zephyr's voice was a low rumble, wrapping around her seductively.

"We do not have time for that." She kicked the truck into first and then second, maneuvering it out of the big parking lot the wolf pack had been storing it at. There were two trucks behind her—one being driven by Hyacinth and another by either Gabriel or Vega. They also had a handful of other vehicles following a few miles behind. They weren't infiltrating this group alone, but with a bunch of wolves as hungry for justice as they were.

"I'm pretty sure we always have time to talk about *that*."

Stupid supernatural senses. She hated that thinking about that kiss turned her on, and that Zephyr could clearly scent it. And she was so not talking about that right now. Not on the first leg of this long trek. *Nope.* "Last time I checked, the navigator for road trips was also in charge of the music. If you slack on the job, I'll make you trade with Ren."

He simply snorted and slid a CD into the player.

She let out a quiet sigh, glad he hadn't pushed her, until he said, "I'm getting you off before this trip is over."

~

ZEPHYR STARED out at the scenery as it flew past them, taking in the barren countryside.

"This is a much better snack choice than what Ren normally picks." Juniper handed the glass container back to Zephyr.

He closed the top on the grapes. He didn't want small talk with Juniper right now, but they had a long drive so he was going to take advantage of every second of being alone with her. "I feel a little bad for the others."

She snorted softly, glanced in the sideview mirror once. "Don't. If he ended up with Vega or Hyacinth, one of them has definitely tossed those Fritos out. Disgusting food choices aside, he is a very entertaining partner for stakeouts or long road trips."

"Yeah?"

"He always comes up with silly games. One time it was just the four of us in an SUV and he tossed Cheetos at each of us to see who could catch the most in their mouth."

"Who won?"

"Griff all the way." She laughed lightly, turning her normally intense expression into something a lot softer.

Zephyr loved seeing her like that. More carefree.

"We were all disgusting orange-faced messes by the end of that trip, but it was fun."

"You guys are a good team."

"Yeah, we are." She cleared her throat and gave him a searching look before returning her gaze to the road.

It was sunny out with blue skies and they hadn't seen another soul on the road. They'd seen a couple dragon shifters flying after about four hours of driving, but the beasts had given them a wide berth. Maybe because Starlena was flying above them.

"Speaking of team," she continued. "Have you thought about what you want to do after this job?"

"What do you mean?" He knew, but she needed to ask him. He was breaking down her walls, and needed to know that she wanted him around long-term.

"Would you like to join our crew? Officially?"

"Are there any rules about not getting involved with crewmates?" He figured there weren't, considering Vega and Gabriel were mated. But…he wanted to get under her skin a little anyway. Remind Juniper that she was the reason he was here at all. Just her.

"No."

"Then yes, I would love to." He would also love to worship her body right now.

The tension in her shoulders seemed to ease slightly, which made him smile. She definitely wanted him.

"If I'd said no, would you have begged me?"

She snorted. "I don't beg anyone for anything."

"Hmm. I don't want you to beg, but I bet I can get you to," he murmured, watching her mouth.

She jerked the wheel slightly as she looked over at him. And her scent was interesting. "What are you playing at?"

"Just thinking of a way to pass this very long drive." One of Finn's people had spelled the trucks so they didn't have to deal with refueling at all. They only had to stop for needed breaks. And they'd just taken one so they had plenty of time.

"What are you thinking?"

His gaze fell to her mouth again and when her tongue briefly flicked out to wet her lips, he groaned. Couldn't help it. The sound just slipped out because, goddess above, Juniper was everything. "I'm thinking I can make you come, take the edge off."

She looked back at the road, her breathing raspier, unsteady now. "We can't do anything while I'm driving a very heavy vehicle."

"I'll do all the work, you just steer. There's no one else on the road in front of us anyway." He looked out the windshield to reconfirm. No vehicles on the two-lane highway, and surrounding them were wide stretches of land in either direction. It was desolate out here.

"That's…"

"Exactly what you need," he murmured. "You've barely gotten any rest. You need this."

Her breathing kicked up slightly and he knew he was on the right path. She was thinking about this, not just shutting him down. And goddess help him, he needed to taste her, needed to bring her pleasure.

"What about your rules from before?" Her voice was a sultry whisper.

Hell yeah. She wasn't saying no. That meant she was thinking about doing this. "I have ulterior motives."

A sharp scent popped off her as she glanced at him. "What?"

"I want to taste your come."

She spluttered for a moment. "That's not…ulterior!"

"It's purely selfish. I want to make you come, want to taste it on my fingers."

She squirmed in her seat, pressing her thighs together. "You make me crazy, Zephyr."

Yeah, definitely not a no—and she'd said his name. He slid closer to her, ran a palm up her jean-clad leg as he dipped his head to her neck, inhaled. Her wild, untamed scent was strong, sliding around him.

She clutched the wheel, her knuckles turning white.

He grinned against her neck, raked his teeth over her sensitive skin. "Is that a yes?" he murmured.

She inhaled sharply and nodded.

"Say it," he ordered.

The scent of her arousal spiked. "Yes."

There wasn't much room in the cab of the truck, but there was more than enough for what he intended to do. He nibbled on her ear oh so gently as he slid a hand up her shirt, slowly, slowly, running his palm against her taut abdomen. He wanted to touch all of her, to memorize every inch of her body right down to her toenails.

Her muscles tightened under his touch and that sweet scent of hers skyrocketed, filling the entire space, making him lightheaded.

Knowing that she was turned on because of him had his dragon right at the surface, ready to claim his female. It was too soon, he knew that, but it didn't change anything. She was it for him and he'd accepted it. He just wished she'd give in to what he knew she wanted, that she would see how worthy she was. How amazing.

Until then, he was going to give her as many orgasms as it took to prove that he was the male for her. But it wasn't just about the orgasms. He was going to be there for her. Show up when she needed him. Because that was what a mate did.

He slid his hand higher until he cupped her bra, tugged it down. Her pebbled nipple was visible through her T-shirt, straining against it. He leaned down, sucked it into his mouth through the cotton.

She let out a yelp of surprise, then arched her back. The vehicle jerked slightly and he grinned against her breast.

"Maybe this isn't a great idea," she rasped out.

"Best idea I've had today." He slid his hand lower even as he continued teasing her nipple. He thought about shoving her shirt up, but there was something erotic about this—and soon enough he planned to have her naked and splayed out for him.

When he freed her jeans button, she sucked in a breath. And when he slid his hand down the front of her pants, right under her black cotton panties, the scent of her arousal slammed into him hard.

"I love your scent," he murmured, pressing his teeth gently around her still covered nipple. He was tempted to tug her shirt completely off, but she was on a wire's edge right now.

And he simply wanted her to climax. Then he wanted to claim her forever. But one step at a time.

She lifted up slightly, raising her ass so that he could easily slide his hand downward. As he did, he kissed upward, raking his teeth over her neck in the spot he planned to bite her when they mated. "Eyes on the road," he whispered when she jerked the wheel slightly.

Her breathing was overly loud as he slid his palm over her mound, cupping her completely. His movements were restrained, as were hers, and there was something about that which had his erection shoving at his pants.

"Such a bad idea," she moaned.

"The worst." He nipped her earlobe, bit down.

She let out a moan as he dragged his middle finger over her clit. His cock reacted to the noise, her scent, everything.

He took his time, slowly teasing her clit in little circles until she grasped his wrist. "You've got to speed up!"

He grinned against her neck, bit down but didn't break the skin. "Is that begging?"

"Fine. Yes. Get me off, *please*." She shifted her hips upward, trying to force him to move.

He didn't need to be told twice, however. He would tease her, but later. She might not realize it, but the fact that she'd asked for this, had made herself so vulnerable with him, told him that he was busting down the cage she'd created around herself. She trusted him. And that mattered.

He circled her clit in tight little moves, wishing they were stretched out on a flat surface and he could thrust his fingers or his cock inside her.

When her breathing grew unsteady, he increased his pace until her legs suddenly tightened, her fingers gripping the wheel harder as an orgasm slammed into her.

"Zephyr!" she cried out as he continued teasing her clit. "Oh, fuck me."

"I plan to," he growled as she came down from her climax, breathing hard, still white-knuckling the wheel. Her phone buzzing wildly on the dash but they both ignored it. She'd been swerving and no doubt someone was checking on them.

"Unzip your pants." Her words were unsteady as she looked over at him, her bicolor eyes dilated as he licked his fingers, savoring the taste of her. "Now," she demanded. "Take your cock out."

Oh yeah. He hadn't planned on this, had wanted this to be about her, but if she wanted to touch him, this was happening. His cock kicked against his zipper at her words, the order she was giving him.

He quickly unzipped his pants and she reached over before he'd managed to shove them down, wrapped her long fingers around his thick length.

As she did, one of her chains shot free and wrapped around his calf. It was an odd, warm pressure, one he found he liked. It was almost as if she was holding on to him, claiming him. Or more likely that was him projecting, but he loved the feel of her gripping his leg almost as much as the feel of her fingers wrapped around his hard length.

"Juniper," he breathed out, needing to say her name. He pulsed in her grip and when she stroked him once, hard, he forgot to breathe, to think. He felt nothing but *her* as she started getting him off.

He was vaguely aware of their surroundings, the countryside flying by as she gripped his length with the right amount of pressure and kept stroking over and over until he couldn't control himself. Didn't want to.

He came with a shout, all over his shirt and her hands, and the sight of his seed all over her was enough to make him hard again.

This had barely taken the edge off for him and he knew it was the same for her. Breathing unsteadily, he said, "When we get back, or when we have time alone, we're taking our time with each other."

She nodded, her eyes still wildly dilated. "Definitely. We're not leaving our room for days. Weeks."

The way she said "our" struck him deep. He didn't think she was even aware of it, but he held on to that word, the possessive way she was looking at him.

She was his other half. Soon, he would make her completely his.

CHAPTER TWENTY-EIGHT

"This is about twenty miles from the drop-off point." Griffin had his arms crossed over his chest as they all talked under the moonlight and stars.

Their convoy had pulled off the two-lane highway onto an exit that had a long-ago abandoned gas station and no signs of life. They were close to where they were supposedly going to find all the vampires behind this trafficking operation. They'd find out soon enough if the information held up. It was a couple towns over from where Juniper and her crew had come through weeks ago, looking for these guys.

The parking lot was gravelly and a good place to wait. There was no foot traffic here, no chance of being seen from the highway since no one was traveling on it, and twenty miles out should be far enough away from a tight grid. Or at least that was the hope, since they knew this crew had dragons working with them. Or, they assumed, since there had been two with them before.

"I want you to recon it," she said to Griffin, then glanced at Ren. "You too. I'll do the aerial scout. Zephyr, you stay here. I need eyes on the sky in case there's danger here." She knew that Finn's wolves were more than capable but she was in charge now and felt responsible for them. And she knew that Zephyr would spot a threat overhead and take care of it. She trusted him.

He nodded, though she could tell he didn't want to be separated from her.

Well, she didn't want to be separated from him either, but that was the way it had to be. "Hyacinth, you're in charge here," she said, glancing at Finn's wolves, who simply nodded. "Vega and Gabriel, I want you scouting behind us and expanding out from where the drop-off point is. Starlena, I want you doing the same, but aerially."

Everyone nodded and she could practically feel the energy from the others in the air. It was the calm before the storm. Whatever was about to happen—there was going to be a fight tonight.

They all knew it. And they were ready.

"Any questions or concerns?"

Everyone shook their head, except Zephyr, who motioned her over to him.

"What is it?" she murmured as they stood by the passenger door of the truck they'd arrived in. The truck he'd recently brought her to orgasm in. The scent of their sex hung in the air, clung to both of them. She'd had to change shirts after he'd sucked her nipples through it. And after getting come on his shirt, he'd just taken his off and left it off—she didn't mind the view.

Surprising her, he cupped her cheek, brushed his mouth over hers. "I know you'll be careful," he murmured. "But I just wanted to remind you to take care."

Her heart squeezed but she didn't know how to respond. Not well anyway. This was new territory for her. She could say she wanted casual all she wanted, but that was a lie. One she wouldn't insult him by saying now. But she was still terrified of a relationship. Because what happened if he eventually saw through her, realized she wasn't good enough? *Ugh.* She had to get out of her head right now, to let go of old insecurities of a dragonling thrust into a pack of wolves where she'd never felt like she fit in.

Juniper grabbed his hip, squeezed possessively. "You take care too."

He simply nodded and they walked back to the others.

"Let's do this." Juniper forced herself not to stare as Zephyr started sliding his pants off, readying to shift and take to the skies.

Instead she turned to find her grandmother watching her curiously. Starlena had the same blades as before strapped to her chest. She wondered if they were magic, and hated her curiosity.

"What?" she asked.

"If it's not a true mating," Starlena said quietly, her voice low enough for only Juniper to hear. "If he's not strong enough to be with a Nova female, it'll break both your hearts."

Juniper wasn't sure what a true mating meant. And now wasn't the time to ask. So she stepped back across the parking lot, readying herself to shift. She'd gotten enough food and rest to recharge and could shift without taking off her clothes, could tap into her magic once again.

Moments later she took to the skies, very aware of Zephyr nearby. She wondered if she should have said something more to him, though wasn't sure what she could have said. Things had shifted between them, but she had no idea what it meant. And she couldn't worry about any of that right now.

She banked to the left, back toward the highway, and let her camouflage fall into place. As she headed toward their target spot, she saw Griffin racing into a shadow of trees that paralleled the highway.

She flapped upward, wanting to get a wide view of the upcoming mountain and surrounding areas below. Homes dotted the area, but not many lights were on anywhere.

A few small campfires flickered in the distance but there weren't many electric lights that she could see. Not like in New Orleans, where the city was still alive and bustling.

An eerie sensation settled in her bones as she flew even higher, the wind slicing over her wings. She'd gotten used to being around so many humans and supernaturals that being up here, looking out over this ghosted area, was unsettling.

The closer she flew toward the nearest mountain, and also their target, voices filtered up now and then. But there were so many trees, so much foliage blocking her view, even in this winter month.

Juniper eyed the mountainside below from her dragon's-eye view, frustrated that there were so many trees in the way. And that was when she realized it wasn't all trees, but a sort of netting.

The way she viewed color was different in this form, but with her night vision she had vivid clarity of heat signatures. And she could see at least a dozen beings that must be shifters—vampires had a different type of signature—clustered together under what looked like a netting.

In the daytime, it would likely be a camouflage that blended with the trees.

The moonlight was on her side tonight at least, the near-full moon unencumbered by clouds.

She shifted upward, and as she crested the current mountain was greeted with a lot more light from the next one. A hotel jutted out from near the top, and she could see a small town below, little buildings clustered together in various formations.

As she angled lower, she heard it. Wings flapping.

Staying alert, she glided, wanting to be as quiet as possible.

A dragon with golden yellow scales suddenly burst up from the stream that cut through the town, as if it had been drinking from it. She tensed, readying for battle, but the dragon didn't seem to sense her, didn't fly in Juniper's direction.

It flew higher and higher before it began a lazy glide, circling around the whole area. So it was part of the security of this region. Knowing dragons were involved with this operation pissed her off to no end.

She stayed low, wanting to remain out of the path of the dragon above so it wouldn't catch her scent. After she finished scanning the town below, and seeing only vampire signatures and no humans, she turned around.

But made sure to keep an eye on her back. The dragon seemed to only surveil the township area below. But he could be on a schedule and could definitely be working with others. Likely was.

She hoped Griffin had fared better than her on the ground. They knew where they were supposed to drop off the trucks, but now that she'd seen a dragon, the playing field had changed. They would have to keep some of them in the air to fight however many dragons while the rest stayed on the ground and took out the vampires.

Then they needed to figure out who the hell was in charge, to cut off the head of this beast once and for all.

CHAPTER TWENTY-NINE

"There are dragon traps in place," Starlena said the moment she shifted to human form.

"What do you mean?" Juniper asked. She'd landed only five minutes ago back at their very temporary home base to find that Griff still hadn't returned.

"Sharp wiring throughout clusters of trees. I've seen it before. It's spelled, made from demonfire. It'll do serious damage to our wings."

"That's what that was," Ren said, his expression dark. "Was it the glowing webbing?" he asked as he looked at Starlena.

She nodded, her expression mirroring Ren's.

"So there are vampires, dragons and potentially demons at play here." Juniper didn't like any of this.

"Not necessarily demons. They could have simply taken the fire from a Hell realm gate and harnessed it with magic."

"That doesn't sound simple," Hyacinth said. "And vampires working with fire? That's… My people don't like fire."

"It's not simple. It takes very specific skills and knowledge," Starlena said, her expression shifting slightly, as if she was racking her brain.

"You know who's behind this?" Zephyr was right next to Juniper, had been from the moment she'd touched down minutes ago.

"No. But the skill set to harness demonfire is something only an ancient like myself can do. So either an ancient is involved or they're working with demons. My money is on an ancient because demons don't play well with others."

"So what's the plan?" Ren asked, looking at Juniper.

Finn's wolves were behind them, watching her expectantly as well. And she wished she had the answer. They needed to bring down this group but this was sounding like it was bigger than she'd originally thought.

"We can recon the rest of the night, then lie low tomorrow, watch them some more and attack." But she didn't want to wait. They were in a strange territory and the longer they were out in the open, relatively speaking, the bigger the chance they'd lose the element of surprise. "But the drop-off time is later tonight."

Griffin appeared as if out of nowhere, fully clothed. Juniper still found herself impressed by how quiet her wolf packmate was, by any standards. "We should hit them before the sun comes up," he said immediately.

Everyone looked at him then. Considering her packmate chose his words carefully, always, Juniper was going to listen. "What did you see?"

"The drop-off point for the trucks is in a huge cave right in the side of a mountain. And it leads to a Hell realm gate. There's no doubt where they're taking the humans. I didn't spot humans anywhere in this territory. Did anyone else?" He looked around, got all negative answers and continued. "I heard enough conversations that they're worried about the boat delivery of the humans in Finn's territory. They don't know we saved them, but they haven't heard from the boat's captain and that had been their contact. And one of the vampires said that their dragon brethren seem tenser than normal, that they lost two of their people but don't know how or when."

That would be the dragons they'd killed over the Gulf waters.

When they'd died, their clan would have felt the severing of their lives. *Shit.*

"The mood in that cave is worried. But they're not on high alert— yet. It's coming, however. If we're going to strike, I say we do it now, rescue any humans trapped and get out of here."

"The only problem with that is getting out of the Hell realm." That was always a tricky thing. She was a dragon, and her kind's blood had been used to open and shut Hell realm doors for ages. But going into one and then actually leaving…sometimes it didn't work out the way you planned. Zephyr getting trapped in one was a prime example of that. She couldn't risk her people being trapped somewhere.

"We don't need to cross the barrier of the door. I can pull the humans out with my magic," Starlena said.

Juniper blinked. "How?" She'd never heard of anything like that.

She patted her blades once as she said, "Nova magic." Her words were so matter-of-fact, as if it was a simple thing.

Juniper had questions but wouldn't ask them in front of the others. Still… "You're sure?"

"Yes."

Juniper looked out at the others as she digested everything, as she went over everything they'd gleaned. "They've got dragons on their side and they have the advantage of being on their home turf. But I think we should attack tonight, free the humans, then close the gate. We'll go in covertly, on the ground, attack the cave first." Since getting everyone out of that Hell realm was the main objective, it made sense to slip into there first. "What do you think our odds are of getting in undetected?" she asked Griffin.

He paused once before he said, "If we go in on foot, I think good. I know we came in with the trucks, but I don't think we need them. They might even hurt our attempts to infiltrate. There were a good twenty vampires inside that cave. Mostly just dicking around, but they're acting as security of that Hell realm gate. I say we infiltrate using our natural abilities and kill everyone in sight before they have a chance to alert anyone else."

Sometimes the simplest plan was best. "I like it. We'll head out in ten." Juniper glanced back at the trucks, frowned.

"We can hide the trucks off a nearby road right off the highway," Zephyr said, clearly reading her expression. "When I was flying, I spotted a place we could drive into and leave them. It won't be a perfect hiding spot but someone would have to be looking for them."

"Do it, then." She nodded once at him and he ordered two of the wolves to start up the trucks. "And if anyone wants to make calls before the mission, now's the time." She knew Griff liked to call his dad before a mission and she wasn't surprised when Ren and Hyacinth both pulled out their phones—Ren likely to call the sweet human Grace, and Hyacinth to call the Magic Man.

Even Starlena stepped away, pulling out her cell phone.

Juniper pulled out her own phone and called her parents. She needed to contact them anyway—needed to tell them about her biological family. But mainly she just wanted to tell her mom and dad that she loved them. That she appreciated them.

Stepping away from everyone, she called her mom first. It rang and rang so she called her dad next. No answer either but she decided to leave a voicemail, something she almost never did. "Hey Dad, just checking in with you guys. I called both of you and no answer so you must be really busy."

She smiled at that. They had to be ridiculously busy not to answer her. Because it could be four in the morning and if she called, they picked up. But they were healers and there had recently been a few pregnancies in the pack. She had a feeling they were dealing with all the preggos right now. Or more likely, the mates of the pregnant wolves.

"Been busy with work," she continued. "But I should have called you back sooner. I love you both more than you'll ever know. And I'll be coming home as soon as I can." She hung up then, not trusting her voice. Then she sent a text to Finn, letting him know what they planned and that Vega was safe. After he responded, she texted August, let him know they'd be going dark. She received a thumbs-up emoji.

Which made her smile. Their boss trusted them to get the job done.

She turned off her cell. They all would before heading out. As she shoved her phone into her duffel bag, she glanced up at Zephyr's approach.

He strode across the parking lot, all long, muscular jean-clad legs and barely restrained energy buzzing through him.

The male was walking sex and raw power. And she could still feel his fingers thrusting inside her. "You call your brothers?" she asked, shoving those thoughts aside.

He nodded, his gaze straying to her mouth. "Yeah. Avery told us all to be safe," he said, his expression softening.

Which just made Juniper's heart flip over. The male should smile more often. And goddess, she wanted all of his smiles. She stepped closer to him, moving on pure instinct, and wrapped her arms around his middle. She knew she'd taken him off guard, but he didn't pause, simply wrapped her in a tight embrace.

She melted into him, just savoring being held by him. She'd never fully trusted anyone other than her parents and crew. Certainly not a lover. This thing with Zephyr that she was afraid to define or even try to put into words had woken her up inside. And she didn't want to go back to sleep.

"As soon as this is over, you're mine for a few days." He inhaled deeply and she knew he was straight up smelling her.

She liked it way too much. "Just a few?" she murmured against his chest. Only a week ago she'd have blown off the thought of a few days. A week ago, she'd been a dumbass.

"How about forever?" His voice was a low growl, hitting her in all the right places.

That should terrify her. And okay, it totally did. They were drag-ons. If they mated, they were linked forever, quite literally, till death do they part. But she didn't want to live half a life anymore. She didn't want to be so afraid of her own happiness that she missed out on something amazing, life changing. She wanted to hold on to him tight, her baggage be damned. "I'm still a mess sometimes. That hasn't changed." She kept her face buried in his chest. This was exactly where she wanted to be. And for the next two minutes, before they had to fly into danger, she was going to stay right here.

His grip tightened. "You're perfection."

"I can be cranky in the mornings," she murmured, keeping her voice low enough for only him.

"I know a good way to put a smile on your face." His low-spoken words were wicked and sliced right through to her core.

Swallowing hard, because she couldn't afford to let her emotions overtake her, she leaned back to look up at him. She didn't know what to say in that moment. Not with words. So she kissed him, lightly, brushed her mouth over his in a claiming. It might be light, but she was doing it in front of everyone. She was making a statement now. He was hers.

Though she hated to pull back, she had to. It was almost go time.

Clearing her throat, she stepped back and found everyone had returned from making their phone calls.

"Thurman says we've got this in the bag," Hyacinth said as she joined the group, a grin on her face. "Let's go kick some ass."

Juniper had known her long enough to know that Thurman hadn't actually said that, but the wolves in the group nodded, their expressions feral and determined as they readied for battle.

She raised an eyebrow at Hyacinth, who simply gave a short shrug. So Thurman *hadn't* said that, but whatever, they *did* have this handled.

"Let's go over the plan of attack. We'll be working in tandem and as quietly as possible." She ran over the plan once, then took input from all the scouts, tweaked it.

Then they went over it again.

Adrenaline jagged through her. She was ready for this and she was glad Zephyr would have her back. Though she would worry about him, she knew he was one of the most capable males she'd ever met.

Capable, warm, giving, and so damn patient he might as well be a unicorn.

And she wasn't going to let him go.

CHAPTER THIRTY

Zephyr crept toward the entrance of the cave opening, his camouflage in place. They'd had to trek up half the mountain and Griff had been spot-on; this place was the entrance to a Hell realm gate. The glow that emanated from the mouth of it had been visible from about a hundred yards down.

And it was clear the cave opening had been created recently, which made sense. Someone supernatural must have blown the mountain open to get to it. Hell realm gates were usually difficult or impossible to get to.

Despite the name "Hell realm," some of them were paradises. If he had to guess, this one might be too, considering the trouble whoever was running this show was putting into trafficking so many humans into it.

Across the cave mouth, a rock was tapped on the ground twice.

Juniper's signal. She and Starlena were moving in from the west of the cave mouth, while he was moving in from the east. Since they were the only ones who had natural camouflage, they were infiltrating the cave. The others were scattered down the mountainside, hiding and waiting—and stopping any potential problems.

They needed to keep things as quiet as possible while they rescued the humans. At least long enough to get them out of the realm. But he knew better than most that things didn't always work out as planned.

Following her signal, he moved inside, watching for traps. The opening was about thirty feet high with a long string of lights hung up along the ceiling. Given the natural blue glow coming from deeper inside, he didn't think anyone actually needed the illumination.

Voices trailed from deeper inside and he paused as a shout went up. There was also a consistent *pat, pat, pat* sound that would stop, then start up again.

"Time to pay up!"

"Man, fuck you," a voice said jokingly.

So he and the others hadn't been seen. Zephyr continued on and nearly rolled his eyes at what he saw. The cave opened up into a wide space with twenty-one vampires in it. Two were playing ping-pong—that was the source of the shouting and pat sounds.

Five were playing a card game around a table.

Three were playing some sort of electronic handheld game.

Seven were lifting weights in an area that had been designated as a gym. Vampires were naturally strong, but it was clear the males in the workout area were practicing their agility. So those were the first he'd attack.

Four were in front of the Hell realm gate—which was a glowing ball of energy. And they looked bored out of their minds.

There'd been no guards by the cave mouth, which made him wonder about their security.

Moving quietly, he edged closer to the vampires working out. Two were doing plyometric exercises, jumping over stacked up boulders.

"That's impressive," one said to the other.

"Nah. What would be impressive would be if we actually got some company in here once in a while," one grumbled.

From the way he said company, Zephyr figured he meant of the female variety. He was going to kill that one first.

"It's bullshit," another agreed. "The old ones are keeping the humans for themselves."

"That sounds like treason," one by the gate called out. "Stop discussing this now. I will not be part of this conversation."

"Forget you!" the one who'd just jumped over the boulders snapped, his fangs dropping as he took a menacing step toward the other male. "You guard that thing but you've never been inside. None of us have! These arrogant dragons keep everything for themselves, treat us like servants."

"We just need to have patience," the male responded, turning his nose slightly up. "We'll earn the right to enter."

"Or we can just go inside, take what we want," the beefed-up one continued.

"Or you could just die," a familiar female voice purred. *Juniper.*

That was the signal. Still in human form, Zephyr released a stream of fire directly at the vampires working out.

Out of the corner of his eye, he saw both Starlena and Juniper drop their camouflage as they whipped their chains out, slicing off the heads of the video game and card playing vamps in quick succession.

Screams filled the cavern as the three of them attacked with savagery, setting vampires on fire or slashing them down with their chains.

He ashed the vampires in the makeshift gym in seconds, their screams fading as quickly as they started. Then he turned on the others but Juniper was faster, her chains reaching out farther than he'd thought possible, whipping straight through the ping-pong players.

He focused on the guards at the realm entrance who pulled out actual guns, started shooting wildly.

Shit. They couldn't afford a lot of noise.

He avoided the wild bullets as he raced at the vamps with super-natural speed, unleashed his fire in a sharp arc, burning them to nothing.

In less than sixty seconds, all the vampires were ash, the cave now silent other than the pulsing from the Hell realm gate.

He let his camo fall and turned to face the females. Neither of them had broken a sweat.

This was the easy part. "What do you need to do to get the humans free?" he asked Starlena.

"Just watch my back," she ordered as she approached the gate, pulled both her blades out, gripped them tight. Her entire body glowed, her eyes pure silver instead of blue as she released her chains. They extended from her hands, wrapping around the entirety of the blades, and surged out straight into the gate. "I won't be able to stop once I start."

"Enemy on the move up the mountain," Ren said through the comm line. "Vamps emerging from a truck… Shit." His voice grew quieter. "Fifty tangos incoming."

"Let them all pass you. Stay hidden until they're close to the entrance, then attack en masse." Juniper's order was just as quietly spoken.

And a good one. Once all the vamps got up the mountain near the cave, they'd be attacked from all sides.

They acknowledged her orders, then… "Three dragons scaling down the mountain." Griff's voice was whisper quiet. "They're in beast form, crawling toward the cave opening. They're moving with stealth. Shifting to human now."

"We've got them." Juniper looked at Zephyr and they stepped forward as a unit.

A shot of adrenaline and raw protectiveness surged through him as they hurried to the cave mouth, keeping Starlena protected behind them.

Then Juniper motioned with her hands for him to move to the side of the cave, scale upward and attack from above.

He nodded, the need to protect her overwhelming, his beast ready to take over, shift. But he couldn't, not in this smaller space. And she was strong. Knew what she was doing.

Distant shouts sounded from somewhere outside the cave, but Starlena didn't stop whatever she was doing.

Rocks skittered downward as Zephyr easily climbed up the face of the wall until he was nearly to the top.

Three dragons strode inside moments later, naked and swaggering. Two males. One female. And they were definitely part of the same clan. They had pale skin and inky black hair and were tall as most dragons were.

"You do not belong in this territory!" The female stepped forward, her long braid swinging behind her.

The males spanned out, not bothering to look up as they all stared between Juniper and Starlena—whose entire body was incandescent now, her chains and blades glowing as well.

"You took something that doesn't belong to you," Juniper snapped, her chains swinging dangerously toward one of the dragons. "Who is giving you orders?"

The female laughed maniacally. "Why do you care about humans? They're good for menial labor and sex, but that's it. We've taken no one who will be missed!" The female started to move toward Starlena, but Juniper moved fast, shifting so that her body was in front of Starlena.

"It's pathetic that you answer to vampires, do their dirty work." Juniper was clearly trying a different tactic.

The dark-haired female laughed again, this time the sound short and sharp. "Those fools work for *me*. Though I'm glad to hear that the rumors of vampires running this show are spreading." She laughed again, the sound bouncing off the cave, mixing with the chaos of shouts and gunfire from outside the cave.

Zephyr knew that was all Juniper had wanted—to know who the leader was—and he anticipated her signal even before she gave it. A quick flick of her chains upward.

He released his grip on the cave wall, his fall quiet as he landed on one of the dragon males. Out of the corner of his eye he saw the female race at Juniper even as the second male turned toward Zephyr and his almost dead clanmate.

Using raw dragon strength, Zephyr punched straight through the dragon's back, ripped the male's heart out even as he released a stream of fire at the other incoming dragon.

The male released his own fire in a blast of fury.

Heat and flames burned over Zephyr's face as he tossed the heart into the dirt, raced at the remaining male.

The male dodged, still shooting fire at him.

Zephyr kept going, his own fire a scorching stream as he attempted to get close enough to take off the male's head.

But the male was quick, moving with an impressive supernatural speed as he raced around the cave.

Trying to tire Zephyr out, he realized.

He turned toward the other threat, spotted Juniper lashing the female dragon across the face with her chains.

The female wasn't fazed, just shot something out from her hands— *Oh shit.* Darts of poison from her fingertips. He knew some dragon Alphas could do this, had a vicious poison running through their system that they used to defend themselves or incapacitate prey. He moved in on the female from behind, hoping it would draw the male after him instead of this stupid game of chase.

He released his fire at the female and a bright blue fire like he'd never seen shot out, skimming the top of the female's head.

She screamed in agony and the male attacked.

Zephyr turned, aware of Juniper lashing her chains around the female's neck as he breathed the same scorching fire at the male, the blue fire slicing an arc right across the male's neck even as he shot fire at Zephyr.

The male's fire stopped instantly, his head falling from his body.

Zephyr turned before it hit the ground, ready to jump into the other fight, only to find Juniper standing over the fallen, headless female dragon, her chains glowing at her side.

"Are you good?" she demanded, looking him over.

"Yeah. You?" He scanned her, looking for signs of injury, that she'd been poisoned. "Did she poison you?"

"No. She missed. Barely. We need to help the others."

He was already moving toward the cave exit when Starlena suddenly pulled her chains back, gasping hard.

They both moved toward her and to his surprise she nearly collapsed. Juniper caught her, steadied her.

"They're coming," Starlena whispered. "The humans. There are only fifty of them alive now. The others…" She shook her head, then continued. "As soon as the humans are out, we have to shut the gate. There's a whole dragon clan in there and we need to cut off their exit. I've used my magic to give the humans a small head start."

"Ren, report," Juniper ordered even as she nodded at what her grandmother said.

"We're picking them off now. Only a few left. How are you guys?"

"Good. Did you hear Starlena?"

"Yeah."

"Get ready, then. Any humans that come out," she said, even as two human females were spit out of the glowing door, "get off the mountain and back to base. We've got to close the gate."

"Run that way!" Zephyr ordered the humans, pointing at the exit. "We're getting you out of here. There are wolf shifters outside who are going to help you off the mountain, get you to safety."

The two females stared with wide eyes. They each had on ragged-looking sneakers, jeans and T-shirts and were covered in fine red clay. Wordlessly they scrambled up and did what he said—they ran.

For the next ten minutes, human after human was spit out of the Hell realm door, each in various states of undress and physical condition. But they all ran to the exit, some screaming, others silent.

"That's it," Starlena said as a petite blonde scrambled to her feet, didn't glance backward as she sprinted away from them. "Now we blast the door with all our firepower," she said, looking between the two of them. "I'll do the rest. Don't stop your fire."

"We won't," Juniper said, even as Zephyr nodded.

The three of them shot their fire—his was normal now, not that blue fire from before—and Starlena released her chains, injecting magic straight into the glowing opening.

Heat surged through his body as the glow grew brighter and brighter around them. He had to close his eyes as Starlena shouted, "Keep going!"

But he kept blasting fire until a ball of heat suddenly ricocheted out, sending the three of them flying back.

He slammed into the nearest wall, winced at the impact, but as he landed on his feet he immediately sought out Juniper.

She was shoving up from the ground, her gaze drawn to his. "I'm good," she murmured as Starlena pushed up on wobbly legs.

"It's done," the ancient said. No longer were her eyes or body glowing, and she looked thinner. And no longer did a glowing gate illuminate the cave. Instead a thick wall of rock remained.

"The gate is closed? Will they be trapped forever?" Juniper asked.

"Probably not," Starlena said, her expression grim. "But the dragons inside there will be stuck for a long while."

"How did you know there were fifty humans in there? And how did you get them out?" Juniper asked, worry in her gaze as she eyed Starlena.

Yeah, Zephyr was worried about her too.

"I can sort of 'see' with my chains. Not literally, but I don't know how else to explain it. And there's a deep magic inside me. It's part of our clan. I used it to call the humans to me. It didn't matter what they were doing, it pulled them free and created a sort of protection around them so they could escape."

"That's amazing," Zephyr murmured.

"As amazing as that crazy blue fire of yours. What the heck was that, by the way?" Juniper asked, her bicolor gaze shifting to him.

"I'm not entirely sure." Though he thought he might know. His brother Mikael had experienced it once before when he'd been protecting his mate. "But right now I think we need to get you some food," he said to Starlena.

She nodded and they all turned as Griff strode into the cave, covered in ash and blood. Zephyr had heard enough over the comm line that he knew that their people had taken gunfire and gotten into full-on fights with vampires, but they were all alive even if some were injured.

"We're currently transporting all the humans back to base. A few vamps escaped and they seem to be scattering, but I want to hunt them down."

"Can we spare you?" Juniper asked.

He nodded. "Finn's wolves are in triage mode, getting the humans to safety. Unless there are more dragons we don't know about, Hyacinth, Ren and I want to finish this and clean out this area for good."

Zephyr rolled his shoulders once, still amped up. "This place needs a purge."

And they would need to search for any additional humans as well, help them get to safety if there were any.

"Okay. Starlena, I want you going with the wolves back to base. We're going to hunt down any straggler vamps tonight but we'll be back to base by daylight," Juniper said.

Starlena nodded once and gently patted Juniper's cheek. "It was a pleasure to fight by your side today."

Juniper's cheeks actually flushed pink—which Zephyr absolutely loved. Hell, he loved everything about her, but in that moment she was adorable. His fierce, brave dragon was so many things. But above all, she was his.

And it said a hell of a lot for how exhausted Starlena must be that she wasn't arguing with Juniper about returning.

"We need to take down all the dragon traps before we leave as well," he said as she headed out of the cave.

Juniper nodded and started giving them orders.

It was going to be a long night, but he was glad to be by her side. They'd done a lot of good here. And now that this mission was mostly over, the burning need to claim his mate was riding him harder than it ever had.

CHAPTER THIRTY-ONE

Five days later

"Ren said he had something to tell me. And he sounded weird about it." Juniper yawned as she headed up the front walk with Zephyr, Hyacinth and Griff. The last five days they'd been going at warp speed hunting down anyone involved with trafficking humans. They'd killed two escaped dragons and a handful of vampires in the Tennessee region.

They'd also ended up saving another fourteen humans, who were now in New Orleans with one of the many healers in the territory. She, Zephyr and her crew had stayed behind for the cleanup. She'd actually managed to convince Starlena to leave a day early, and her grandmother had taken Ren back to New Orleans with her. They'd been working to get a lot of the humans settled.

Now, she wanted to take a shower, eat and have sex with Zephyr. Maybe even shower and have sex at the same time. They hadn't had a moment alone the last few days and then they'd flown straight home without stopping.

"You're gonna be mad at him," Hyacinth murmured. "But I think you should cut him some slack."

Juniper paused at the top of the steps, turned around to look at her friend. "What did he do?"

Hyacinth winced and didn't answer.

Zephyr took her hand in his, linked their fingers together and squeezed. "Whatever it is, I'm sure he has your best interests at heart."

She looked at him sharply. "You know what he did too?" And he hadn't told her?

Zephyr shook his head. "Nah. But I don't want you to waste time killing him when we can be getting naked." His eyes were all dragon in that moment.

Heat surged through her at his words—and tempered some of the tension in her shoulders. Goddess, this male was actually trying to handle her. And it was working.

Griff snorted out a laugh behind them and patted Zephyr on the shoulder once. "Can you guys wait to get naked until we're inside? I'm exhausted."

Juniper frowned at him, but opened the front door and stopped in her tracks.

August, their boss, was waiting. He was a big male with red hair and he was a giant teddy bear. Well, to them.

Her mouth dropped open for a second before she raced at him, threw her arms around him. "I can't believe you're here!"

He laughed in that hearty way of his and patted her back once. "Mira wanted to visit her twin and I wanted to let you guys know how proud I am of you." He then gave Griff and Hyacinth a hug before he shook hands with Zephyr in the way of warriors and said, "I'm glad to meet you in person. Welcome to the team."

Zephyr nodded and shoved his hands into his pockets, content to let everyone talk.

She grabbed Zephyr's hand, dragging him to her side because she wanted to make a clear statement to August. Her boss and friend glanced at their linked hands and grinned. Then he said, "I know you've been traveling for hours and need rest. But Ren's out back. He needs to talk to you. Don't kill him."

Oh hell. What had that cat done? Sighing, she looked at Zephyr. "Give me a few minutes? I'll meet you upstairs in just a sec."

He nodded and brushed his lips over hers. She leaned into him, but forced herself not to get carried away. Not yet, but soon. So very soon. Heat pooled between her thighs as she thought of just how soon. Mere minutes.

The male was so damn steady, so damn perfect for her. It scared her, but she was managing the fear that came with loving someone. The alternative was to live without him and that wasn't an option.

She stepped outside, breathed in the cool air. It was still a couple hours until sunset and the sun was at the right angle to highlight most of the lush yard. There wasn't much color other than green, despite the cooler month.

Ren stood on the back deck, hands shoved into his jeans pockets. He straightened as soon as she stepped out, shutting the door behind her. "Hey, how was the flight?"

"Good weather. No rain. What's up?" She got right to it because she wanted to be upstairs naked at the moment, not dealing with whatever this was. Though Zephyr was right, Ren always had her best interests at heart. He was her brother in all ways but blood and she loved him.

"Your mom called a couple days ago, said she'd been trying to call you back but couldn't get through. I accidentally told her about Starlena. It just slipped out! I wasn't trying to go behind your back but your mom is like a word ninja. I told her everything then, just vomited it right out! And now she's here with your dad and—"

"My parents are in New Orleans?" She stared at Ren in shock. She hadn't had much service when they'd been up in the mountains. None of them had. They'd sporadically checked in with King and August, but that had been it.

"Yeah, they just arrived yesterday. They're currently at Starlena's place and…they've met your biological mom."

Juniper's mouth dropped open. *What. The. Hell.*

"Are you angry at me?" Ren whispered, the feline looking guilt-stricken.

"No."

He blinked in surprise. "Seriously?"

She sighed and pulled him into a big hug. "Yeah, seriously. I'm actually kind of grateful I don't have to tell them. They just know now. But...they're actually there? They've met my bio mom?" She'd planned to call Starlena and tell her that she was back, but only after she'd gotten settled. And had some real alone time with Zephyr. "Have you met her?"

"No. But Starlena rolled out the red carpet for your parents apparently. I thought about introducing myself to your bio mom, but I've been too busy with everything, and honestly, I would have felt weird meeting her before you. I really am sorry I told your parents—"

"Don't be. I'm...glad they're here." Because the thought of meeting her bio mom scared her. Yeah, she said it. Absolutely scared her. And she wanted her parents here.

Ren shoved out a sigh, looking relieved. "Good. They're excited to see you and they brought a bunch of baked goods sent from the pack. There's plenty of room for them here and I figured they'd stay here after you got back."

Even though she wasn't mad at Ren, tension bunched in her shoulders all the same. She needed to call them, to go meet her mother.

My. Mother.

But...she scrubbed her hands over her face. Zephyr was her priority. "I'm going to go shower. Do we have any food here?"

Ren blinked. "You're not going to..."

"What, rush over there? Hell no. The first time I meet my...Soleil, I'm not going to stink." And truth be told, she needed to mentally prepare herself. "I'll call my parents soon, let them know I'm in town. Do *not* tell them I'm back."

"I won't!"

Shaking her head at him, she headed back inside and raced up the stairs. No one was waiting in the kitchen or foyer and she'd catch up with August later. Right now, she only wanted Zephyr, to lose herself in him.

She followed his scent straight to her room. Both their small bags were at the foot of the bed and the shower was running. She pictured him standing under the spray in all his naked glory, waiting for her.

Heat surged through her even as her abdominal muscles tightened in anticipation. After this there was no going back.

Who was she kidding—there was no going back regardless for her. Zephyr was her person.

She was secure in that more than anything else.

She quickly stripped, tossed her clothes onto the floor and absently noticed that his were neatly folded on a chair, his shoes tucked underneath it.

Steam rolled out as she stepped inside the bathroom. Not bothering to announce herself because he'd have heard and scented her by now, she tugged the shower curtain back and stepped inside to find a god washing his scarred-up, ripped abs.

He was pure power.

Jets of water pounded against his shoulders, rolling down his body in little streams, highlighting each cut and striation of his muscles. Her dragon might as well have been carved from marble, his thick thighs powerful—and what was between them was a hell of a lot better. His long, thick cock jutted out, all for her.

His vivid gray eyes swept over her, hunger rolling off him in a sharp burst of wild need.

And she felt like she was coming home in that moment. She'd tell him what Ren had said later. Now was only about the two of them.

He reached for her, grabbed onto her hips even as he pinned her to the slick wall. He ran his fingers through her unbound hair, cupping the back of her head.

Heat flooded between her thighs at his possessive touch, at the feel of his thick erection between them. She arched her back, brushing her breasts against his chest, the skin to skin almost not enough. She wanted to wrap herself around him, to drown in him, to devour him.

Her chain snapped out, latched around his ankle immediately.

She wondered why her magic was so damn erratic around him, but couldn't bring herself to care when he rolled his hips once against her, his cock sliding up against her stomach.

Her inner walls clenched as she imagined him sliding it between her folds, pushing deep.

"I like that you're not hiding your hair now." He tightened his grip slightly, his gaze searing hers. "And you and me, this isn't temporary," he growled out, keeping her pinned in place as water pounded down around them.

"I know." Her words were barely above a whisper as she looked at the male who'd stolen her heart. "I'm not letting you go."

"Good. Because I love you. And if you run, I'll follow you to the ends of the earth. To other realms. You're my person, Juniper."

Her throat thickened with emotion as his words mirrored her earlier thoughts. She slid her hands up his chest and around his neck, held tight and pressed herself fully to him. They were a perfect fit in more ways than one. "I love you too." The words came out as a whisper again because she was almost beyond words at this point. She'd never told another male that before and the moment felt monumental. As if she was releasing something inside herself, letting him in. Literally and figuratively.

He slanted his mouth over hers, his kiss anything but soft as he claimed her.

She lifted a leg, slid it around him and pulled him even closer as he pressed her up against the cool tile.

As she teased her tongue against his, as they finally got to be alone, to just be together, he slid a big callused palm between their bodies and cupped her mound.

Her inner walls clenched again, desperate to be filled by his fingers, his cock—later, his tongue. She wanted all of him. Everywhere. Right freaking now.

When he slid two thick digits inside her, she moaned into his mouth and reached for his erection.

She wrapped her hand around him and stroked once as he added a third finger, then arched her back into him. "Inside me now," she demanded. Not his fingers, she wanted more.

Gripping his thick length, she balanced against the tiled wall. He grabbed onto one hip as she centered herself over him and then he thrust up even as she slid down, their two bodies joining in the most intimate way possible.

She sucked in a breath as he completely filled her. "You feel amazing," she managed to rasp out.

His neck muscles tightened as he gripped her hips, held her still as his cock pulsed inside her.

Goddess he was thick, stretching her to the hilt.

He let out a low growl as he reached between their bodies and began teasing her clit. And…the earth was definitely rumbling somewhere. That wasn't her imagination.

When he suddenly pulled back and thrust into her hard, she groaned, gripped his shoulders tight. They'd been building up to this since the day they'd met. Since the day he'd shifted in front of her and stretched out his wings, showing off for her alone.

As he stared down at her, he pulled out again, slowly, then thrust back inside her. Each time he thrust all the way home, her body trembled, her chain tightening on his calf. She was going to come soon, probably too soon.

But she didn't care. They deserved this, deserved to climax and then do it all over again. Because this was just the beginning, would only take the edge off.

He slid one hand around her hip and then down until he was cupping her ass, his big palm spanning it. When he squeezed, her inner walls tightened again.

He gripped her hard, as if he never wanted to let her go—that was fine by her.

When he slipped a finger between her cheeks, she stilled for a moment as he teased his finger against her tight entrance. "This okay?" he murmured against her mouth before nipping her bottom lip between his teeth.

She nodded, her breath catching as he slowly pressed his finger inside her. She jerked against him. The sensation of his thick cock thrusting into her while he buried his finger inside her was going to shove her over the edge.

Keeping his finger pushed inside her, he pulled his hips back, then thrust into her hard.

She wrapped her legs tight around him, her entire body trembling now. Her inner walls tightened around him faster and faster and when he pulled out again, her climax started.

The dual stimulation was too much.

"Touch your clit," he growled even as her orgasm started to build, pleasure punching through her.

He had her held in place against the wall as he continued thrusting so she reached between their bodies and rubbed her finger over her swollen clit.

The instant she began teasing herself, her inner walls convulsed out of control as she came with him buried inside her. The moment she did, he squeezed her ass again and as he started to withdraw his finger, he let go.

Growling, he began thrusting harder, pinning her in place as he lost himself inside her, coming hot and hard, the friction against her G-spot prolonging her orgasm. She bit down on his shoulder as he thrust again so she wouldn't scream out her pleasure. This was all for him, for them. She didn't want anyone overhearing them. Though she didn't care if they had.

Eventually, his grip on her hips loosened and he lifted his head to look down at her. Water sprayed all around them, but it was just background at this point. All her focus was on him.

She kept her legs wrapped firmly around his waist, savoring the feel of his half-hard length inside her. She knew it wouldn't take him long to rebound and they could do this all over again. Maybe on the bed.

Or maybe they'd just make it to the bathroom floor. She didn't care which.

"I really want you to sit on my face," he murmured before he brushed his mouth over hers.

Oh hell yeah. Her inner walls fluttered around him, making him grin against her mouth.

"You like that idea?"

"Oh yeah." She nipped his lip, arched into him to stimulate her nipples even more. She loved that she had the right to touch him anywhere and everywhere, kiss him, pleasure him.

There was so much she needed to deal with, to worry about, but for right now she was going to savor this quiet time with him. And hold on tight.

Reaching out, he turned the shower off and shoved the shower curtain back. "Then let's get started."

She shivered at the way he growled the words, the heat in his gaze that said he was going to take great pleasure in eating her out. She couldn't believe she'd held out against him as long as she had.

Never again. He was hers and she was his.

CHAPTER THIRTY-TWO

"I can't stop sweating." Juniper raised her arms slightly, not joking. She was a ball of nerves and literal heat as she and Zephyr approached the house where Starlena, her parents and her biological mother were. Only a few hours ago she'd been naked and sated in the shower with Zephyr. Now…she was a mess. "What if…I don't know. What if she takes one look at me and—"

"Stop." Zephyr tugged on her hand so that she turned to face him. He cupped her cheek gently. "She wants to meet you. You know that. You're her daughter, she loves you. And given that she's a dragon, she'd probably set the actual world on fire for you. Get out of your head, my love."

She smiled softly at the endearment. "I love you," she growled. She was so happy he was with her now, grounding her as too many emotions ricocheted through her.

He grinned slightly. "I love you too." The ground slightly rumbled beneath them and he sighed. "And unless we want to start an earthquake…" He nodded once in the direction of the little pathway that led to the front door.

He'd told her that the earth rumblings she'd been feeling had definitely been him, his mating manifestation. So there was no doubt that she was his mate. She just...wondered why hers hadn't shown up. But she wasn't going to spiral, to go all negative. Zephyr was hers with or without a mating manifestation. She didn't need it, she just needed him.

She took a deep breath, nodded once. "Okay, let's do this. And also, I should warn you about my parents. They'll get you to confess all sorts of things if you're not careful," she said as they headed up the walkway. "You'll be talking about your feelings and childhood stuff before you know it."

He gave a full-body laugh as they reached the front step, and man, she felt that laugh, wrapped his happiness around her and held it close. Before they could knock, the door opened and her parents were there, all smiles and tears as they rushed out to attack her with hugs.

Milana, her petite, pixie-like mother, reached up and cupped her face. "My baby!" Then she peppered kisses all over her face, making Juniper laugh.

Her father, Andre, stepped in then, wrapping his arms around both of them and holding them close. A couple inches shorter than her, he was rangy in the way of wolves. Rangy, strong, fast. And so incredibly patient and kind. "You have found *more* family and we are so happy for you, our sweet, wonderful child."

Oh, his words hit the mark. They were her family too, no matter what. "Mom, Dad," she managed to rasp out. And that was it, because her voice stopped working. She loved them so much.

It didn't matter; her mom picked up the thread immediately. "Your birth family is wonderful. We are so happy to have met them. They've welcomed us with open arms, and while we want to catch up with you, there is someone I know you want to meet." Milana cupped one cheek again. "Take your time and open your heart, sweet girl. Don't be afraid to let them in."

"I'll be open. Promise," she whispered. Because she couldn't disobey her mother. *Nope.* Feeling suddenly nervous, she cleared her throat and motioned to Zephyr. "Ah, Mom and Dad, this is Zephyr. My mate." They hadn't officially mated, but that was just semantics.

They turned to him, both reaching out to hug him. "Let's get you inside and fed," Milana said, linking her arm with his. She looked so small next to him, but her mom was fierce when she needed to be. "You find us when you're done," Milana said over her shoulder as Juniper stepped into the foyer after her.

Oh goddess. So what happened now? She didn't follow them, because she could scent Starlena, could feel eyes on her from the living room to her left. She took a breath. Then another, and turned left, her heart thundering in her ears as she found herself looking at Starlena and a woman who was definitely her mother.

She stared into bicolor eyes the same as hers—one gray, one blue-green. Her hair was draped over one shoulder in a long, silvery braid.

The female in front of her was dressed not like she'd expected, but in form-fitting clothing that looked leathery and battle worn. A blade was strapped to one thigh and her hands were trembling slightly as she stepped forward.

Juniper was aware of Starlena murmuring something, but she couldn't hear the actual words. Her grandmother walked past her, patted her gently on the arm, but Juniper couldn't take her eyes off Soleil.

Something pulsed in her mind, a flash of memory as pain spiked inside her head. *This female sitting by Juniper's bed, reading a story. A big male with dark hair was next to her, his hand on the female's thigh as she read, as if he couldn't stand to not touch her. A silver-haired girl tucked up against Juniper, already asleep as the female read.*

"You're bleeding." Alarm laced Soleil's voice and it broke the silent bubble around them as she hurried forward in a couple long strides, a tissue in hand. Her voice was lilting, comforting.

"Thank you," Juniper murmured, taking it even as she inwardly cursed and pressed it to her nose.

"Perhaps we should sit...outside?"

She shoved out a sigh of relief, nodded even as she stopped the bleeding. Being stuck in this sitting room was too much. It didn't matter how huge it was, the outdoors was the only place big enough for her emotions. Overcome with everything, still slightly trembling, she followed Soleil outside and sat on the same bench in the front yard she'd sat on with Starlena.

"Did you read to me when I was a child?" she asked, tucking the tissue away.

Faint surprise flickered in the female's eyes, but Soleil nodded. "Every night. Until war broke out and I was called to battle. But even then, I read to my babies. I want to respect your space," the dragon queen blurted, "but I want to touch you to make sure you're real."

Juniper held out her hand without pause and Soleil snagged it, held it tight as she brought it up to her face.

Closing her eyes once, Soleil inhaled. "I knew you weren't gone," she rasped out. "And I searched endlessly for you. You must know that. Scoured the world."

Swallowing hard, she nodded. "Starlena told me." Until that moment, she hadn't been sure she believed everything her grandmother had said about Soleil, but it was clear this female loved her, would have done anything to find her. More pain, a different kind, ricocheted through her as she grieved all their lost time. So many lost years. And the agony she felt for a woman who'd lost her child... "Did she tell you how I was found?"

"She did. And so did your wonderful parents. I...thought I would hate them, was actually prepared to," she confessed. "But they are such kind people. They brought my mother and me photo albums filled with pictures of you growing up. And when I cried, your mother held me and comforted me as if I was one of her own. I can't hate a female like that."

Juniper smiled at that. "They are always thinking of others."

"I'm grateful they found you. But..." She cleared her throat and her dragon flickered in her gaze, the warrior peeking out at her. "I will find out what happened to you. Who stole you from us."

Juniper nodded. She'd expected nothing less. "Starlena thinks I need to see a dragon healer, have someone look closer at my memories."

Soleil nodded. "I've brought two healers with me. I don't want to bombard you, but when you're ready, and if you consent, I would like them to look at your mind."

"You trust them?"

"With my life, your life. My entire clan's lives."

"Then I might trust them too." She wouldn't commit just yet. Having someone dig into her mind required great trust. And she would want Zephyr there the whole time. "I...have so many questions." And she didn't know where to start.

Soleil squeezed her hand, not letting go. "And I will answer anything I can. I would also ask about your mate. He has a familiar coloring. I think I know who his clan is. Or...was."

Juniper cleared her throat. Zephyr had told her that most of his clan had died, been killed by an evil dragon mage. "We're not technically mated." Though they were headed that way.

Soleil gave a soft snort, the sound at odds with her queenly persona. "Yet. My mother has assured me he's a strong mate, one who will fit in well with the Nova females."

"She certainly didn't tell him that."

"No, she wouldn't. But she likes him."

"What is the Nova clan's...mating manifestation?"

Surprise flickered in Soleil's gaze but she quickly masked it. "It varies, but for the royal line, the females of your line, our chains make it very clear who our dragon half chooses. Mine chose your father at a very inopportune time." Her expression turned dry, though there was a hint of amusement in her eyes.

That made so much sense. And now she realized her mating manifestation *had* appeared with him. Juniper wanted to ask what had been so inopportune, but instead blurted, "My father?" She knew he was in Hibernation, but wanted to meet him too.

"I've sent mental messages to him. He's currently waking up and I have instructions that a message is to be delivered to him once he does. He will either come here or, perhaps, by the time he's awake, you'll decide you want to visit your home realm."

"I...would like that," she said carefully and realized she meant it. "Zephyr will come with me." And it wasn't a question.

"Of course. Your family, friends, everyone is welcome."

Soleil's words eased even more of the tension bunched in her shoulders. She could relax now and ask all the questions she wanted. Spend time with her mother.

JUNIPER WASN'T sure how much time passed but the sun had fully shifted directions in the sky, the shadows growing longer around them, when a female with similar silvery hair wearing a long, fancy dress stepped out onto the lawn.

Soleil's expression tightened slightly and Juniper had a feeling it had to do with being interrupted.

The female nodded respectfully as she carried out a tray with two steaming drinks and assorted treats. "Starlena insisted I bring you food," the female said, her lips curving up slightly. "And she needs to speak to you about something in private. I believe it's about the dragon eggs."

Soleil looked as if she was going to decline but Juniper shook her head. "It's okay, go talk to her. I'm not going anywhere." She thought she should probably check on Zephyr too, but wasn't actually worried about him. Her parents had probably grilled him a bit, but then made him feel welcome.

As Soleil stepped away, Juniper stood, stretched slightly. As she did, her nose started bleeding again, and this time she didn't bite back her curse.

"Here, my lady." The female who'd set the tray on the little table next to the bench held out a handkerchief.

My lady? Oh no, that would have to stop. "Thanks." Goddess, would her nose stop bleeding, please? She tilted her head back and pressed the handkerchief against her nose.

"I'm Astra, by the way. We're cousins." The female had a lilting voice and delicate features. Now *she* looked like what Juniper thought of as royalty. "Is it true you don't remember us?"

"Yeah," she said, her voice slightly garbled.

"Well, we're all looking forward to getting to know you again."

"Me too." She pulled the cloth away, then pressed it to her nose again but there was no blood. "Sorry about this, I'll wash it."

The female's smile was serene as she shook her head. "No need, you can keep it. And please enjoy the tea and pastries. We'll be serving dinner soon, but I know you must be starving."

"Thanks." Her stomach was actually still knotted up, but the gesture was nice so she picked up the stupidly small teacup. They were dragons, why were they drinking from such small dishes?

She started to drink, but paused when she realized Astra was still standing on the front stoop. Watching her. Way too intently.

Tension buzzed at the back of her skull as she set the cup down on the tray and stood. Angry bees swarmed inside her as she stared at the beautiful female.

Going on instinct, she took a step forward. "You stole my memories," she snarled. It was just a guess, and if she was wrong, she was going to feel really stupid.

"I knew you remembered," the female hissed, her delicate features twisting into something ugly. Moving lightning fast, she whipped out her chains at Juniper.

Moving faster, Juniper dodged to avoid them.

Astra took her by surprise and shifted, jumping into the air in a few quick wing beats.

She planned to run? *Oh hell no.* Juniper released her own chains and snapped them at the dragon, wrapping them around one of her wings.

The beast screeched, blasting out flames.

Zephyr, Soleil, and Starlena all burst out of the door, her parents right behind them.

They didn't ask questions; her mother and grandmother released their own chains and snapped them out at Astra, completely immobilizing her wings and snout by the time Zephyr had fully shifted—and wrapped his jaws around Astra's neck in a display of raw power.

Yeah, this female wasn't going anywhere.

"No! Don't kill her." Juniper hurried forward and placed a hand on

253

her male's wing. Not because she cared about the female. But she wanted answers. Wanted to know why this female had wanted her dead. Why she'd likely killed a baby sister Juniper couldn't remember. "I need answers, Zephyr."

He bit down slightly, making Astra whine, but he finally let go and shifted to human form. "She wanted to hurt you," he snarled, his beast still in his eyes. He was dangerously close to shifting again and finishing Astra.

"I know." She looked at Starlena and Soleil. "I think she's the one who did something to my memories."

Starlena's eyes were glowing now, the power punching off her actually visible in the air around her.

And Soleil tightened her chains around the dragon, her face a mask of barely restrained rage. "We will thoroughly question her. Then she will know my full wrath."

"And mine," Starlena growled.

Heart racing, Juniper nodded even as her parents hurried to her side, their expressions worried as they closed ranks around her and Zephyr. She loved that her healer parents were trying to protect them in that moment.

As Soleil shouted out, "Shift now!" to Astra, a huge beast with shimmering white scales appeared from above, arrowing straight toward the street.

Juniper went into fight mode, about to shift. Zephyr and her parents tensed beside her and she knew Zephyr was about to shift until Starlena growled, "Damn it. That's your sister, Juniper. Don't attack her," she called out as a burst of magic filled the air, sparkling everywhere.

A beautiful female with a shockingly petite build for a dragon but the same silvery hair and bicolor eyes as Juniper's raced across the lawn at them. She took in the scene in moments, and to Juniper's surprise snarled at Soleil. "Can't believe you heifers tried to leave me at home!" She barreled toward Juniper, arms wide. "Seren!" The female threw herself at Juniper with abandon, and hugged her tight.

Juniper didn't even think to defend herself. She knew bone-deep this female meant her no harm. She stumbled back under the impact of the female's hug and realized her cheeks were wet with tears as she hugged the small female. A surge of memories slammed through her, of her and this female. They'd flown together always, snuck out of the castle at night together far too often, and this girl had almost always crept into her bed at night, demanding stories.

"Stella," she whispered into the female's hair. She remembered her, her mischievous little sister.

A scream rent the air as Astra was forced to shift back to human form. She screeched and hissed hate-filled words at all of them until Soleil knocked her out with a bone-rattling punch that might have broken her jaw.

"I hate to do this now, but the dragon eggs are hatching." Cosmo stood on the front porch in the frame of the open doorway, staring at the bloody melee on the lawn as he wrung his hands in front of him.

"I'll take care of this trash," Starlena snarled, tightening her chains around the prone, unconscious Astra. Her entire body was wrapped in Starlena's chains—she wasn't going anywhere.

"I always hated that bitch," Stella muttered as Zephyr moved in, wrapped his arm tight around Juniper's shoulders.

"Breathe," he whispered to her. Her wonderful, steady rock.

She forced herself to take a deep breath, then another. So much was happening at once and she was having a hard time processing it all. So she took another steadying breath and leaned into her mate's hold.

Whatever happened next, at least she had him at her side.

CHAPTER THIRTY-THREE

Two days later

"Thank you for meeting with us." Juniper smiled at King as she and Zephyr sat across from him at the outside patio table on his pack's property. She and Zephyr had been inseparable the last two days, especially after what had happened. He'd gone into hyperpossessive mode.

Hunter, King's dragonling, was currently floating on his back in the huge pool, his wings spread wide and a look of pure bliss on his adorable face. The size of a small elephant, his gray sparkling wings glittered under the sunlight and every so occasionally he would burp out a puff of orange flames.

"Of course. I'm very grateful for all you and your crew have done," King said. "You have a standing invitation to live in my territory. We would be proud to call you one of our own. Though I have a feeling you might be leaving soon." He looked between her and Zephyr.

"Ah…maybe." Her mother had asked her, Zephyr, her crew and her parents to visit the Nova realm. And she really wanted to go. "I actually wanted to talk to you…ah, to just ask you something."

Hunter flapped to life then, the little dragon showering water over the sides of the pool as he started chirping animatedly.

"He wants you to play fetch with him," King said to Zephyr. "That metal pole by the bar area is his."

Zephyr simply laughed, kissed Juniper on the forehead before he hurried over to grab the pole—and started playing fetch.

"He's too cute," she murmured, watching the dragon animatedly catch the pole and then do a sort of bow, midair.

"He's a pain in the ass." King's tone was dry as he turned back to her. "So."

"So...I feel weird being here but you're the only person I know who's been in a similar situation to mine."

He raised an eyebrow.

"Discovering your long-lost family. Family that's also royalty. I'm in a weird position and I have no one else to talk to about it that will understand."

King paused, then a grin spread across his face, making him look youthful instead of the battle-scarred Alpha that he was. "Yeah, you're right. Hell. So what do you want to know?"

"How has your adjustment been? Did you consider moving to the fae realm? Or... I don't know what I'm asking. I'm just trying to wrap my head around having a new sibling and parents and...everything."

He gave a short sigh. "I never once considered moving. This is my territory to protect. But I have been enjoying getting to know my father and sister. It's...a lot to process. But they've never pressured me to be anything I'm not. I don't know that I'll ever call Sorgin 'Dad,' but I'm enjoying getting to know him and my sister as people. My sister doesn't hold back. She's made it clear that she wants a relationship, and she's so kind. It's hard not to want to build one with her."

She nodded slowly, thinking of how welcoming her family had been. Especially Stella—who was a bulldozer wrapped in a small package. She'd basically been Juniper's shadow the last couple days, wanting to spend all her time with Juniper. And Zephyr by extension because he hadn't left her side. And...she really liked it. Liked having more family. "I hope you'll thank your father for me. For reaching out to my grandmother." Without him, Juniper might never have met her blood family.

"Of course. How are you feeling since having your healers mend your mind?"

Her clan's healers had looked into her mind, found a very thin, almost indiscernible trap of sorts. It had caged her memories, blocking out everything from that fateful night. She'd seen her cousin Astra murdering the children in the nursery. Anyone who'd been in line to rule. Astra had planned to come after Seren—Juniper—and Stella, but had wanted to take out the weakest first. Juniper had caught her in the act, had been beyond horrified.

Astra had been working with an ancient member of their clan, one who'd wanted Astra in power eventually. Because the weak dragon Astra had been malleable, a corrupt dragon who simply wanted power and all it offered. The ancient had blasted Juniper's mind, placed a trap in it as she'd tried to escape and tell her parents what was happening. Then she'd cast a spell sending Juniper to the human realm. The plan had always been to hunt her down later, but the ancient and Astra hadn't been able to find her.

By the time the ancient and Astra had been able to sneak away to the human realm, there had been no trace of Juniper anywhere. And they hadn't had a lot of time to search for her. So they'd simply returned to Nova and tried to return to life as normal. They would have eventually gone after Stella, Soleil, and Juniper's father. But after what happened, they'd tightened security and it had never loosened, even after her father had gone into Hibernation.

According to Starlena, the ancient was now in chains and would be executed as soon as Soleil returned to the realm. Astra was dead —Soleil killed her—and Juniper was glad the dragon was gone. It wouldn't bring back her lost years, her murdered baby sister and cousins, or anything else, but at least Astra couldn't hurt anyone else.

"I feel whole. My memories came back in a rush and it's a lot to process. The dump of information, knowing that I truly had a life before. A family I was torn from."

He nodded, his expression thoughtful. "How are your two families getting along?"

"Amazingly. It's hard not to love my parents, which is probably a big reason why everyone is meshing so well. And they do want to ally with your territory. My grandmother has said that I can be the liaison."

King nodded once. "I think that's a great idea."

"What you said about us living here...we're going to be visiting my family's realm for a bit, but Zephyr's brothers are here and I know they're not leaving. So we would like to call New Orleans home as well."

He gave her another nod. "We will need to discuss your relationship with August."

Yeah, she'd been expecting that. "Right now, everything is still so unknown. But I would like to continue working for him. I love what I do. But I also realize that my loyalties would also be divided, so to speak."

"That's not necessarily true. I understand that in black ops you're loyal to keeping all supernaturals safe. Yes?"

She nodded once, glad he got it. It was a simple way of looking at it, but that was it in a nutshell. She'd taken an oath to defend supernaturals, to keep them safe from anyone who wished them harm. That hadn't changed since The Fall.

"As long as you never spy on my territory, never betray anyone in my territory for your own gain, I'm fine with you and your crew living here. And I understand that I won't be your Alpha. Not technically."

Goddess, he really was a good Alpha. "I can promise to never spy on your territory, never to betray anyone here, and if we suspect someone of, well, anything suspect, we'll come to you with it. You've proven to all of us that you're the kind of Alpha we want to live under."

He gave her a small smile. "Good, then. I don't think we'll have a problem. And hopefully I'll be able to ask you for help if the need ever arises."

"Absolutely."

He glanced over at Hunter and Zephyr—who were now rolling around on the grass together. Zephyr was still in human form and play-fighting with Hunter, who kept cackling and falling on his back in mock surrender before attacking Zephyr again.

Speaking of dragonlings... "My grandmother is taking two of the hatched dragonlings back to the Nova realm, but I believe that Avery is keeping one. It's bonded with her."

To her surprise, King snorted in amusement. "I'm glad to hear that. I tried to give her Hunter once but he wouldn't stay."

Hunter looked over at them and chirped loud and long at King. The dragonling was definitely scolding the Alpha.

"I know, I know. I didn't realize how amazing you were back then." King's tone was dry, but his mouth curved up slightly at the corners.

Hunter sniffed once, then looked back at Zephyr and blew smoke at him before pouncing.

"Do you really understand him?" she asked.

"Somehow, yes. I'm not even sure when it happened, but I speak Hunter now."

She laughed at that, then looked back at Zephyr and Hunter, roughhousing. And the image of him doing the same thing with their future kids popped into her mind with such a suddenness, her heart rate kicked up.

She'd never once even thought of having kids—and she didn't want them for a while. But as she looked at Zephyr, she realized that she did want a family one day.

With him. It didn't matter where they made their home either, as long as they were together.

CHAPTER THIRTY-FOUR

Three months later

"You look so stunning I want to cry." Hyacinth dabbed at her eyes as she stood in front of Juniper.

Her crew was in the bridal waiting room at her biological family's palace. Natural light streamed in from the multiple stained-glass windows, all depicting dragons in various states of battle. Her clan was definitely mostly of the warrior class and they wanted everyone to know it.

"You can't cry. You're my rock!" Juniper glanced past Hyacinth to the trio of huge, gilded mirrors and said, "Though I do look stunning."

Which made Hyacinth laugh—Juniper's intent. She could not deal with tears on her wedding day. *Nope, nope, nope.*

"She's right, you're gorgeous." Ren stepped up then, a big grin on his face. He was wearing the traditional clothing of her dragon clan since he was one of her attendants for the biggest wedding in the Nova realm's recent history. His pants were a loose silk type of material and his tunic was similar in style, though he had a loose belt around his waist. The embroidery on the belt matched the embroidery on the cuffs of his tunic and pants. It was an intricate hand-sewn stitching depicting her clan members over the millennia. "The most beautiful dragon bride to ever walk the face of the earth. Or any realm."

"You guys have to stop."

"No way. It's our job to tell you how amazing you are." Griff, her normally quiet wolf, stepped up, looking similar to Ren. "And you are. Though I won't say that in front of Zephyr because I value my head."

She snickered slightly. Zephyr loved Griff and Ren like brothers now, but he still got growly with them sometimes simply because they were male and his dragon viewed all males as rivals for her affections. She'd learned a lot the last few months in Nova, and weddings were apparently a huge deal for some dragon clans, especially those in different realms. And the Nova clan hadn't had a wedding in centuries. Add on that she was quite literally the long-lost daughter—aka princess—of Soleil and Ares, and this was quite the big deal.

She and Zephyr were already mated, and if she was being honest, this official and very public ceremony was so over-the-top and a little scary. But it meant so much to her clan and parents so she'd gone along with everything.

The door to the waiting room—which was lush and as over-the-top in luxury as the rest of the palace—opened and Stella slipped in, her face lighting up when she saw Juniper. "Goddess, you're gorgeous!" Her petite sister was a ball of constant energy, she'd learned the last few months.

She and Zephyr had spent most of that time here, with two quick trips back to New Orleans. Her parents had taken a leave from their pack and had been here with her as well. It had helped immensely to have them here, especially when the wedding talk had started.

"How's Zephyr?" she asked. Because she'd asked Stella to check on him. There was a stupid tradition that said they couldn't see each other for three *days* before the wedding and she did not like being separated from him. Her dragon half was one cranky, very horny bitch. She missed him too much.

"As cranky as you," Stella said pointedly. She was also in the clan's traditional garb, a flowing, loose, long-sleeved dress that reached her ankles. It was the same luminescent sparkling marble white as their dragon scales. There was intricate embroidery down the front of her dress in two separate columns and stitching around her cuffs.

The comment made Hyacinth giggle. "I could have told you that. I saw him snarling at one of his brothers last night. Threatening to remove all sorts of body parts. He was quite descriptive."

Juniper frowned, missing him even more. Over the last few months they hadn't been separated for more than an hour or so at once. As a newly mated couple, they were essentially banging like bunnies, multiple times a day. Or "banging like dragons" as Stella liked to say.

The door opened again and both sets of her parents stepped in. Milana and Andre—her wolf parents, as she'd started thinking of them—had expressions of pure excitement and love. Her dragon parents had commissioned them new, custom clothing for the wedding so that her father had on the same tunic and pants as every other male in her clan, and her mother had on the same dress. The only difference was in the embroidery. They had wolves sewn in with the dragons, representing them as part of Juniper's line.

Starlena had explained it all to her—as she'd been explaining a lot the last few months—and said that it was a very big honor. Her biological parents truly had welcomed Milana and Andre into their clan. They'd even invited them to live with them permanently. Juniper knew it was because they wanted her to live here permanently. Something she hadn't quite decided on yet. And she didn't want to have to yet.

Her biological father, Ares, quiet and reserved, stepped forward first. "It is almost time, dearest daughter."

Juniper smiled at the endearment. Her huge, scary-looking dragon father called her dearest daughter almost every chance he got. It was like he was making up for lost time. And she was so okay with it. "I'm ready."

Ready to see Zephyr again, to be in his arms. To publicly seal their vows to each other before her family and people.

"We have one more thing for you." Soleil's long dress swished slightly as she moved forward, all elegant and powerful as she carried a glittering tiara. "If you would like to wear it."

Juniper stared, confused for a moment, until she realized it was for her. Dragons' wings that looked just like hers swept back from the metalwork as if in flight, and in the middle was a huge, bright, glittering blue sapphire. "It's beautiful."

Soleil set it on Juniper's head with excruciating gentleness before she gently cupped her cheek. She didn't say anything, just kissed her on the cheek with tears in her eyes before she turned to the others and clapped once. "It is time!" Now she was in full-on queen mode.

Which made Juniper smile. Her dragon mother was a total badass.

"I APOLOGIZE FOR BEING SO GRUMPY," Zephyr said stiffly to his brothers as he turned away from the mirror. He'd been a bit of a jackass the last few days.

Mikael snorted. "You are sorry for threatening to disembowel me?"

"And for threatening to cut off my head?" Ivyn asked.

"At least he didn't threaten to cut off your dick," Cas muttered, though he had a grin on his face. "Jo wouldn't have been happy with you."

"I'm sorry for all of it." He missed his mate, as simple as that.

His brothers all laughed and converged on him, pulling him into a big hug. The last few months had moved at warp speed. He and Juniper had been in her family's realm most of the time but they'd returned to New Orleans twice.

To his surprise, his brothers had all made separate, multiple trips to the Nova realm to visit him—thanks to a magical dragon from Juniper's clan who had been helping with travel. He felt like he was getting back years he'd lost with them. And he was glad to know that the last few days of his bad behavior hadn't ruined that budding relationship with them.

"It is understandable," Mikael said as they all stepped back. "You miss your mate. Mine is downstairs waiting and I already miss her."

"According to Jo, Juniper's just as cranky as you are, so it is safe to say she misses you too," Cas said.

"Of course she misses me!" They were mates, they belonged together. Forever.

His brothers just snickered again.

He took a deep breath, getting his dragon under control. He would see Juniper in just a few minutes. He could wait that long. Probably.

"So are you going to be a prince now?" Mikael asked as he straightened Zephyr's belt and dusted off nonexistent lint from his tunic.

"I…don't know." They hadn't even talked about it. He wasn't sure if Juniper even knew. There was so much she was still learning, and mostly her parents were still trying to convince her, subtly, to move here.

"Are you going to live here?" Ivyn asked as he leaned against one of the open balcony doors.

"I don't know that either. I think Juniper wants to but is afraid to make such a big change."

"What do you want?" Mikael asked.

"For her to be happy."

His brothers all murmured their understanding.

He'd made it clear to her that he would do whatever she wanted to do, but maybe he needed to be clearer. And *maybe* he needed to see his mate again. Right now. To put eyes on her, to know she was safe. Which he technically knew because they were mated. He could sense it along their mating link. He was simply being a ridiculous, over-the-top—

A sharp knock sounded, then one of the dragons from Juniper's clan popped his head in. "It's time," he said, nodding at Zephyr, an encouraging smile on his face.

His brothers all clapped him on the shoulder once before they headed out first. Then he followed, anticipation buzzing through him as each step took him closer and closer to Juniper.

His mate. His forever.

He followed after his brothers, knowing what to expect thanks to so very many instructions from Starlena. His brothers would walk down an aisle that had been created in the castle's courtyard, set up between far too many rows of chairs. They'd walk alongside Juniper's attendants—Hyacinth, Stella, Ren and Griff. Then both sets of her parents would walk down the aisle, then her grandparents.

Then he would meet Juniper under the archway and they would walk down the aisle together where they would be officially blessed by one of the healers of her clan. It wasn't like human weddings, but there was a bit of tradition involved.

His dragon didn't care for any of it, but this was Juniper's family and he could admit he wanted them to accept him. Mostly because it would make her happy above all.

He stood where he'd been instructed, at the bottom of a huge staircase that flowed up into the second story of the palace. Juniper's attendants all strode down and joined his brothers. He might have nodded or smiled at some of them, but he couldn't stop staring up the stairs, waiting, waiting, waiting. He needed to see her, to hold her.

Her parents came next, then her grandparents and then…

Zephyr sucked in a breath at the sight of Juniper. She had on a long, shimmering gown the same color of her dragon scales and it glittered under the glow of the chandeliers. Much the same as the small tiara on her head. She looked like a queen in that moment.

Her long, silvery hair was in a thick braid draped over her shoulder, intertwined with various gems and sparkling ribbons. And the intricate stitching at her wrists and along the hem of her gown were the same shades of gray and blue-green as her eyes.

Before he was consciously aware of moving, he raced up the stairs, desperate to get to her as he skipped multiple steps at a time. He knew he was supposed to wait and that they would walk through the doors together, and out in front of what was likely her whole damn realm. But he couldn't wait.

She grinned as he reached her halfway up the stairs. "You look amazing," she murmured, her gaze falling to his mouth. "You even trimmed your beard a bit."

Goddess, she was stunning. And all his. It was still hard to believe. "Mikael said I looked like I should be living in a cave with feral bears."

She snickered and leaned forward. "I like you either way," she murmured as she brushed her mouth against his.

"It's time!" someone called up and that was when he realized the door had already been opened and everyone had already proceeded outside.

He could hear music playing, a gentle melody, but all his focus was on Juniper as they descended the stairs together and out the huge double doors.

Gasps of delight went up from the crowd as they headed down the long aisle filled with sparkling gems and flower petals—these dragons really were over-the-top—but he couldn't see anyone else but Juniper.

Her eyes were bright with joy as she clasped his hand tightly. "I love you so much," she whispered.

"I love you too." And he could feel that love every single day, even the three days they'd been separated. It sang to him on a fundamental level, their mating link connecting them so that he could feel what she was feeling.

And right now, all he felt was a pure, bright happiness.

EPILOGUE

Juniper curled up on Zephyr's bare chest, exactly where she wanted to be. "I didn't think it was possible, but I think you finally tired me out," she said around a yawn.

He slid his hand down from where it rested on her lower back, then grabbed her ass once. "No way, we're not done tonight."

She yawned again, unable to stop herself. "Pretty sure it's morning now." After the wedding celebration, they'd flown in dragon form away to a remote chalet on a mountainside near her parents' castle. Yeah, castle. That was still a weird thing to think. Or say out loud.

They weren't leaving this place for an entire week, per her parents' instructions. It had been fully stocked for them, and all her friends and Zephyr's family—her family now too—had been given the option to stay at the castle as long as they wanted, or they could return home. As far as she knew, mostly everyone except August was staying. He had business to deal with, something she understood. But even her friend Christian and the Magic Man had opted to stay in the Nova territory.

"What are you thinking right now? I can hear your brain working."

She sat up slightly so she could see his face. He was watching her intently with those gorgeous gray eyes, the nearby fire from the fireplace reflecting in them. "The future. Now that our wedding is over, I don't know if we should stay or go. I thought I knew what I wanted, but now...I don't know. And you haven't been very helpful in deciding." She pinched his side playfully.

He tugged her so that she was splayed fully on top of him. Her braid fell over her breast, brushing over her nipple. She'd decided to leave her braid and gems in because it had taken hours to complete and she loved the way it looked. She was going to keep it for a bit longer.

"I just want you happy," he said as she sat up, straddling him, her knees digging into the sheets.

She looked down at him, ran her hands over his chest, tracing over each striation. "That's not an answer." She couldn't make this decision alone. "I want you happy too, so I need your actual opinion."

"I think it would be great to live here for a while."

"Really?"

"Yeah, really."

"What about your brothers?"

"I love my brothers, but they're more than capable of living without me. They're all mated, happy. As they should be. And they've all carved out lives for themselves in New Orleans. I'm happy knowing how settled they are. When I was stuck in that Hell realm, that was all I wanted for my brothers. To start families of their own, to live their lives."

"What about you? You really want to live here with a bunch of strangers?"

"I'll make friends. I'm not worried. What is it you're worried about? How your crew will react if you decide to stay here?"

"Kind of, yeah. I've been working for August for so long and I thought that was what I wanted. I'd been so sure of it. If...I'd never met my biological family, I would have been happy kicking ass for the foreseeable future. I believe in all the work we've done and I'm proud of it. But..."

"You want to get to know your family."

"Yeah. The more time I spend with them, the more I want to stay. Is that selfish?" she whispered.

He sat up suddenly and wrapped his arms around her, their faces close to each other. "Hell no. Your life was stolen from you and you made the best of it. Hell, you flourished in spite of everything that happened. But you don't have to keep doing the same thing simply because it's what you've always done. We're dragons. We're going to live a very long time. If you want to start a new chapter of your life, I'm right by your side."

She nodded, digesting his words because he was saying what she'd been wishing for in her heart. To start a new chapter, to get to know her family. But guilt swamped her at the idea of leaving her crew behind.

"Your crew will be happy for you. And they can visit anytime they want. And we can visit them anytime we want. We're not moving to the moon and we're not prisoners here."

She smiled at his words, some of the tension easing off her chest and shoulders. "And you're really okay with moving here?"

"Sweetheart, you are my home. I will be happy anywhere as long as you're with me. And your father and grandfather have already made it clear they would like me to take over one of their battalions. I'll be a very busy dragon here, doing what I like."

"I won't be able to hunt down bad guys anymore," she murmured, thinking on how much her life had changed.

"Says who? Because I'm pretty sure Soleil will let you do whatever you want if you stay. The females in your line are all warriors. So stop coming up with excuses and make the choice. Let's stay."

Juniper bit her bottom lip as she thought of actually staying, making such a huge change. She didn't feel an obligation to serve her people here...but she wanted to. Deeply. She'd been doing so much good for supernaturals for decades and she wanted to do the same for her realm. She wasn't sure if Milana and Andre would stay—though she desperately hoped they would—but she knew she could visit them as much as she wanted. And the truth was, she did want to stay here, to learn more about her family, her heritage.

If it didn't work out, she would have at least taken the chance. And she really wanted to. But only if Zephyr was by her side.

"Let's do it," she said.

"I'm in." And the joy she felt along their mating link was enough that she knew her mate was as excited as she was.

She leaned forward and kissed him hard, but he took over in seconds, flipping her onto her back. His hard length was thick between them and she realized she wasn't tired anymore.

Not one little bit.

Dear Readers,

Thank you for reading Ancient Retribution and going on this adventure with me! If you'd like to stay in touch and be the first to learn about new releases you can:

Sign up for my monthly newsletter at: www.katiereus.com

Follow me on Bookbub:
https://www.bookbub.com/profile/katie-reus

Find me on Facebook:
https://www.facebook.com/katiereusauthor

Follow me on Instagram:
https://www.instagram.com/katiereusauthor/

Also, please consider leaving a review at one of your favorite online retailers. It's a great way to help other readers discover new books and I appreciate all reviews.

Happy reading,

Katie

ACKNOWLEDGMENTS

I owe a big thanks to my readers for reading this series! I'm able to continue writing it because of you. I'm also (always) grateful to Kaylea Cross, the best friend and critique partner this writer could ask for. I'm also thankful to Julia, editor extraordinaire. For Sarah, thanks never seems enough but I am incredibly thankful for all your behind the scenes help. Jaycee, once again you knocked it out of the park with this cover. I'm absolutely in love with it. For my family, especially my mom who has been a huge help the last year, thank you for everything you do. Last, but never least, for my sweet pups who keep me company while I work.

ABOUT THE AUTHOR

Katie Reus is the *New York Times* and *USA Today* bestselling author of the Red Stone Security series, the Ancients Rising series and the MacArthur Family series. She fell in love with romance at a young age thanks to books she pilfered from her mom's stash. Years later she loves reading romance almost as much as she loves writing it.

However, she didn't always know she wanted to be a writer. After changing majors many times, she finally graduated summa cum laude with a degree in psychology. Not long after that she discovered a new love. Writing. She now spends her days writing paranormal romance and sexy romantic suspense. If you would like to be notified of future releases, please visit her website: https://katiereus.com and join her newsletter.

Complete Booklist

Ancients Rising
Ancient Protector
Ancient Enemy
Ancient Enforcer
Ancient Vendetta
Ancient Retribution

Darkness Series
Darkness Awakened
Taste of Darkness
Beyond the Darkness
Hunted by Darkness
Into the Darkness
Saved by Darkness
Guardian of Darkness
Sentinel of Darkness
A Very Dragon Christmas
Darkness Rising

Deadly Ops Series
Targeted
Bound to Danger
Chasing Danger
Shattered Duty
Edge of Danger
A Covert Affair

Endgame Trilogy
Bishop's Knight
Bishop's Queen
Bishop's Endgame

MacArthur Family Series
Falling for Irish
Unintended Target
Saving Sienna

Moon Shifter Series
Alpha Instinct
Lover's Instinct
Primal Possession
Mating Instinct
His Untamed Desire
Avenger's Heat
Hunter Reborn
Protective Instinct
Dark Protector
A Mate for Christmas

O'Connor Family Series
Merry Christmas, Baby
Tease Me, Baby
It's Me Again, Baby
Mistletoe Me, Baby

Red Stone Security Series®
No One to Trust
Danger Next Door
Fatal Deception
Miami, Mistletoe & Murder
His to Protect
Breaking Her Rules
Protecting His Witness
Sinful Seduction
Under His Protection
Deadly Fallout
Sworn to Protect

Secret Obsession

Love Thy Enemy

Dangerous Protector

Lethal Game

Secret Enemy

Saving Danger

Guarding Her

Deadly Protector

Redemption Harbor Series®

Resurrection

Savage Rising

Dangerous Witness

Innocent Target

Hunting Danger

Covert Games

Chasing Vengeance

Sin City Series (the Serafina)

First Surrender

Sensual Surrender

Sweetest Surrender

Dangerous Surrender

Deadly Surrender

Verona Bay Series

Dark Memento

Deadly Past

Silent Protector

Linked books

Retribution

Tempting Danger

Non-series Romantic Suspense

Made in United States
Orlando, FL
30 March 2022

16326999R00174